Talking With The Dogs

A Vet Speaks With His Patients

By
Dr. Louis Vine, D.V.M.

airleaf.com

© Copyright 2005, Dr. Louis Vine, D.V. M.

All Rights Reserved.

No part of this book may be reproduced, stored in a retrieval system, or transmitted by any means, electronic, mechanical, photocopying, recording, or otherwise, without written permission from the author.

ISBN: 1-60002-000-3

ACKNOWLEDGEMENT

I am indebted to many people for guidance and assistance with this book. However, I am especially beholden to the dogs and their "guardians", the owners that I've worked with for more than 40 years. They have provided me with many opportunities to observe their behavior which I have attempted to describe in this book.

CHAPTER I

It had been a busy day in the Chapel Hill Animal Hospital and Dr. Zebulon was eager to go home. As he finished writing orders to his staff for his ailing patients, his office door flew open and his golden-haired receptionist came in.

"Oh, good, you're still here. UPS just left this package," she said as she handed him a small packet. Zeb tore it open and pulled out a little crystal disc which he dropped into his pocket. He found a note folded inside the box and began to read it. But again he was interrupted. This had been a day when he hadn't been able to finish a thought. His mind was tangled with unfinished sentences and ideas.

"Dr. Zebulon! Dr. Zebulon!" Someone was yelling from the reception room.

The weary doctor straightened his shoulders, dropped the note into his pocket with the disc and hurried to the reception room to answer the frantic call.

"I wish you'd looked at that note, Zeb," his big dog Bridget said to him as they went out together. "That was important stuff."

In the past, Zebulon talked to Bridget exactly as though she could understand everything he said. In fact, he had been forced to spell a few words in front of her until she learned what they meant. Then he would substitute a new word. Her intelligence surprised him but he attributed this to their close association. He had read in veterinary journals that the average dog understood about 200 words and commands. He knew Bridget understood more.

In the six years they had been together, Zebulon and Bridget had become kindred souls. There was a spiritual connection between man and beast. Zebulon attributed it to their co-species meditation. They would sit quietly staring into each other's eyes, probing each other's thoughts. Bridget became his medical assistant, accompanying him on veterinary rounds, displaying an uncanny ability to empathize with all the animals in the hospital. Zebulon realized that Bridget was a remarkably intelligent and gifted animal in whom the natural canine instincts were developed to a supranormal degree. He knew that

Dr. Louis Vine, D.V.M.

Bridget was equipped with a lot more senses than the basic five. Her twitching nose and bristling whiskers could sense danger and uncover hidden truths. Her sixth sense served Zeb and herself well in time of need.

Even before Zebulon attained the canine vernacular, he and Bridget always seemed to be on the same brain length. They understood each other with meticulous precision. He could watch the critical tilt of her ears, and the reproachful contour of her tail. He could read her body language- especially her tail language. A dog uses its tail as an expression of their emotions. Zebulon believed it is the responsibility of their guardians to understand what they are saying with their tails.

As this story opens, Zebulon looked down. Bridget had spoken to him in perfectly understandable English. They had always understood each other but in recent months, the two of them had become even closer than ever before because of his new found ability to comprehend the dog's vernacular. For some strange and unexplainable reason, he could understand what dogs said ever since the Westminster Dog Show in New York. At that time, he had hit his head on the trunk lid of his car while rummaging for medical paraphernalia and accidentally cut his hand on a broken bottle The resounding whack on his noggin caused him to see stars and black out momentarily.

When he fully regained all of his senses and bandaged his hand he went into Madison Square Garden where the dog show is held every year. There he discovered his ability to understand the vernacular of dogs and to have conversations with these previously 'dumb beasts'.

During his three days at the dog show, he had learned a great deal about the relationships between dogs and their owners. Some dogs were happy with their so-called masters while others were not. Zebulon heard lots of unflattering stories about owners' private lives. However, he realized that he couldn't reveal that dogs had divulged this information to him.

People knew that Dr. Zebulon was very close to his patients but he didn't want to be branded an eccentric nut. He treated each dog as a distinct personality as well as a patient. He had worked diligently through the years building an excellent reputation and he didn't want to lose his good name. Therefore, he was very careful while conversing with dogs. Any nearby people would only hear Zebulon's words. The dogs' voices were a variety of grunts, growls, groans and snarls.

Only his two closest friends knew the truth- dog show judge Daniel Clancy and the newest love of his life, Sallie Predino. Both were sympathetic and helpful in keeping him out of trouble with the public. He realized that not all people would be as understanding as his two friends. Although Sallie and Clancy did not know what the dogs were saying, Zebulon oftentimes translated their grunts and growls for his friends.

In one way, Zebulon had come to accept, even enjoy his newfound ability to converse with dogs. It would help him become the world's best veterinarian. Obtaining the symptoms right from dogs' own mouth would help him with the correct diagnosis of these normally silent animals.

However, the people who had seen him talking to dogs were causing him some problems. Some of these critics believed him ready for the men in the white coats because he was having conversations with dogs. Zebulon shrugged off these skeptics as uninformed and ignorant of his unlimited talent for healing dogs. He reasoned that since nine out of 10 owners admittedly talk to their dogs, he was the only one who had the God-given ability to understand what the dogs were saying to him. He had finally accepted his anointed task in life and decided to help as many dogs as he could.

His mind at peace, he proceeded to bring his thoughts back to the reality of the daily routine of a veterinary practitioner. As he entered his reception room, he was met by a tall, bony young man holding an injured spaniel in his arms.

"Doctor, doctor," he said. "This little fellow was struck in front of your hospital. It was a hit and run!"

Zebulon ran his weary hands through his tawny hair and bent to take the dog from the young man. "Is it your dog?"

"No. I was just passing by and saw it happen. He looks badly hurt."

Dr. Louis Vine, D.V.M.

A glance at the motionless dog confirmed that fact to Zebulon. He leaned over the victim of yet another thoughtless driver. Gently he patted the dog's head. The pain-filled eyes looked up at him. Feebly, the dog wagged his tail. Zebulon leaned close to the dog and murmured softly, "You'll be all right now, boy."

Carefully, gently, he lifted the dog into a more comfortable position. As he carried him to the surgery room, he glimpsed the sympathetic faces of those seated in the waiting room.

The young man who'd brought the injured animal in wondered why the beautiful big red dog was allowed to go with the doctor.

Zeb's dog, an Irish Setter Bridget McGuire, had a coat of hair the color of a perfect Bloody Mary with an excess of Worcestershire stirred in. She seemed perfectly at home in the hospital and went everywhere her beloved doctor went.

As Zeb walked down the hall, he began to call for his kennel man. "Tyler!" he yelled. "Nurse Nelson has gone home. I know you can help me with all of this." Bridget settled down in a corner of the surgery to watch the doctor work.

Zeb had owned the hospital for years, ever since old Dr. Nolan had died. His first job out of veterinary school had been right here as the old doctor's assistant. He had loved every minute of it. Even as the business grew and he worked long and tedious hours, he enjoyed caring for the little animals.

Finally, he had to hire extra help. Now he had nurse Nelson, a veterinarian, Dr. Peters and Tyler Steele, recently from Jamaica. Zeb was truly impressed by the tall, brown man who had come to his door asking for a job. He wondered what had brought this bright and unusual man to the little college town, Chapel Hill, North Carolina. Tyler's brown eyes looked directly into Zeb's gray eyes and simply said that he was new in town and would like to work with animals since he loved them so very much.

Zeb looked intently at Tyler. His skin was the color of a darkly roasted almond. He wore a little moustache and had elegantly styled hair. His accent was definitely British and his voice like honey. Zeb told himself there would be time enough to find out what had brought

Tyler there, so he simply told what was required of a good kennel keeper and asked if he felt he could do the job.

Tyler said he was ready to work hard and learn anything that he needed to know. "I learn fast, Doctor. And I hope to be with you long enough to become good at the job."

At this moment the doctor needed Tyler. Bridget spoke up "I bet Tyler can do it, Zeb." He agreed with her. Tyler showed lots of basic intelligence and had learned his chores well, in record time.

The two men went to work. Zebulon administered injections to combat shock and suppress pain to the injured dog on the table. Tyler set up a blood transfusion which Zebulon inserted quickly into the venous system of the waiting patient—a routine treatment for auto accident cases. "It's fortunate that dog blood doesn't have to be matched," Zeb said. "That could slow us down."

They took X-rays and Zeb found several ribs were broken. He skillfully tightened surgical bandages around the dog's chest while quietly comforting him. Then he pulled back and stood tall, stretched his tired back and studied his work. "Thank God I'd taught Tyler these procedures," he thought. He mopped his brow. Perspiration darkened his tawny hair and he tousled it with his fist. Tyler left the room to finish his other chores.

"You'll be all right, now," he said to the little dog.

"Wh-what? Did you speak to me?" the little spaniel mixture stammered in a tiny voice.

"Of course he spoke," Bridget answered from her corner. "Dr. Zebulon has learned to speak our vernacular," she explained to the little dog.

"Has the good doctor lost his mind?" the injured dog asked.

"Of course not," Bridget answered. "He's the sanest human I've ever known. He is destined to help all of us dogs that he can and he is the only one on earth that has the gift of gab with us."

"Wow, I'm impressed. I never liked any of my vets before now but I'm beginning to like you, Doctor. You have a good bed side manner."

"Thanks for the compliment. I wish all my patients feel the same way you do."

Dr. Louis Vine, D.V.M.

"I promise I'll spread the word around, Doc. That is, if you pull me out of this ran-in I had with that car."

"I think you have a good chance to make it. Relax and I'll be back in a little while and check you again."

Happy that Tyler had left for the kennels and not overheard any of this conversation, Zeb smiled at Bridget. He quickly put the drugs safely away in the refrigerator and assured himself again that his patient was comfortable and out of danger.

Zebulon left the surgery room followed by his ever present companion, Bridget. She spoke first. "Zeb, you really must look at that disc again. And read that note. It's important."

His fingers reached for the little disc that he'd dropped into his pocket. It was still there. He looked at it once again. It just looks like a four leaf clover, he thought. But it's a shamrock—one with four leaves. I never heard of such a thing. He knew that the national emblem of Ireland was a three-leaved cloverlike plant, but a four leaf clover was rare indeed.

"Come on, Zeb. Let's read the letter that came with it," pleaded Bridget.

"Okay, Bridget," he said at last.

The opened box was still on his desk. It smelled of a perfume that he dimly remembered. He took the note from the box and read it aloud:

Dear Dr. Zebulon,

You've been so kind to me and my beloved Persian cat, Abdullah, that I wanted to show my gratitude. I saw this amulet in an Irish folk market and felt you should have it. They say that as long as it is on your body you will be able to understand dog language. You almost could before. Now it'll be true.

                      Please, I do hope you enjoy it,
                      As ever,
                      Mary Burke

"Really, Zeb! That's great." Bridget said approvingly.

Little did Mary Burke realize that Dr. Zebulon had already attained the dog's vernacular. Zeb's intelligent face broke into a sardonic smile. "It sounds like a lot of balderdash to me, Bridget."

"Hey, we've been talking, don't forget that. It sounds like some kind of magic to me," Bridget nodded her beautifully shaped red head wisely. She'd been shocked at first when Zebulon returned from the Westminster Show with his ability to converse with her. But her astonishment was soon overcome with joy to know that she could talk with 'the one person in her life.'

"Well, don't forget I'm a scientist. This doesn't sound like anything I've heard of before."

Bridget answered. "There are some amazing things in the world such as thought transference and telepathy. My grandmother used to tell me lots of stuff."

"Everyone will think I'm crazy. We'll have to hush up about this."

"'It'll be our secret, but you'll be the greatest vet in the whole world," assured Bridget.

"Nobody in their right mind would believe this. How come you accept this?"

"Don't forget that I'm Irish. Pity you aren't." Bridget gave Zebulon a superior, teasing look. "In the country where my parents came from they say that if you wear a four-leaf shamrock you can talk the language of dogs as long as you wear it. As everyone knows, a three-leaf shamrock is the official emblem of Ireland but a four-leaf one is very rare and priceless. You're a lucky man, Doctor."

The amulet was a strikingly beautiful piece of jewelry. It had been dried by a new method that made it look freshly picked. Mounted in a crystal disc and hung on a golden chain, it would be worn forever by Dr. Zeb.

"I remember that Mary Burke's cat wasn't always really sick when she brought her to see you," Bridget added." Mary had a crush on you and you didn't even guess it."

"Yes, I suppose you're right," Zeb agreed. He bent his long body down to Bridget.

"I'm just a logical old scientist who depends on three dimensions and five senses. But you're right. I never could find much wrong with that cat. Abdullah ate many a sugar pill."

"Yeah, Mary was gone on you.

"That's enough, Bridget. Back to work."

They trudged back to the white-tiled surgery where the injured dog waited.

Zebulon leaned closer to the patient and said in a quiet and calm voice, "I'm sorry, fellow. The young man who brought you in didn't know you. We've got to find out where you live and who your humans are."

"My name's Jerry," came the answer in a faltering voice. The little dog looked at the doctor, amazed that they were actually talking together. "I live over on Greenbrier Avenue with the Edgertons."

"I'd better give them a call. They're probably looking for you." said Dr. Zebulon.

He sat down at his desk, still feeling shaky because of his recently-acquired ability to talk to dogs. Am I hearing voices? He wondered. Yes, I certainly am. After obtaining the number from the information operator, he dialed the Edgerton number with shaking fingers.

"Yes? Came a woman's voice.

"Mrs. Edgerton?"

"That's right."

"This is Dr. Jacob Zebulon, the veterinarian. We have your dog Jerry here at my hospital. He was hit by a car."

"Oh, no!" Mrs. Edgerton interrupted shrilly.

"Don't worry. I've treated him. His injuries were bad, but not critical. He is going to be all right." He almost told her that Jerry had insisted that she be called, and scolded himself - "Zeb, you're really nuts."

"Oh, doctor!" The lady's voice rose higher. "Thank the Lord! I've been worried sick about him. Can I come over?"

"Not just yet," Zeb cautioned her. "I must keep him under observation for a while. Accident injuries are difficult, you know." Then to calm the frightened woman, he added, "You can come when he feels better. So do call me tomorrow and lets hope for the best."

"Oh, thank you, doctor," she breathed. Then, after a pause: "How on earth did you know to call me? We haven't lived here long enough to get a name tag for him."

"Oh," Zebulon said lamely, "A friend told me." He quickly hung up the telephone and sank limply into his big leather chair. He shook his head to clear it as Bridget shoved her nose against his hand.

"Let's talk," she said.

"Later. First we've got to put Jerry to bed for the night."

Jerry's dreamy brown eyes followed Zebulon as he worked. "I don't remember much about this. I saw a car coming lickety-split and tried my damnedest to get to the curb. I guess I didn't make it."

"No, you didn't" said Zebulon.

"Well, I sure do thank you for looking after me, and also whoever brought me in."

"Right," Zebulon said. "I was glad to help. Now to bed with you."

The doctor placed Jerry on an electric heating pad and covered him with a blanket in a freshly scrubbed cage. He filled a dish with water. Then, he wrote Jerry's full name- Jerry Edgerton, complete with a full medical history, on a card and fitted it to a plate at the front of the cage. Next he quickly wrote a history of the injuries and further treatment for the information of the night staff.

"I'm leaving you now," Zeb told Jerry. "Try to have a good sleep. Dr. Peters is on duty tonight and if you need anything just grunt real loud and he'll come running."

"Okay. Thanks again, Doctor, for saving my life."

Zebulon gently closed the door behind him and returned to his office. He pulled the disc from his pocket and looked at it again.

"It looks like an ordinary four-leaf clover."

"Not exactly. It may look like one, but it isn't."

"Yeah?"

"That's a genuine, Irish four-leaf shamrock, Zeb. I've only seen a few of them. They're very rare and mighty valuable. Most shamrocks in Ireland are three-leaved."

"Never heard of them," Zeb said shaking his head.

"Well, they're hard to find," Bridget explained. "It's funny about Mary Burke. She's a cat person. But this won't let you talk to cats.

I'll help you out them. My ancestors knew about these things and they knew that you could talk to dogs if you wore one. You must believe me."

"As of today I believe you. Now let's tell Tyler good night and give him final instructions."

Zebulon changed into a tweed jacket and they went to Tyler's cottage. Again he wondered why this man had left Jamaica and come to such a little town. As they got into Zeb's car Bridget settled down comfortably besides him in the front seat. Zebulon drove down the steep driveway that was lined with its false red fire hydrants and rose bushes.

He was especially proud of the hydrants since his patients frequently lifted their legs and deposited their scents on them. At the bottom of the hill, they were on the main road of Chapel Hill, Franklin Street, driving toward a little sandwich bar.

The street was vacant except for a pair of college students strolling hand in hand up the road towards town. Inside the little sandwich bar, Zeb ordered two hamburgers, one with onions, one without. Bridget didn't like onions. They enjoyed their meal, then drove to Zebulon's cottage behind the hospital. The doctor pulled the disc from his pocket again and said. "I'll go to Charlie Beatty's store and get a chain for it tomorrow, so I can wear it around my neck."

"Good," Bridget said. "And you jolly well better wear it all the time. I mean all the time!"

"Okay, boss, okay. All the time."

When they arrived at the cottage, Zeb sat down with a copy of a new book he'd recently acquired and was soon engrossed in the fascinating subject of dog behavior. The first chapter of the book, Training Problem Dogs, brought a smile to Zebulon~s face. It said: *Most dogs are not born problem dogs but become that way as a result of human mismanagement.* "How true," he thought to himself. Turning to Bridget, he told her of the statement in the book about human mishandling of their pets, to which she readily agreed. He then added, "However I want you to know that I also know that some of you dogs are headstrong and contrary. You figure out what we owners want and then you do the opposite." Bridget shook her head to show her disagreement.

Zebulon leaned back in his chair and put his feet up on a large ottoman. After a short period of reading, he dozed. He was awakened by a ringing telephone. It was Dr. Peters advising him that it might be necessary for him to take a look at Shelia, the Irish Setter because she had not produced any puppies after being in heavy labor for quite a while. He told Peters he would be right down and decided to call Tyler in case they needed his help.—No rest for the weary, thought Zebulon.

He hurried to the recovery room, where the hurt dog, Jerry, was lying quietly in a cage. Nearby in an enormous cardboard box was one of the most beautiful Irish Setters he had ever seen. Her swollen belly made him fairly ache to help get those puppies out into the world. She had been in labor several hours. Her eyes, dulled with pain and bewilderment at the thing happening to her, said plainly, "Can't you help me?" Zebulon leaned over the box, and with rubber gloves, examined her internally. "Yep, just as I suspected, a breech presentation."

"Dr. Peters, I'm afraid we'll have to do a Caesarian operation. Let's get everything ready. We have to get all those puppies out of her. One of them is trying to get out butt first and he's stuck in the pelvic canal." He leaned over the setter and spoke in a low, soothing voice, "Sheila, now don't you worry, we'll have your babies out in a short time. I'm going to give you some shots to relax you and we'll get you ready for surgery," He gently rubbed the places penetrated by the needle. The big dog gave the doctor a grateful, although weak, wag of her tail - a vote of confidence. Tyler arrived and the three of them placed the waiting mother on the prep table. "Easy now," he said, stroking her beautiful head, "over you go, Shelia. Good girl." They rolled her on her back. She scarcely seemed to feel the electric clipper as he shaved her abdomen. Then one of the puppies kicked, kicked hard. Zebulon exclaimed," Although I've often had the experience it never fails to thrill me. One of those little Irish fellows is in a hurry to get out now."

Dr. Louis Vine, D.V.M.

Dr. Peters administered the anesthesia by passing a tube down her trachea and the gas soon had her in dreamland.—Now the incision.

This was Shelia's first litter. A champion in her own right, she had been bred to one of the finest Irish Setters in the country. She and her puppies were worth all the effort and skill he could give to them. The thought passed briefly through his mind as he reached for an instrument, *that poor little mutt hit by a car in the other room will get everything I can give him, too.* Then he forgot all else in the struggle to bring those small creatures into the world.

He handed the first puppy over to Tyler. "There's the troublemaker," he murmured. As he had supposed would be the case, the breech pup was too large to pass through Shelia's pelvis. Tyler received the puppy, rubbed off the surrounding sac, held the tiny body head down, and gave it a shake.

An outcry soon told them that another Irish Setter would live to make the world a richer place. He placed the puppy in a makeshift incubator lined with electric heating pads to keep the newborns warm and cozy until their mother was ready to feed them. There were 10 more puppies. These would have come into the world head first, as they were supposed to. One by one they were rubbed, held head down, and given a shake. Each responded with a yelp. Each umbilical cord was ligated with suture material. At last it was all over. Tyler cleaned up the surgery while Zebulon did the same for himself. He looked into the incubator. Eleven tiny blind puppies with tags for ears and buds for tails, no larger than Vienna rolls, but every one containing the promise of vigorous doghood. Each puppy was bedded down where it was soft and warm to wait for mother to come back from wherever the anesthetic had wafted her.

"I'll stay with them until Shelia regains consciousness," Zebulon told the men. "I want to keep my eye on that injured dog, Jerry, anyway. And I also want to watch the Schnauzer who swallowed the corsage pin. Thank you for coming. And good night."

Tyler responded by saying, "I'll check her later after you leave." Zebulon nodded his head in appreciation.

With a "good night, Doc," they were gone. Soft little sounds came from the incubator. He checked the injured dog Jerry and glanced at the Schnauzer, Griffin Lou, usually gay but just now shaky and unhappy after having had a corsage pin dredged out of her throat. Maybe she won't be so eager and anxious to gulp down orchids when they're really meant to grace the trim bosom of the lady of the house.

Then he looked at Shelia. Beautiful Shelia heard nothing, though. She was still in some far-off place where puppies, head first or tail first, were of no concern. Zebulon sat in the near darkness, surrounded by dogs who depended on him for curing their sickness and keeping them alive.

After a long time of thinking quietly he arose and slowly went around the different rooms, turning out most of the lights. As always when he was there late at night, he was deeply aware of the hospital's night atmosphere. During the daylight hours there is excitement about the place. The boarding kennel dogs bark with vigor. There is the constant coming and going in the waiting room, where both dogs and humans talk things over and wonder what will happen when their turn comes to be seen. Cars, large and small and of all ages and in every conceivable condition, arrive and depart from the parking spaces.

There are the serious moments in surgery; the joyful times when dog and human are reunited after an absence of days or weeks; the tragedy of emergency cases; the sadness of a beloved pet's death. From early morning to dusk there is movement and sound and sometimes fury. But it is quite a different story as one day merges into another. Then the sick dog lies still in his cage. The boarder sleeps, dreaming perhaps of that absent one-person-in-the-world. The lights burn low and, all too often, life burns low, too.

The clock over at the University struck the hour. Twelve strokes. "I'd better take a look at the new family."

Shelia was awake and looking around for her puppies. She heard their crying in the nearby box. Her maternal instincts began to take over. Zebulon picked up each puppy, one by one, and put them on her breasts. Hungrily they attacked a waiting nipple that was already dripping with milk. Eventually, all eleven pups were scrambling for their milk. Meanwhile, mother licked and cleaned each pup. "Too many of them to nurse, I'm afraid, girl," he told her. "You really went overboard on this thing, didn't you? Never mind, we'll fix up a good formula that'll take care of everything and help you out."

As if she understood the problem, Shelia gave an encouraging wave of her plumy tail. When you think of it, a tail is rather a remarkable thing, Zebulon mused. The dog does so much with it. It can be a badge of courage; a battle flag; a meek sign of surrender; and can express more eloquently than any words, welcome, gratitude, or love. One misconception that he tries to clear up is that a wagging tail means a dog is happy. Not always. If the tail wags high and is arched slightly over the back, the dog is saying, "I'm top dog, and I'll fight to prove it."

Meanwhile, the repentant ingester of corsage pins has perked up. She lifts her head and looks. A while back she was swearing at Zebulon and his sheaf of instruments, but she seems to feel more normal now. Her eyes are friendly as she watches him. She is thinking things over. What is there in that venerable argument that a dog can read your innermost thoughts and judge you by them? Zebulon shrugged his shoulders. He didn't know the answer, either.

He had just finished his chores as the big university clock informed a sleeping and uninterested town that it was one o'clock. It marked the small hours of the night when life ebbs low. He stood by the injured dog's cage. The spaniel had not moved. His eyes sought Zebulon and again he saw a small dog with pleading eyes that had looked in vain for kindness and understanding. He remembered another small dog years ago whose fate had done more to set the course of his life than any single factor. As Zebulon rubbed the spaniel's ear, the brown eyes closed, but not before the dog's tail had given a gallant, if feeble, thump.

When Zebulon was a young lad in Brooklyn, he had seen a luckless mongrel run down by a speeding car. A crowd had gathered quickly. The dog had pleaded for help with his eyes. But a burly policeman, hardened by many accidents, had sent a bullet between the anguished brown eyes of the injured dog. It was at that moment that Zebulon swore that he would become a veterinarian. So after a baccalaureate degree, magna cure laude, and a D.V.M., he came to Chapel Hill to assist Dr. Noland, and finally to own the hospital.

As usual when Zebulon had time to meditate, his thoughts went to his patients and their relations with their owners. This night, with three critically ill dogs to care for, was no different. *Here I sit in the recovery room of my hospital on the edge of town. It's so late at night that it's almost early, but I'm here where I need to be, watching, hoping that my patient will be all right after the Caesarian she underwent at my hand.*

It has been my observation that certain people have a much closer relationship—kinship is perhaps a better word—with dogs than the majority. I'll go farther and say this special kinship extends to almost any kind of animal. It may be that these are what I think of as essentially 'lonely' people. I don't mean 'lonesome.' Most who are in this category like to be with others. At the same time they are more than content to have no other companionship than that of a dog, or some other animal. This relationship may be especially close between the person and one certain dog, or cat, and not exist at all where other dogs and cats are concerned. For the most part, though, it is communication between the person and all dogs and cats.

When such a person comes to me with me with a very sick dog or cat, I feel that I must do everything in my power, not only for the animal but for the owner. The callous person would say that no one should permit a dog or cat to mean so much. The truth of the matter is that he cannot help himself. Probably I should say 'herself,' for in many cases the affected one is a woman. She may be a widow, or childless, or in some situation where a human being cannot fill the place in her affections that a dog or cat can. Or she may simply be one of those who is born with a special understanding of and feeling for animals. Monetary value does not enter into it. I've known of cases where a dog or cat may not be worth five dollars, but it is invaluable so far as its owner *is concerned.*

The other day, for instance, a man and his wife brought in a small mongrel dog. It didn't take much examining to determine that the trouble was bronchial pneumonia. As I prepared medication I glanced at the couple, standing together beside the table. They were middle-aged and plain country people. But the look both of them gave the suffering animal was filled with significance for me. I recognized it as that special one reserved for a greatly loved dog.

"Will she be all right, Doctor?" asked the woman.

The man let his eyes speak for him.

"She'll need special nursing care, Mrs. Plummet," I replied "I wonder if you wouldn't like to leave her in the hospital for a few days."

"No." The man's voice was harsh with something he was trying to hold back. "I mean-the wife and I'll nurse her. She'll get good care."

Ordinarily I should prefer to have such a case under my personal supervision, at least for a few days. I knew, though, that this was one of the cases involving more than the dog. To the two people before me she had brought not only a return to a good life, but a return of a self-respect they had supposed gone forever. Josephine had done for them what no amount of preaching or lecturing or scolding could ever do. And she did it in her own doggy way, by giving them all the love a dog can bestow—by requiring of them love and care in return.

They had been alcoholics for years. I'd known them because George Plummet had done odd jobs for me around the place. They were childless and poor. Life was drab and becoming more so. Like many another person with few, if any, inner resources they began drinking. They drifted apart. The farther they drifted the harder they drank. Then, a year or so ago, they found a small nondescript dog. The starved creature followed them home. The man threw it some food. Soon it came on the porch. Then into the house.

Once again those two human derelicts knew what it meant to have a living being look upon them with admiration. Once again they felt the urge to take on responsibility. Within six months they found that other urge, that to drink until everything became nothing, was fast disappearing. They were needed! To Josephine went all the affection they had held back for so many years. She was more than a mongrel dog to this man and woman. She was a way life. And now she was desperately sick. No, they wouldn't leave her to be nursed by others. This was one time, I knew, that to cure my patient I must let her go. I gave directions as to her care. Josephine's two bright eyes saw *nothing but her beloved human companions. She knew they would not fail her. And they did not.*

Finally, when Zebulon returned to reality from his reverie, he saw that the mother and her brood were content and out of danger, he headed for his cottage to rest his weary bones. Zebulon prepared a cup of coffee and carried it to his favorite comfortable chair, propping his feet on an ottoman. Bridget promptly took possession of his lap in an attentive position. They were both ready for some quality time with each other.

CHAPTER II

A mocking-bird singing noisily under Zeb's bedroom window woke him much too early the next morning. He sighed, stretched lazily and decided that he might as well get up. The injured Jerry had been in his thoughts much of the night and his sleep had been restless. He stepped out of the warm bed onto a chilly floor and reached for a robe. Then to the kitchen to make coffee. A plate of breakfast for Bridget and strong hot coffee for Zeb were the morning ritual. Both came awake. Soon, he opened the door and they went into the misty woods on their way to the hospital.

The reception room was dimly lighted when he entered. Chips, a small South American Owl monkey, greeted him from his tall wrought-iron cage in the corner of the room. Chips had become quite popular and famous among the clients entering the veterinary hospital. They brought him all kinds of fruit and other goodies, but his favorite was chewing gum. He relished the taste of all kinds of sticky stuff but was partial to bubble gum. Chip's picture was in the Chapel Hill Newspaper quite often and many articles appeared about him. He was definitely a town character.

When Zeb entered the room, Chips scrambled towards him and pursed his lips to receive his daily morning kiss. "Good morning, old boy," he said, and kissed him back. Chips looked as if he would like to speak. Maybe some day, Zeb thought, I'll be able to speak to cats, monkeys and all other animals.

The doctor handed him a bright yellow pear and he and Bridget went on their way to the recovery room.

"Good morning, Jerry," the doctor said.

Jerry opened sleepy brown eyes and looked up at Zeb. "Hi," he murmured.

"How do you feel this morning?" Zebulon asked with real concern.

"Well, I just woke up. But I think I'm better. But my chest hurts pretty bad, doctor."

"Yes. You'll have to take it easy for a while. Sorry, but you've got some broken ribs, and internal bruising." He gave Jerry a gentle pat on the head. "Now let me look you over. Open your mouth, please." Zebulon touched the disc in his pocket in gratitude. Jerry opened his mouth. "Well, you've more color in your gums. And your pulse is normal. Great! You've done better than I'd hoped for." He was glad to comfort the little dog. "But let's lie quietly for another day and see what happens. Okay?"

"If you insist. I won't mind a little peace and quiet," Jerry said. "My missy, Mrs. Edgerton is nice, but she's a talker and drives me crazy with all her baby talk. I'm her only child- so she says- and treats me as one. That's why I went for a run yesterday, to get away from it all for a while and do what a male does naturally- look for bitches in heat."

"I understand. All that sweet baby talk can be hard to take sometimes."

Zebulon turned towards Sheila and her eleven hungry offspring. All of them were fast asleep. He knew that a quiet puppy was a contented one with a full stomach and so all was well with the new Irish Setter puppies. Sheila waved her tail to let him know that she appreciated what he did for her. The Schnauzer that ingested the corsage pin was also up on its feet and barking for some attention. Zeb wanted to pat himself on the back for a night well spent saving three critically ill patients.

He finished his rounds of the surgical ward and went on to check the sick dogs in the other rooms. He stopped at a squeaky clean cage. "Good morning, Hero," he said to a doleful looking German Shepherd inside.

At that moment Nurse Lib Nelson came into the room. She was smart, but with no imagination. He hushed at once. He wasn't sure that she would understand his predicament of being able to converse with dogs. He decided that he would be careful of who knew about his new-found ability.

Lib was a well-built woman. He thought of her as motherly looking. She was his gifted medical technician. Zebulon quickly gave her a list of the coming day's duties. She left.

Zeb turned back to the German Shepherd. "Good morning again, Hero," he said. "Your fever's down. How do you feel?"

"Oh, better Doc, much better." Hero showed no surprise that he and Zeb were speaking. "Good enough to let you in on something kinda funny. I'm sure glad you've learned to talk like me. Bridget broke the news to me."

"Oh?"

"Yeah, Doc, you may not believe this. My human isn't exactly a heavy thinker," Hero said. "You remember, you told her you needed a urine specimen to find out what was wrong with my kidneys."

"Yes, I remember."

"Well, my lady spent several days following me around with a quart jar in her hands. Every time I lifted my leg, she'd get right under me with a jar. And she didn't stop until she'd caught about a quart of it."

"Yes. I know that lady." Zebulon tried not to chuckle.

"It was humiliating- embarrassing- terrible," Hero said. "Just how much of that stuff did you really need?"

"Oh, just a few ounces." Again Zebulon stifled a laugh. "Don't let it bother you. That kind of thing brightens an otherwise dull day."

Zeb's last patient was a Collie who lay sprawled out in an oversized cage. "You're looking better today, Mac," the doctor said.

The big dog looked up at Zebulon, "I sure hope so, Doc. But I still feel pretty awful. That mean old stomach pump you used made me sicker than the stuff I ate."

"Sorry. But if you insist on eating your lady's nylons, I'll have to do it again." The Collie quivered. "I don't know why I do that. I just get so hungry for nylon that I can't resist eating it!"

"You'd better learn to withstand your desire," Zebulon spoke almost angrily. "You were on the verge of gangrene of the bowels when they brought you to see me. Try eating bread and gravy for a change."

Zebulon and Bridget returned to the office. Norris Martin, the receptionist, came swishing in wearing a very short blue skirt that exposed handsome legs in the sheerest of hose, and high-heeled sandals of the same shade of blue. She always wore matched outfits. Yesterday everything had been in shocking pink. Zebulon smiled broadly, enjoying her good looks. She is in her early 30's but her clothes and makeup are designed for the early 20's. Norris had fixed her sights on Jacob Zebulon. But they had nothing in common—so it was hopeless. Zeb reads and likes Russian music. Norris reads only romances and listens to rock and roll. However, Norris is a charming young woman and makes the patients and their humans feel very important and sees that they are shuffled in and out of the examining rooms as efficiently as possible.

"You're going to have a full day, doctor," she announced. "Lots of old clients have called and a special lady- a Miss Predino."

With the mention of Sallie Predino's name, Zeb smiled and a warm sensation rumbled through his body. Ever since the Westminster Dog Show in New York a few months ago, Sallie and he had been dating regularly. The 47- year-old bachelor had fallen in love.

"That's great," Zebulon responded, thinking more of Sallie than the other clients. "Bridget and I are going out for a late breakfast, Norris. Be back soon." They left by the front door, through the reception room lined with pictures of cats and dogs and a large oil portrait of the good doctor holding two dogs. One of his admirers, a talented artist, had painted this tribute to him. Norris followed them and gently closed the door.

The ride into town was pleasant. The mist had lifted and the morning air was fresh and clean. Beautifully kept old houses lined the street. Flowering bushes grew lush at the edges of neatly trimmed green lawns. Oh, so peaceful, thought Zebulon. Much of the morning traffic was headed towards the University where most Chapel Hill residents worked. The academic atmosphere nurtured its inhabitants' historical and cultural pursuits. And educated their young. As usual, students were walking, hand in hand, toward the campus and their morning classes.

The University of North Carolina had many famous alumni but Zebulon knew a few personally because they brought their pets to his hospital. Betty Smith of "Tree Grows in Brooklyn" fame and Thomas Wolfe of "You Can Go Home Again" were just a few celebrated authors to frequent the streets of Chapel Hill. Kay Kyser, the famed bandleader, was the alumnus who so aptly named Chapel Hill-"The Southern Part Of Heaven." James Taylor, the singing sensation was reared in Chapel Hill where his father was a doctor on the University staff. Andy Griffith was another famous alumnus who made the big time.

Zebulon saw the big sign, Matt's Pub, ahead and turned into the parking lot. The doctor was no friend of Matt Dye, but he thought that the restaurant served the best breakfast in town. The scrambled eggs were creamy and the toast crisp—and there was real butter. Matt scorned a local law and permitted Bridget to join Zebulon at the table.

Matt had been deep in conversation with a good looking dark-skinned cashier when the two entered. After he pointed Zebulon to a table, he hurried back to continue whispering to her. Zebulon remembered something he'd heard about Matt- how he's been absent from Chapel Hill for several years. Matt said he'd been in the West Indies on business; but rumor had it that he was hiding from the law. Recently, Matt had begun breeding dogs. But, since he'd never used Zebulon for his professional services, the doctor had never seen his kennels.

Their table, this morning, gave them a view of the whole room. The dark, timbered ceiling held a long rack of brown kegs. The bar across the room sparkled with all the bottles necessary for mixing drinks. The paneled wall facing the bar showed a handsome tapestry of an English hunter killing a deer with bow and arrow. Blood flowed from the deer's mouth. Bridget looked away.

A mix of early customers lingered over coffee. Some were students in ancient jeans and untidy hair. Others were neat looking business men and workmen. Bridget thought a couple of them looked like thugs and whispered to Zebulon. "His customers are a strange bunch."

As the two finished their eggs and country ham, Matt Dye strolled over. "Here's another plate of biscuits," he began. "Stick around a minute," he drawled in a scratchy baritone voice that hurt Bridget's ears. "I'd like to talk with you. I'm always glad to see you and that fine dog of yours."

"I can't do it. Sorry. I'm already late. Gotta go," Zebulon said crisply. He brushed his tawny hair out of his eyes and looked directly into Matt's craggy face.

Talking With The Dogs

"I often jog past your place," Matt went on, unperturbed. "Next time, I'll drop in."

"Call Norris Martin for an appointment. Good day." Zebulon knew that he sounded curt and Bridget nudged his hand with her cold nose.

Outside the pub, Bridget looked at Zebulon with soulful brown eyes and said, "That's a weird man."

"You're right. What do you suppose he wants?"

Bridget used her extra sensory knowledge and said. "I don't know what he wants. But he is weird—that's the only word I know for it. I also have the feeling that he is not trustworthy." She nodded her head wisely. "Call it canine intuition."

****

Charlie Beatty, the jeweler, showed Zeb several handsome chains. He chose a lean one of intertwined gold and silver links and quickly strung his shamrock amulet on it. The jeweler watched with curiosity showing in his brown eyes.

"That's a mighty strange little thing," he finally said. "What exactly is it?"

"It's something a client gave to me. I thought I'd enjoy wearing it." Zebulon fastened the clasp of the chain, tucked the shamrock inside his shirt and left the jewelry store.

"Don't ever forget to wear that," Bridget warned him as they climbed into the car.

The usual syrupy music and the babble of voices greeted him as he opened the door of the hospital. He fervently hoped that no unpleasant surprises would spoil his day. He was preparing to see the routinely ill patients and their two footed companions. Most of those waiting were old friends; a blind student from the University, his uncomplaining Seeing Eye dog at his feet; a faculty member, with a bouncy Boston terrier sitting wide-eyed on his knee; a prominent town businessman, trying to soothe a shivering Boxer. The only stranger was a large woman with a Cocker Spaniel. As he entered the waiting room, all the human and canine eyes turned towards him. The big woman with the spaniel stroked the dog's soft ears. The others, it seemed to him, all drew nearer to their own dogs.

He wondered again, as he had so often during the years, which were really his patients. In most instances the anxiety in the dogs' eyes was reflected in those of their owners. Owners? Does one really own a dog?

Zebulon didn't think so. It had always been his feeling that in any good relationship there is no thought of indebtedness. Whether it be friendship, or marriage, or the sometimes very close bond of dog and man, whatever is given is given freely and with love.

Zebulon proceeded to see his waiting patients. First came Gypsy, the blind boy's dog, who had a bad throat. "All right now, girl," he said to her, putting his head close to Gypsy's. "This won't bother you much and soon you'll feel a lot better." Quickly he gave the antibiotic injection, withdrew the needle, and rubbed the sore place with his hand very tenderly. Then Professor Randolph's Boston terrier, with a tiny spot of fungus showing at the base of his tail. Mr. Morgan's Boxer's shivering stopped when Zebulon examined the injured foot with a broken toe. An X-ray showed the new patient, a cocker spaniel, to have an intestinal obstruction. She would have to spend the night for an enema to correct the impaction.

Zebulon reflected on all the different types of dogs and their reactions to being in a veterinary hospital. Most dogs going into a clinic are apprehensive, to say the least. Some are downright scared of what might happen to them. Then he thought, I feel the same way when I go to the dentist. As for the dogs, there is sometimes the exception, the extrovert who is fazed by nothing and wants to be the center of attraction. One of these is a big female Samoyed named Trina. As you know, an examining table is high enough so that it is convenient for the veterinarian's use. As a rule, the patients shy away from it. Some of them, when being placed on it, try their best to get down again. But not Trina. When she is taken into an examining room, she braces herself. Then with a mighty leap, she jumps on the table without any assistance whatever and is ready for the doctor's ministrations.

Norris Martin came to his office to tell him that his friend, Sallie Predino, was waiting for him. "Now I know why you like her, Doctor," she assured him. "She's a beauty."

"I bet Mary Burke wouldn't like her then," quipped Bridget.

"Beautiful women aren't so rare here in Chapel Hill," Zebulon said.

"You just wait till you see her new dog. It's probably the ugliest dog in Christendom." Norris added.

"Where will you put them?"

"In room one."

"Okay."

Zebulon waited impatiently beside the examination table until the door opened. In walked a tall, willowy woman who had a cap of blonde curly hair that lit up the room and skin like peach petals. Her hair shone like a rosey sunset over her fair skin. Her eyes were so blue that it almost hurt Zebulon to look at them. He felt exhilarated and charged with electricity every time he looked at Sallie Predino.

The red leash in her hand held a classically ugly copper-colored dog, dressed in a black leather collar with gold workings. Zebulon saw at once that the dog was a Chinese Shar Pei and probably priceless. Its skin was wrinkled like a suit of ill-fitting clothing. Its face was like that of the better class of bulldog, tiny eyes peering out from between the wrinkles. A beautiful example of a rare and expensive breed. Zebulon knew that Shar Peis were smuggled out of China so that the world could share the wonders of this exotic breed. The more wrinkles the dog exhibited, the more of a perfect specimen it was considered.

Zebulon's eyes finally left the dog and he looked at Sallie. He looked again. He felt tingling sensations up and down his back. Bridget could read his thoughts. She felt his excitement. "Oh God," she thought, "I'm afraid he's going to go all sloppy."

After giving the expected kiss to the doctor, Sallie exclaimed, "This is Lili Tu, my new dog that my uncle gave me. As you know, Collies are my preferred breed but I didn't want to hurt Uncle Milt's feeling by refusing to accept one of his prized possessions as a gift. He raises these dogs and has lots of luck in dog shows with his brood."

"It's so wonderful to see you again," stammered the doctor. "I haven't seen you for such a long time. I believe it was two nights ago."

"How quickly they forget," giggled Sallie.

"Sallie, that's a spectacular dog that you have there. Is she sick? How can I help you with her?"

"What I want is for you to spay Lili Tu," Sallie simply stated.

Zeb looked at the hideously expensive dog and his eyes grew wide. "Oh, no!" he said. "You mustn't do that. Don't even think of spaying this dog. She can be a champion in the show ring. She can have puppies that will bring you lots of money."

"But Jacob, ugly little puppies full of wrinkles?" she protested.

Bridget looked up in surprise after hearing her call him Jacob. Bridget knew that only Zeb's mother called him Jacob. Hearing this young lady call him by his given name made Bridget finally realize that he was falling for her. He was allowing this woman to call him Jacob. She admitted this fact to herself with a twinge of jealousy. She had always been Zebulon's first love. Now she was being replaced by someone else. While she was brooding over this fact, Zebulon continued the conversation about the new puppy.

"Beauty's in the eye of the beholder. She's a fine specimen. And she's an unusual color—that copper tint is rare. Most Shar Peis are a softer beige."

"To be honest with you Jacob, when I first saw this little dog, she looked as if she was wearing a suit of long scratchy underwear several sizes too large for her, had wrinkles beyond measure, and little slits of almond-shaped eyes. However, even though I've only had Lili Tu for a few days now, I've fallen for her sweet disposition. She's a darling dog. I guess I'll get used to all those wrinkles. And maybe you're right. Maybe she is valuable," Sallie finally agreed. "There's a man here who's been making an awful nuisance of himself ever since I got her.

"Oh?"

"Yes, he owns a restaurant. He's been following us when we go walking. I despise him. He frightens me. I try to avoid him. But he keeps turning up."

"You can't mean Matt Dye?"

"Yes, that's his name. How did you guess?" Sallie asked in surprise. "Yes. One day he offered to buy her from me for three hundred dollars."

"Three hundred dollars!" Zebulon was horrified. "That's a pittance for your dog."

"I told you that man was a crook," Bridget whispered.

"Yes? Well, even if it was a lot of money, I couldn't sell Lili Tu. My Uncle Milt gave her to me." Sallie explained.

Lili Tu cozied up to Bridget for a private conversation. "A dog friend told me that Mr. Dye raises champion dogs. And he seems to like my style." She noticed that Zebulon had seemed to understand her and turned a surprised face to Bridget. "Can he understand me?" Bridget replied proudly, "He most certainly can. Everything you say.".

Sallie looked at the two dogs. "What do you suppose they're whining about?"

"I'll tell you later," Zebulon said laughingly. He brushed his stubborn forelock out of his eyes. He had already told Sallie of his new-found ability to understand the vernacular of the dog several months before at the Westminster Dog Show. She and his friend Judge Clancy were the only people in the world who knew his secret. Many people were suspicious that Dr. Zebulon had a very unusual close relationship with dogs but since his success rate in treating patients was so high, they put up with his eccentricities. However, they all agreed that he was a veterinarian to whom all dogs were personalities as well as patients.

"Let me make a suggestion. Leave Lili Tu with me tonight. I'll give her a thorough examination, any shots she might need, all of that. Then we'll plan her diet. You may come back tomorrow to pick her up and we'll have another talk about her. Be sure to leave her health chart with me."

"That sounds all right," Sallie agreed. "I'll drop by after school. As you know, besides raising Collies, I teach music at the University."

"Okay. See you then." He gave her a goodbye kiss as a parting gesture. Bridget looked at Lili Tu in disgust.

Dr. Louis Vine, D.V.M.

Zebulon knew how to win a dog's affection real quickly. He opened a can of beef stew and put a large platter in front of Lili Tu. She responded by circling the dish dubiously, first clockwise and then counter-clockwise, before commencing to nibble.

"I suppose you'd prefer a rare filet mignon," Zebulon said.

Lili Tu looked at him while her long pink tongue licked first one side of her muzzle, then the other. She managed to say between gulps, "This will do, thank you."

****

Zebulon's last client was a local trumpet player accompanied by his little terrier, Danny. He complained that his dog had developed the shakes. "Every time I bring out my horn, he begins to tremble."

The doctor stood over the little dog, who muttered under his breath, "Have you ever been shut up in a little room with a blatting horn?" he asked. "It's enough to shake your teeth loose. He's busting my ear drums."

Zebulon then turned to the horn player and asked. "Have you ever tried shutting Danny out of the room when you practice?"

Danny looked at Zebulon in astonishment. This man sounded as he'd understood everything the little dog had said.

"No," responded the horn player. "He goes everywhere with me."

You must realize how sensitive dog's ears are."

"You may be right. The old horn doesn't exactly whisper."

Zebulon looked sternly into the man's questioning eyes. "If the horn sounds loud to you, you must realize that it sounds ten times as loud to Danny. It's driving him crazy. Why don't you practice away from him? Are you willing to try that? I believe that if you do, his nervousness will disappear."

"Oh, sure. I'll try anything. He's gotten so he jumps even if I slam a door. I'll try anything that you think might help." He seemed to feel consoled as they left.

"I'm beginning to be right hungry, Bridget. How about you?" Zebulon said as he went out the door. "Let's go to our humble cottage and have a snack."

Talking With The Dogs

They ate hungrily of sausage biscuits and coffee and returned to the hospital, feeling able to handle any problems. The short walk to the hospital and a close look at his beautiful rose bushes renewed Zeb's energy for the afternoon.

"Look, Zeb. There goes Matt Dye. He's jogging right past the hospital."

"I think he needs to exercise that pot belly of his," Zebulon said with a grin.

"Yeah. He probably swills plenty of beer," Bridget agreed.

"However," Zebulon said in a serious tone. "I'd just as soon that he stayed away from my hospital."

The doctor washed his hands in preparation to see patients. A great hubbub came from the reception room. He hurried to investigate.

Puggy, hysterical Mrs. Respass appeared to be performing some ancient tribal dance before Chips' cage. The waiting clients were chattering and trying to suppress laughter. Chips had snatched Mrs. Respess's long blonde wig from her head and revealed her tightly knotted brown hair beneath. Her crimson face worked in furious grimaces.

"I was trying to give the little beast a lollipop," she screamed at Zebulon, "and look—look..."

Zebulon stopped beside the monkey cage. Chips blinked at him innocently, in high good humor and cuddled his ringleted treasure. As the doctor neared, Chips backed to the farthest reach of the cage. Zebulon knew that pulling girls or women's hair was the only bad habit this lovable creature had. It was just fun and games for him.

"I wanted to buy a flea collar for my cat and bring Chips a present," Mrs. Respass sputtered. Tears splashed her fiery red cheeks.

"Give the lady back her hair, Chips," Zebulon ordered quietly. Chips looked at him, pleading to keep his prize.

"No Chips. Give it to me," he sternly said as he opened the front door of the cage. Zebulon put his head inside the cage and bent closer to the monkey. "Give me a kiss." It was a ritual for the past 15 years for Chips to give Zebulon a kiss every morning when he entered the hospital.

Chips pursed his lips, kissed Zebulon and wistfully held out the wig. The doctor handed it to Mrs. Respass.

"Well!" she cried, and ran awkwardly out the front door.

Zebulon sighed and went to the desk. "That's a client we've lost forever, Norris. Who's next?"

Everything was quiet. The canned music played another sugary tune. Zebulon went to an examination room where a Mrs. Morris waited for him with her large Airedale. The wife of history professor Tully Morris, she was well known about town. She sat, lost in the big office chair, quietly staring about the room and nervously stroked her pet, talking in a soft, apologetic voice.

"I'm truly embarrassed, Doctor," she began. "I hardly know how to begin."

"You can tell me anything, Mrs. Morris," Zebulon assured her. "You know that. Or you should know it. I like to make friends as well as save patients. But I don't think we've met before?"

"No. I've been going to Dr. Roberts. I think someone in town recommended him to my husband."

"I see. How may I help you?" Zebulon nodded.

"Well," she continued. "Dr. Roberts told me that Buster's illness was incurable. He's been getting older and failing, you see. So we thought he shouldn't be asked to suffer any more- that we should let Dr. Roberts put him to sleep."

"Thanks a whole heap," groaned old Buster. His voice was a muffled bark, and he looked surprised when he realized that Zebulon had understood him.

"So I left him with Dr. Roberts and went home," she said. "I felt terrible. I cried and cried. I couldn't bring myself to tell the family- thought I'd wait until the next day. But when I was cooking breakfast the next morning, I heard a scratching at the kitchen door and there was poor Buster. At first I couldn't believe my eyes."

"Poor Buster, indeed," repeated the Airedale. "You can say that again! I returned from the dead."

"Had Dr. Roberts really administered the injection?"

"Yes. He said he'd given him enough to kill a horse."

"Well, it gave me a nice refreshing nap," countered Buster sardonically.

"Mrs. Morris, it happens sometimes to every doctor. On rare occasion, a patient can be particularly resistant to the effect of a certain drug. That's probably what happened in this case. The toxic dose of barbiturate that Buster received was not sufficient to euthanize him. It's a scientific oddity that occasionally occurs in animal medicine."

"Let me keep Buster overnight and give him a thorough examination," Dr. Zebulon said in a very serious tone. "Let's give Buster every benefit of the doubt."

"Thanks Doc." Buster whispered. "I needed that."

"Okay, Doctor." She sounded grateful and gave the doctor a big smile. "I'll do anything to make it up to Buster. I'll never let him down ever again. I love him so much. Why, he's part of the family."

"Roberts is a lousy vet," Bridget whispered to Buster. "I'd call him a shoemaker, but that's an honest trade. He's a vet who is only out for the money, doesn't care much about animals, and is a blatant manipulator of people's affection for their pets."

"Really. He gave me the shot and put me in his back yard. Then he never looked at me again. So I woke up during the night and went home."

"Great," Bridget agreed. "And now Zeb's going to take care of you, so everything will be hunky-dory."

CHAPTER III

Tyler had gone home for the night and Dr. Peters was in sole charge of the hospital. They took turns on alternate nights to be available for any emergencies. Things appeared to be quiet. Dr. Zebulon had left the ailing dogs content in their cages and the cats were sleeping. Nevertheless, Dr. Peters made rounds once more and looked in each cage. Two of the cats were having a whispered discussion, but everyone else was lying quietly. The dogs appeared to be resting comfortably.

Dr. Ken Peters was young, but he prided himself on being a good vet and worked hard. Dr. Zebulon had discovered him mowing a neighbor's grass for pocket money and longing for a college education. With his usual generosity, Zeb helped him get his degree and brought him in to his own practice. Ken Peters was good looking, slender and clean shaven. His fair hair was cut rather long in a fashionable semi-bob. The younger clients asked for him, the ladies under thirty, that is.

Having completed one o'clock rounds, Dr. Peters headed for the office to get a cup of warming coffee. Suddenly his ears were assailed by barking that sounded more like human screams. A frightening sound was coming from the kennels. He ran towards the uproar. His rubber soled shoes gripped the slippery floor and he was in the kennel in seconds.

King, the pet of the hospital and long-time boarder, was fighting for his life. A German shepherd mixture, King was a large dog who had the run of the kennels since he boarded there most of the time. He never was confined to a cage. He was everybody's friend, animal and human alike. He was attacking a man who hovered above him with a large machete-type knife in his hands. When the intruder saw Dr. Peters enter the room, he turned quickly and jumped out the open window, from which he had entered.

The young doctor turned to follow. But when he pulled the door open to step outside he could see nothing. He could smell a stench in the air like the smell of hell. It was nothing that Dr. Peters had ever experienced- a combination of rotting cabbage and burned-out fire. He covered his tortured nostrils and pulled himself back into the room with King. He examined King and found several cuts on his body. He felt confident that he could treat the wounded dog, but aware of Zebulon's love for the old boarder, he thought it best to call him to treat the poor old boy.

Zeb came, stifling a yawn. His concern for King overrode his weariness, and worry about what might have happened to Lily Tu. He bent over King, murmuring words of sympathy. There were wounds in his neck and body with chunks of fur, skin and muscle torn loose. The two men carried the big dog to the surgery and laid him on the operating table. First, they gave him a shot to ease the pain and relax him. Then came the sutures after carefully cleaning the wounds. Each layer of muscle and skin were sutured by both men to expedite the procedure. It required many stitches and much careful thought. At last all the wounds were closed. King was a good patient.

Although slightly drowsy by the mild anesthetic given, he was completely aware of what was going on and occasionally looked up at the doctors working on him. Zeb talked to King while they worked, telling that he was going to be all right and expressing his pride in King's heroic defense of the hospital intrusion. Although Dr. Peters could hear Zebulon talking to King, he didn't realize that King understood everything that was being said to him. After all, most everybody talks to dogs he rationalized. He did himself so he he didn't think it improper for his idol, Dr. Zebulon, to hold such lengthy conversations with his patients.

When they were finished, Zeb gave the first in a series of antibiotic injections that would continue while King healed.

When the doctors had completed their surgery, they put the wounded dog into a clean cage. Zebulon asked Dr. Peters to check some of the dogs in the other wards. He wanted to be alone with King so that they could talk. After Dr. Peters left, Zeb told King that it was important not to disturb the tube in his neck as it was needed for drainage of the severe wounds. He then asked King to tell him what happened.

King answered slowly, still under the effects of the sedatives. "I heard strange noises in the kennel. When I went to investigate, I was met by a big ugly man carrying a big blade. I attacked him and was losing the battle until Peters appeared on the scene. That's when he fled out the back window. Lucky for me the doctor showed up. He saved my hide."

Zebulon told King to sleep and let the mending take over. He turned to Bridget and asked, "What do you think of this new development?" She murmured an ambiguous reply, her attention fixed on the bushes outside the window, where the large creature had recently been standing. She wanted to make sure the beast was gone for good.

Zeb decided to call Tyler into his office. "It's really late to have a conference, Tyler," he apologized. "But this is so serious. Have you any explanation for what has happened? Why would anyone try to break into our kennel?"

Tyler replied by saying, "I checked the window before I came here and it looks like someone pried it open with a knife. It smacks of the kind of thing a Voodoo man could make happen. I've heard of stranger things than this going on back in Jamaica where I come from. People say that you have to be a believer for a Voodoo man to work his magic on you. King didn't have any lessons in magic."

"So right. And those wounds were damnably real."

"Are there any Voodoo people here in Chapel Hill?"

"I can't answer that."

"I've heard that Matt Dye spent a few years in Jamaica some time ago."

"I've heard that too." Tyler looked puzzled. "But why would he do this?"

"He's been trying to buy Lili Tu. Remember? He seems obsessed with owning her."

Tyler replied, "Oh, I didn't know. Well, he could have taken some lessons from an Obeah man when he was in Jamaica. Perhaps he has learned West Indian diabolism. We might look in to that."

"It's too much for me to take in, Tyler. This is such a little town. I can't see Voodoo working here." Zeb thought long about the village, inhabited by intellectuals and serious-minded business men. The students were pretty far out, but how could they learn this sort of magic? Then he remembered seeing Matt as he jogged past the hospital this very evening, casting his eyes toward the place as he passed. He was apparently giving the kennels a good hard look so one of his henchmen could break in to the hospital that night. It was a good possibility, he thought.

"Do you believe that Matt knew we were keeping Lili Tu overnight? Tyler asked.

Zeb turned towards Tyler with a deep frown between his glazed gray eyes. He remembered too much of the conversation with Sallie about Matt's efforts to buy Lily Tu. "He offered the lady a trifling sum, and she was insulted. She wouldn't sell Lili for any amount of money."

Tyler nodded his head solemnly. His thoughts went back to the place of his birth, where strange things could happen and nobody questioned their possibility.

Zeb thought about Matt for a moment. He finally grinned at Tyler. "This is just too far off the wall for me, Tyler" he said. "Go on to bed. We'll try to thresh it out tomorrow." Zeb decided to go home and get some rest.

Dr. Peters promised to keep an eye on King and let the doctor know if anything changed. The two doctors walked through the hall past every room to see that all was serene. They checked the outer door to the kennel once more. The screen in the window would have to be replaced. It was ripped to shreds. The rank and putrid odor was still in the air. Convinced that the place was secure, Zeb left. Dr. Peters was in sole charge.

Zebulon and Bridget walked to the hospital the next morning through soggy woods. Birds sang to them from their nests. The morning was misty gray. Silver spikes of rain stroked their faces and streaks of lightning brightened the sky. "I love it," Bridget said. "It'll keep the snakes away- safely asleep."

A dim light shone at the receptionist's desk and there sat Tyler. His little gray cat, Henry, lay curled up beside the telephone. Lili Tu arose from a corner of the room and stretched luxuriously. She greeted Zebulon in her subtle way and Zebulon responded by rubbing her ears and saying, "Wow, am I glad to see you safe and sound. We had a rough night around here. Somebody came looking for you but you had a good man, Tyler here, to protect you. You were safe as in your mother's arms."

Tyler straightened his long legs in front of him. "I came over early, Doctor," he said.

Zebulon thought again how lucky he was to have this young Jamaican to assist him at the hospital. He had the cleanest kennels in the states and his patients were lovingly attended. He was adroit at soothing frightened, homesick animals. They loved and respected him as he did them. Zebulon knew that the most valuable asset a veterinarian can have is a person in his hospital who is gentle and understanding with his patients. Such a one is Tyler. To get the dog's or cat's confidence, you must prove you are trying to help them. Tyler has an uncanny ability to do just that. Should a dog refuse to eat, Tyler will pet him, talk to him. If the animal is small, he is more likely to end up on Tyler's lap. Sometimes he takes a sick and lonely dog into his own small house. Before he is finished with the dog it is literally eating out of his hand. That's the sort of communication with animals not everyone possesses. Zebulon realized he was indeed fortunate in having Tyler at his side.

Tyler's skin looked dark in the half light but his smile was bright.

"Good morning, Tyler," Zeb greeted him.

"You can call it good if you want to, Doctor," Tyler countered. "I hate the gray sickness. I long for some hot sunshine."

Zeb stopped beside the monkey cage and breathed a kiss toward Chip. The little fellow held out a hand for whatever goodie might be coming. Zeb gave him a section of orange. Chips crammed it into his mouth and held out a beseeching hand for more.

"Later old man," Zeb said in an affectionate voice, and strode into his office. Tyler followed. Henry, Lili Tu and Bridget fell into formation and went along.

"Lili Tu's a fine dog, Doctor," Tyler announced. "She wasn't happy in a cage, so I took her with Henry and me."

Talking With The Dogs

"I appreciate that, Tyler. Her lady's coming in today. She'll be glad you gave Lili special care. And I want to tell you all right now," Zeb said with a smile on his face and a twinkle in his eyes," I really like Lili Tu's missy very, very much."

Bridget turned to face Lili Tu and whispered, "That's what I was afraid would happen all along."

Tyler reported to Zebulon, "All the patients seem to be doing okay. I'll put out their breakfast after you look them over. But first you'd better check King."

Zeb gave him a strange look as if he resented this nudge. "Of course," he said.

King was still groggy from the drugs and gave Zeb a tiny grunt of welcome. "Good morning, King. I sure wish you could tell us more about that fight and identify that man who broke in."

King replied in the vernacular, "Doc, if I ever see him again, I'll be sure and let you know. He was a mean looking SOB. And I'll surely never forget that odor he was carrying on him. It was awful."

Zebulon turned to Tyler who had just returned. "There's one thing I want to talk to you about. That nasty odor that the man had. Is there any significance in that?"

"Yes, there is. Before an Obeah man or woman does a Voodoo deed of some kind, they perform a ritual, wearing long colored gowns, chanting over a fire which has all kinds of magical herbs and branches which give off unforgettable fragrances. The ceremony is performed with the heads of chickens being one of the main ingredients. That is what Dr. Peters and King had the pleasure of smelling. Other animal heads such as goats, ferrets, rats and snakes can also be used to cast evil spells on people. However, if there is a special rite requested For an important person, the head of a black cat is the main component."

"Let's us hope he doesn't come back!'

"With people like that, you never know. They usually keep trying to cast their Voodoo power over you," Tyler added.

After the doctor completed rounds, he and Bridget went to his office where nurse Lib Nelson waited for them in her crisp white coat. She held the coffee pot in her large capable hands and was pouring two cups of coffee, one black and the other with sugar and cream. She knew that Bridget was hooked on sweet coffee. She had dusted and straightened all the diplomas on the walls and made neat piles of the papers on his desk. Zebulon wondered wryly if he would ever be able to find anything again.

Lib Nelson had been with Dr. Zebulon for many years. She was familiar with his procedures and his perfectionism, She was as tall as Zeb but much larger—had big brown eyes and brown hair, cut short and turning gray. Her muscular arms were freckled and strong. She could handle the large dogs easily to give them necessary shots. Lib really preferred animals to human beings. She felt that they were more honest and that dogs were the most faithful of all God's creatures. She began her career as a registered nurse but became disillusioned with humans and switched to veterinary medicine. She treated Zebulon like a motherless child and looked after his welfare without being offensive. He felt secure with her; knowing he could depend on Lib's doing her duties well and efficiently.

"Please give Lili Tu some extra attention today," he told Lib as he eased himself into the big leather chair. He patted Lili on the top of her wrinkled head as he spoke. "She's a pretty girl."

"Special maybe. But hardly pretty," Lib grinned. "Save that for the lady who brought her in."

"You're too right," agreed Zeb. Sudden warmth flowed through his body as he thought of Sallie. He decided it was time for a break. "Bridget and I will go for some breakfast." They went to his big car.

Rain still fell in large silver drops, dimming the center line. A typical spring downpour. Bridget sat quietly, letting Zeb concentrate on his driving. They pulled into the restaurant parking lot and stopped under the huge sign that read MATT'S PUB. They sat for a moment, listening to the rain and willing it to stop.

"I'm afraid we're going to have to run for it," Zeb finally decided. "A good breakfast is just what the doctor ordered. Go!"

"Okay. It'll build up my muscles."

"Right. And get me ready for any emergency those reckless college students can make for me." He wrinkled his blonde eyebrows. "They drive too fast for dogs and children. Parents look after their

Talking With The Dogs

kids, but dogs have to look after themselves." He shrugged his shoulders at the thought of all the auto accident victims he'd treated.

Inside the richly paneled entry, Matt Dye greeted them with a beady smile. "Good morning, Doctor Zebulon," he said in a sharply abrasive voice. "Good morning to your Irish friend, too. Your dog can join you because we have drag with the law. Is this booth okay?"

Zeb's ears hurt from the rasping voice and he remembered a friend calling him, "Hissing Matt Dye"

A pretty waitress in a perky red apron came to take their orders. Zebulon requested scrambled eggs and bacon. He ordered sausages for Bridget, warning her that her love of the greasy stuff was depraved and destructive. They were still eating when Matt Dye slid into the seat next to Zebulon.

"Listen," he said, conspiratorially, pushing his hairy face close to Zebulon. "I'd like for you to be my guest at dinner one of these nights."

"Thanks, but no thanks," said Zeb, pulling back from the thrusting beard and nasty breath. "I'm pretty well booked for the rest of the week."

"Well, sometime soon, then," Matt Dye insisted. "I have a proposition that just might interest you." He left to greet a couple just entering the room. Zebulon and Bridget finished their breakfast and hurried back to the car. The rain had ceased.

"Boy! Are you a good liar!" Bridget complimented him. "But I bet you'd like to know what he has up his sleeve."

"He makes my hackles rise. And don't forget what Sallie said about him following her."

"I'd almost forgotten," Bridget said. "Weird's the word for him. I've said it before and I'll say it again."

"I must admit I agree with you."

****

An uproar of voices drowned out the melodious music as Zeb opened the door of the hospital. The main reception room for dogs was full and there were several cats with their humans in the smaller room reserved for them. Chips was obviously putting on a show. Zeb's clients had sought shelter from the rain and had obviously been bored enough to welcome any entertainment. Chips stretched out a hand toward the doctor and jumped up and down with pleasure at seeing him. Most of the clients brought Chips his favorite tidbits, especially fruit and gum. He loved to eat chewing gum although he would suck a lolly pop for hours.

Norris Martin handed Zeb a list of the clients in the order of their arrival. "Give this one and this one to Dr. Peters" he said, pointing his long slender finger at the names. "Send Mrs. Rasmussen and her little dog to me." He knew Mrs. Rasmussen well. She was pudgy and twittery and held the leash of a plainly troubled dog.

As Zeb lifted the dog, Susie, onto the examination table, Bridget managed to whisper to the dog the news that the doctor could understand their vernacular and that she must tell him everything.

Mrs. Rasmussen began to babble excitedly. "I don't know how to tell you, doctor. One minute she's shivering with chills and the next she's panting. And—she's having- a vag…"

"A vaginal discharge?" Zebulon asked helpfully.

Susie decided to speak up. "You won't believe this, doc," she began. "She gives me a pill every day—she's been doing it for weeks—and I don't know why. But I think it's making me sick."

"Did you hear that, Doctor?" Mrs. Rasmussen giggled. "It sounded exactly as if Susie was trying to talk."

Zeb nodded. "Tell me this. Have you made any changes in her diet lately? Or have you given her any new medication?"

"No, not much. Just my birth control pills, is all."

"Your birth control pills! My dear lady!" Zebulon spoke loudly enough to rattle the glass door of the medicine cabinet. "I thought I'd heard everything. Those pills aren't for dogs. It's a wonder you didn't kill her!"

"I was only trying to keep down the homeless dog population," Mrs. Rasmussen nodded her head so that her curls shook. She congratulated herself heartily.

"I must tell you there is a better way," Zeb said. "She should be spayed. Then your worries would be over."

"But I don't want to hurt Susie."

"Yes, how about that?" Susie piped up.

Zebulon stroked his shamrock amulet with his thumb.

"No, it wouldn't hurt. She's young and would recover quickly. But first we must cure her from the use of those nasty pills." He looked sternly at Mrs. Rasmussen. "Just now she's overstocked with hormones and has a uterine infection with a very high fever. If the antibiotics do not cure the infection, then we shall have to do a hysterectomy to save her."

"Okay, doctor. I'll do anything you say."

She left with a pocket full of prescription medicine and hurried out to her car.

Almost before the door closed behind Mrs. Rasmussen, Norris brought the doctor another patient. Miss Turner came bouncing in, leading a little white poodle by a turquoise leash. The lady was what Dr. Peters would call 'stacked'. She reminded Zebulon of a movie starlet, all paint and posture.

"What seems to be the trouble?" Zebulon asked.

"Why," and Miss Turner giggled prettily, feigning embarrassment. Zeb couldn't help but remember Sallie's lovely laugh. "I don't quite know," Miss Turner continued. She shook her shoulder-length black hair back from her face and twinkled her hazel eyes at Zeb. "Tammy scratches and bites herself. But I can't find any fleas."

Zebulon lifted the little dog to the table. "Let me look at you, he soothed. "Don't be afraid. I won't hurt you." He patted the fluffy head gently.

Tammy seemed to sense that the doctor could understand her, so she spoke to him. "I sure hope you can cure me, doc."

"Please lie still," the doctor coaxed. He brought a magnifying glass with a bright light into play. He pushed the thick hair aside in several places and studied the skin carefully. Then he looked up and casually said, "Lice."

"Lice!" echoed Miss Turner, hazel eyes wide in astonishment.

"Not to worry. We'll give her a bath with a special shampoo." Zebulon rang for Tyler Steele. "And I'll leave a bottle at the desk, so you can bathe her at home."

Dr. Louis Vine, D.V.M.

"But doctor! I have a rash too!" Miss Turner began to tear at her blouse, trying to remove it. "She sleeps in bed with me. Maybe I've caught it from her."

Zebulon stopped her from taking off her blouse saying that it would not be necessary to remove it as he could look at her arms for the rash. Blood rushed to Zeb's cheeks as she held out her arms and he held them. Then he noticed a strange-looking wrist watch on one of her arms. It looked almost like a tiny tape recorder. But why would Miss Turner want to record her visit? He must be imagining things. "No need for this," he said almost gruffly. "When you get home, use this shampoo on yourself too and if it doesn't get rid of your rash, go see a dermatologist."

"Dog shampoo?" she cried angrily. She grabbed her dog and the shampoo and turned on her heels and left the room without a word. Zebulon drew a deep breath of relief and looked at Bridget.

"How do I get mixed up with these people?" he muttered.

"I don't know. But Tammy told me that her lady is Matt Dye's girl friend. So maybe he likes weird women." Bridget nodded her head wisely. "But then again, maybe Matt sent her here to try and blackmail you. That wrist watch sure looked like a tape recorder to me. She probably was waiting for you to make a pass at her and say something foolish. It proves one thing, Zeb. It proves that you can't trust women."

"Thanks for that advice, Bridget. I'll try to remember that the next time I'm with one." He smiled as he uttered these words in anticipation of Sallie's impending visit.

As Zebulon busily washed his hands to prepare for the next patient, he heard a chilling scream from the reception room. He rushed from his room. He saw Norris backing away from her desk, her face contorted in a look of extreme horror. Her blue eyes were wide and her pink baby-like skin was green under its makeup.

"Look out, Doctor," she said, her voice shaking. "I opened Sam Jones box and a horrible snake reared its ugly head."

Sam Jones protested, "It's my pet snake, Oliver, and he is not a poisonous one. He is a very friendly snake who likes to be held. But I brought him to see you because he's got worms. Can you help him?"

Talking With The Dogs

Zebulon moved cautiously nearer. A chubby, long squirming snake peered up at him unhappily. Sam Jones was holding the snake down. It was a boa constrictor and a powerful one.

Zeb recognized Sam as one of Matt Dye's bus boys and wondered why he'd brought his pet here and not to Dr. Roberts.

"Well, that's hardly my idea of a household pet," Zebulon conceded. "But I'll see what we can do." He remembered an ancient method of ridding worms in snakes by feeding worm medicine to a mouse, then the mouse to the snake. Too clumsy. Also, you could insert a stomach tube into the mouth and send the worm medicine directly to the intestinal tract of the snake. But who would hold the snake? 'Not I,' thought Zeb. Maybe Tyler could use some of his Jamaican magic, or was it obeah- or voodoo? Too chancey.

Then he had the answer. "Dr. Peters will take care of Oliver for you. He specializes in treating exotic animals." He walked guiltily from the room.

****

Zeb was glad to be in his cottage again, where he could relax for a moment and forget the stresses of his professional life. "I could certainly use a little rest, old girl," he said to Bridget. "How about you?" He gently ruffled the red hair in back of her ears as he spoke.

"You can bet your boots, I could." Bridget agreed.

The doctor decided to have a peppermint ice tea with his dull peanut butter and jelly sandwich. It would refresh him for a busy afternoon. The house was quiet. The only sound came from a bird singing outside his window and what sounded like a tree frog. He stretched himself out in his big easy chair and thought about his life at the hospital and his clients- some of them so strange. There were women who fed their dogs the same food they ate themselves. An English woman who shared her afternoon tea and 'biscuits' with her little dog regularly every day at five. He knew farmers who fed their dogs gunpowder to make them fierce. Another one of his clients, a thrice divorced woman, had given up on men as untrustworthy and accumulated ten dogs of various breeds to live with. Every night all the dogs jumped on her huge round bed with her where they slept. She had an overhead mirror so that she could watch all of her family with pride and joy. Other dogs, like Bridget, had become addicted to a morning cup of coffee rich with cream and sugar. A parade of madness. But now he had met Sallie Predino. Her kind made it all worth while. Her beautiful blue eyes fascinated him. And her voice was music to his ears. Soon he would see her again, perhaps get to know her much better. But first, he must give Lilli Tu her physical. That shouldn't be difficult—the dog looked to be in fine condition.

Bridget suddenly broke the silence. "She jolly well better be good enough for you, Zeb."

"Wh-what? Miss Predino? Bridget- are you reading my mind?"

"That's not too hard. After all, I've known you all my life! In fact, you saved me when no one else wanted me. That's why I love you so much."

"You're probably right about reading my mind. I hope my staff can't read me that clearly. I do like Sallie very much." He looked at Bridget with wonder in his eyes and then as an afterthought, said, "But I love you too, Bridget."

My Bridget McGuire of happy memories. So I have called her. And so she was in spite of the less than happy circumstances that brought us together in the first place. There's something about an Irish setter, something about an Irish name, that calls for singing and laughter. But the small bit of dogdom brought to the hospital door that long ago night was more likely to move one to tears than to laughter.

Bridget suddenly interrupted his thoughts. "I owe you one. You saved my life several years ago. Remember?"

"Yes, I certainly do. I remember every time I look at your beautiful coat of hair you have now. When I first laid eyes on you, you were a scrawny mangy puppy with the worst case of demodectic mange I have ever seen. Your owners brought you to this hospital for me to put you to sleep. They had been working on you with all kinds of concoctions and medications that their neighbors and friends had suggested. Nothing seemed to work and you were a walking festering monstrosity. Your owners gave up and left you with me to dispose of anyway that I wanted. I asked them if I could try and cure you since I always wanted an Irish Setter. They agreed. I worked on you in my spare time for over six months and you finally made it to become 'my one and only love'."

"Oh yeah," Bridget answered, "You're kind of sweet on Sallie and I have to admit it, I'm kind of jealous."

"Don't feel that way, Bridget, there's enough love in me to keep you and Sallie both happy. After all, I need a few heirs to run this hospital some day. Be reasonable, will ya?"

"Okay, as long as you have honorable intentions with the young lady, I'll relent and accept her as *our* own."

"Thanks, Bridget, I appreciate your vote of acceptance because I've really fallen for that gal. Come on. We've got to get back to work."

As they neared the hospital, Bridget spied Matt Dye walking in front. "There he is again! What's that old so-and-so up to any way? He didn't used to be here so much of the time." Bridget sounded worried and a frown grew on her brow.

"I don't understand it either. We'll put Tyler to work on it. Nothing escapes him that goes around here."

This was the day that Zebulon became a clock watcher. He treated sick patients and neurotic patients with their eccentric owners. But one eye seemed to know what time was all that afternoon. Every now and then he would rub his amulet in gratitude as it helped in a diagnosis simply because an animal could tell him exactly where it hurt.

At precisely five o'clock, Norris Martin ushered Sallie Predino into the examination room. Norris gave him a knowing, sly look and a wry smile. 'Do you suppose I'm really so transparent?' wondered Zebulon. Tyler Steele arrived with the coppery-beige Lili Tu, who showed joy at seeing Sallie. She licked her hand and Sallie bent and kissed Lili.

As soon as Norris and Tyler left the room, Sallie rushed over to Zebulon and gave him a resounding kiss on his lips. Bridget turned to Lili and said, "Here they go again, getting all hot and bothered over each other."

The rain had stopped and it had grown quite hot. Sallie was

dressed in a summery pink blouse and her cheeks shone with the same rosy hue. Zeb stared. Sunshine had come into the room with Sallie. Zebulon brightened and Bridget looked at him critically.

"Lili didn't like her cage, so Tyler kept her with him and his cat, Henry, in the office. She adjusted beautifully."

Lili leaned towards Bridget and whispered, "Yes. That's a sure thing. Who ever invented cages ought to be put in one."

"I agree with you there, Lili," Bridget said. "But they insist that sometimes cages are necessary."

"Tyler tells me that they heard a commotion during the night. Some strange noises in the patch of woods behind the hospital." Zeb hesitated a moment. "They went out to investigate. They didn't find anything. But there was a strange odor back there. Anyway, Lili Tu joined in the search and seemed to enjoy herself," Zeb explained. He purposely neglected to tell her about King's fight with the intruder in the kennel. He didn't want to alarm her unnecessarily.

"It was fun," Lili Tu told Bridget.

"I've been giving you and Lili a good deal of thought lately," he conceded. "She's a wonderful specimen- a rare color, fine lines. She really has it. You could train her for the dog shows." His gray eyes were serious. "If she were a champion, she'd be worth a good deal of money. And if you bred her, the puppies would be worth much, much money as well."

"Hmmm?"

"That could be why Matt Dye's so eager to buy her."

"I've heard tell," whispered Bridget, "that old weirdo will do anything to make a buck. I hate him."

Sallie flushed with anger. "I'll never sell Lili Tu," she said. "She was a present from my uncle- Uncle Milt Porter."

"Milt Porter?" Zeb gasped. "They say he's one of the wealthiest men in the state and he's a top breeder."

"Yes. He lives in Woodbine. And he could make Christmas fall on the Fourth of July over there. Everybody loves him." She was smiling at Zeb in a way that made his ears hum. "The people there would do anything for him—and he'd do anything for them. It's mutual adoration."

"He sounds great."

"He's a love. Just a great big, friendly old bear. He never had children of his own. So he says I'm his favorite niece and that's why he gave Lili to me. How could I possibly sell her?"

"No. Of course you couldn't. Let me fill you in about Shar Peis. They're a fairly new breed and maybe you don't know much about them."

"Please do. I really know very little."

They were raised in China to be fighting dogs. They were taught ferocity and their skins were toughened by scarring to protect them from bites. The meaner they became, the more highly valued they were. Then Communism came to China. And the government ruled that owning pets was forbidden. Food must not be wasted on animals. People began stealing Shar Peis from each other for their cooking pots and sometimes hungry people even ate their own pets. Before long there were only fifteen or so Shar Peis left."

Sallie shuddered becomingly. "What an awful story, Jacob," she said.

"You can say that again," Lili Tu whispered.

"Yes, it's pretty terrible," agreed Zebulon. "But now American breeders began importing Shar Peis whenever they could find one and brought them here to breed them. At this time there may be several thousand of them in America and their numbers are growing at a rapid pace. They are becoming very popular."

"Boy, that was quite a lecture," Bridget said to Zeb. She noticed that Lili Tu had turned pale and comforted her. "Thank God nobody ate your ancestors, Lili."

Sallie frowned becomingly and said to Zeb, "That makes Lili Tu pretty rare, I guess."

"You're so right. That's why we should train her for the shows."

"But Jacob, as you know, I'm a collie breeder and I don't know much about the finer points of showing a Shar Pei. Won't it be difficult?"

Bridget snorted and said to Lili, "Difficult indeed! It's a piece of dog biscuit. And kind of fun too. We'll all work together. But of course, I can't compete because I've been spayed."

"You're not to worry," Zebulon assured Sallie, "If you'll permit me I can show you the basics about Shar Peis and with your experience in showing dogs, it will be easy."

"We'd best meet in a more private place," Zeb suggested. "Would my house be okay to start the lessons?"

"Yes. Or mine," agreed Sallie. "Come to my apartment tonight, about six o'clock and I'll cook you a steak- that is if you don't have a previous engagement."

"I'd be delighted to come. May I bring Bridget? She could help with the training."

"Does she always go with you?" Sallie asked.

Bridget gave an angry grunt. "Well, how do you like that? She's the new girl on the block so she'd better check things out with me before she tries to take over. I'm afraid that Zeb is falling into her trap. Cooking him steak with all the extras and I don't mean beef. Men are so gullible!"

Lili Tu looked soothingly at Bridget. "Take it easy, friend. Don't forget—they're humans! And thank God, we're dogs."

CHAPTER IV

Zeb thought six o'clock would never come. The hours stretched miserably. The sun was sinking in the west more slowly than Zeb had dreamed possible. He ran his strong surgeon's fingers through his tawny hair, rumpling it again and again.

He'd been intrigued by women before, but never dazzled as he was by Sallie. The blue sky outside made him remember the blue of her eyes. He must stop watching the clock, it was a new sensation to him. He shook his head to bring the hospital back into focus.

Norris Martin came to the door with a favorite patient. It was a handsome Kerry Blue terrier named Eric who lived with a physician about a mile up the hill from the hospital. He had come scratching at the front door of the hospital until Norris had heard him and brought him inside. Eric held out a gashed paw to Zebulon. After Norris left, Eric began, "Nobody was at home, so I came down the hill by myself."

"I'm glad you did. It's a nasty looking cut and needs a few stitches," Zebulon said as he cleaned the cut and put a few sutures in it under local anesthesia. As he was bandaging the paw, he glanced over at Eric who was watching the procedure closely and Eric notchantly said, "Doc, word has spread all over town amongst us canines that you understand our vernacular. I already knew about it because Bridget told me so."

"Yes, I've learned how to understand you all," Zeb explained. "You mutts will have to be careful what you say about me, now. As for your paw, I'll tie instructions and your follow-up medication to your collar. Your lady will find them. Now go on home- and by all means be careful crossing the street out there."

"Okay, Doc, but before I leave I have a question or two for you since you and I can talk to each other."

"That's what I'm here for, Eric, to help you in any way that I can. What's your problem?"

"It's not my problem, Doc, but my owners are beginning to worry me. Ever since their kids grew up and left the house, they've been referring to themselves as 'Mommy' and 'Daddy' to me. Is there something wrong with them or is it me?"

"No, Eric, it's not you. That's the way of life these days. I recently read in a veterinary journal that 84% of people admit to referring to them self as the pet's 'mom' and 'dad'. And to make matters worse, 72% of married people admit to greeting the pet first when they return home."

"What is this world coming to? It's about time we pets were appreciated."

"And that's not all," Zebulon continued. "The survey also showed that the majority of people sing and dance with their pet; that most of them celebrate and recognize the pet's birthday; that the preponderance turn on music or TV for their pet when they are away from home and most people cook something special for their pet. There are many churches throughout the country who celebrate on St. Francis day for all the animals in the community and allow the people to bring their pets into church on that day for a special blessing as being part of God's creatures."

"Just what I thought," Eric exclaimed. "We pets are part of the family!"

"You sure are. We couldn't do without you."

"You can say that again," Bridged added.

Zebulon watched Eric leave with instructions and medication attached to his collar.

He turned to Norris Martin. "I wish all my patients were so willing to be treated. When I was a kid, I never would go to a dentist unless my mother forced me to do so. Eric is certainly different from Dr. Bloom's dog, Gretel. She crosses over to the other side of the street whenever she sees me coming. I have the feeling that she doesn't like me. That hurts my feelings, did you know that?"

"Yes," Norris agreed. "But she probably remembers a time when you hurt her during your treatments. You shouldn't let it bother you." She laughed suddenly. "Do you remember Tish? She was that shepherd who bit the hand of a traffic cop."

"Tish shouldn't have had her head out the window. And the cop shouldn't have waved his hand so close to her. Two mistakes don't make a right." The doctor grinned. "If it had happened anywhere else but Chapel Hill, someone would have had a citation but fortunately this town is a dog town. Dogs rule the roost. Why, we even have a few town mascots. One of them, Gimpy, gets all over town, holding one paw up to get more sympathy and more goodies. She's at every important town function such as football games and town meetings. And I happen to know that there's nothing wrong with her paw. She's just a fakir."

"We have lots of canine characters in and around town. Some are serious-minded dogs, some are clowns. But none of them will ever hold a candle to George when it comes to a colorful and checkered career. Among the townspeople, the faculty, and the students who knew George no one was likely to forget him. For years he was undisputedly Chapel Hill's own dog. No one knew whether or not he had ever had an owner. Probably he started life with some family. Then, being an individualist and an extrovert of the first order, he struck out for himself. He was undeniably a Collie, and a handsome one. He learned early in life that the University students were pushovers so far as a dog was concerned. Nor did the other residents of Chapel Hill ever let him down. He lived a good life."

"During George's tenure as Town Dog, the Rathskeller Restaurant was chosen by him as his official headquarters, as befitted the top dog of a cultural center. It was in the center of town and was a meeting place for campus and town. The shop's customers became adept at stepping around the great dog. They had to. Otherwise, they could not get into the restaurant at all. In summer he lay just inside the door, so that he might be out of the heat. In mild weather he took up his position just outside the door. In winter, of course, back inside he went, further from the door, to be sure, but still a hazard to be carefully walked around on the way to the dining room."

"Every once in a while the urge to greater learning overcame George. Carefully crossing the street, he would favor one of his favorite professors by attending class. He was always so well behaved, no one dreamed of sending him away. Having done his stint at the University he returned to the Rathskeller for a slight repast. After his snack it was his habit to saunter leisurely along Franklin Street. At other favorite restaurants he often stopped off for a meal in the afternoon where students could always be counted on to treat him to a beer. Since even a Town Dog couldn't quite handle a can or bottle George had his in a saucer."

"No football game was quite complete without George's presence. Sometimes the excitement proved too much for his equanimity. If he thought his University boys weren't getting a square deal he trotted out to the field to lend them his moral assistance. That usually ended up by one of the ushers lending him some assistance in getting off the field, to the accompaniment of roars of laughter and yells of "We want George." He had been known to crash a commencement ceremony. There, too, it was found necessary to put him in his place."

"All in all, George led a good and satisfying life. Everyone, or nearly everyone, liked him. The students saw not only that he was fed but also that he received medical care when he seemed to require it. People learned to walk around him without disturbing his reflections. What more could any dog desire? Unfortunately for George, he had one habit that proved his downfall. He loathed, despised and hated motorcycles. He couldn't abide the flashy, ear shattering things. He chased them. Having caught up with one the next logical step, to him, was to bite the rider of the devilish machine, particularly since said rider had been kicking at him during the chase. Twice he bit motorcyclists. Each time he was sent down to me to be quarantined for fourteen days as a safeguard against Rabies. As soon as he was freed he appeared in all his old haunts. All was forgiven and he seemed destined to reign as Town Dog for the rest of his life."

"Then came the third bite, followed by the third quarantining. Someone, perhaps the bitten one, complained bitterly to the town authorities about having a savage dog running around. The upshot of that was an order from Town Hall. "George is to be executed." Word went around the town and the campus like the proverbial wildfire. Faster, I think. Before long the students had organized a great public meeting on the campus. Speakers in behalf of George spoke long and eloquently. At the end of the meeting a petition was circulated. Everyone there signed it. It was taken through the town. Before night several thousand people put their signatures on that petition. At last the time came to present it to the authorities. The students formed into a loud and noisy parade, led by the University brass band and at the head of the parade was Mrs. Jordan with her 200 pound Newfoundland on a leash. This 95 pound woman was the hallowed leader of the local Humane Society and fought like a tiger when any of her beloved animals in town were abused."

"There were many big banners: SAVE GEORGE. WE WANT GEORGE. Thus did George's friends come to his rescue."

"In the meantime, Mrs. Jordan was hard at work. I can well imagine that the authorities found it difficult to withstand the pleas of this tiny, gentle-spoken woman. Sometimes I wonder which turned the trick-the parade outside the Town Hall, or the little woman inside. Whatever it was, and it was probably both, the authorities finally relented. The death sentence was rescinded. But-and it was a big but, for the officials brooked no disobedience to their order this time- George was to leave town. It is not known how much dismay this sentence brought to George. To his admirers and adherents it spelled the end of a colorful personality. Not ever to have to step over or around George; not to treat him to a saucer of beer; not to escort him from the stadium; not to see him sitting solemn-eyed in class; never to watch him mooch a meal from one of his restaurant friends. The very thought of all this was enough to make any Georgite weep in his beer. However, so thankful were they to have their favorite spared an ignominious death they set about finding a good home out in the country for him."

"Several years older, and probably a much wiser collie, George still lives on a farm not far from the pavements of his beloved town, the green campus of his dear University. I hope he knows he has never been forgotten in Chapel Hill. To this day whenever a conversation turns on the subject of dogs someone is sure to say, "You remember the time when George......?"

When Zebulon finished, Norris said quickly. "Gee, I wish I had the pleasure of meeting that dog. He certainly was top dog in this town, alright."

Zebulon headed back to his office where Bridget waited for him.

"Look here, Zeb," Bridget said, pouting. "Are you getting serious about Miss Sallie?"

Zeb wished he could ignore Bridget's question. "I just don't know," he confessed.

"Well, I remember some of your girl friends. There was Mary Lee Hopkins who couldn't stand the smell of antiseptics."

"I try to keep it washed off these days."

"And there was Nola Healy," Bridget pursued. "She was a real dish. The boys used to whistle 'Frankie and Johnny' when she entered a room." Bridget uttered with a sardonic laugh. "She couldn't stand it when you left her for a sick dog when she was all puckered up for a kiss."

"Stop worrying," Zeb hugged Bridget and kissed her smooth mahogany forehead. He insisted that it was safer to kiss a pet than a girl friend—fewer germs- but he reluctantly admitted that it sure wasn't as exciting.

Almost six o'clock at last. Zeb called Tyler Steele to his office. Several dogs required special medication and some were on special diets. Lib Nelson reported on the day's lab tests. David Smith checked in and was told several things that he should do and most importantly, things that he must not do. David was a college student who worked only a few hours a week. "Dr. Peters will be in charge tonight," he announced.

"Okay," he said at last. "Good night, everyone. You and Dr. Peters have control now, Tyler. I'll look in later. I'll see the rest of the staff tomorrow."

Zeb and Bridget walked back to his cottage. It was tucked into a circle of shade trees which clung tightly around his yard. Zeb loved the quiet of his little house. He took a shower, soaping himself energetically to remove the strong hospital odor. He brushed his unruly hair, shaved, and put on gray slacks and a blue blazer. He strapped a bright blue collar on Bridget. They went out, got into the car and drove away.

"We'll stop at the pet store and get a present for Miss Predino."

"Presents already," Bridget drawled.

"Well, it's for Lili Tu also, you know."

"Okay. She's not such a bad dog. We might even become good friends," Bridget conceded.

The chatter of a big white minah bird greeted them as they entered the pet shop. Puppies whimpered softly and Persian cats stared from their cages in utter boredom. The walls were hung thickly with collars, harnesses and other pet paraphernalia.

A plump dark-haired lady greeted them.

"May I see some nylon show leads." Zeb asked. The clerk brought a handful. Zeb selected a turquoise colored one. "This is the one. It'll look great on Lili's copper colored fur," he decided.

Sallie opened the door to Zeb's soft knock. She gave him a great big and lasting kiss which made him feel good all over. When he recovered from his initial exhilaration, he entered the large, airy living room. Its white walls were hung with pictures of Collies and their blue ribbon winnings. Sallie had been on the dog show circuit for several years and had been in the winner's circle many times. Teakwood lamps with creamy pale shades were spotted here and there about the room. There was a sofa, one comfortable lounge chair and several black sling chairs.

"Please take the big chair," Sallie urged him. "You must be tired after your busy day. Will a martini help?"

"Much," he said gratefully, although he was a bourbon drinker. She poured from a shaker into a frosted glass.

"Thank you," he said and gave her another kiss which she gracefully accepted and embraced him very warmly.

Bridget turned to Lili and remarked, "I hope they don't get mushy tonight."

Sallie poured one for herself and they both drank after clicking their glasses and looking into each other's eyes for a long tantalizing time.

Bridget had joined Lili Tu by the fireplace, where embers glowed. "I hope your Sallie deserves my Zeb," Bridget said.

"Well, I hope your Zeb deserves my Sallie," Lili countered.

Zeb handed the turquoise lead to Sallie. "We'll need this for tonight's training walk," he told her. "Are you ready to begin?"

"Yes. Hadn't we better start before it gets dark?"

Zeb made a loop in the lead, one that could not tighten, and set it around Lili Tu's neck. "Sallie, this training session is not for you since you're an old pro in the dog show business. It's for Lili's benefit. We want to make her a champion, as she so obviously deserves.

Listening, Lili smiled at Bridget. "This will be a piece of cake," she said as the four of them walked out into the evening.

"Thank God for that four-leaved shamrock Zeb has," Bridget said to herself. "May he never lose it."

Outside, they practiced the different gaits for quite a while until Sallie decided that Lili had done enough. "Maybe she better rest now and we all must be getting hungry. I take it that you prefer your steak rare, Jacob."

"Right," replied Zeb, and 'right' whispered Bridget.

Sallie turned to Lili and complimented her on being a bright young future champion and in a very warm voice, added, "Lili Tu, you are beautiful. I love you."

Lili understood. She walked over and licked Sallie's hand.

Katie served dinner on a polished teak table. Tall candles made the silver and the happy faces shine. The steak, rich brown outside and rich red inside, sliced into buttery-delicious portions. The salad was bound together with a splendid oil and vinegar dressing with just a hint of garlic. Zeb luxuriated. Bridget and Lili shared the scraps from a gleaming pan, sitting comfortably together in a corner.

Zeb went to the window when he had finished. "Look at that moon," he said, as if he had never seen it before. "We should take another walk and after that Bridget and I must leave."

"Yes. Lets," Sallie agreed.

The moonlight painted the sidewalk. Zeb thought of many things he'd rather be doing with Sallie than walking dogs.

"Look who's coming, Zeb," grumbled Bridget and Lili made woeful sounds under her breath.

The two dogs strained their eyes into the darkness. The hackles on their backs rose. There was something strange in the air and there was that unmistakable pungent odor again. It was the same odor that Tyler mentioned as being synonymous with voodoo.

Lili Tu wrinkled her nose. "Whatever it is smells kind of funny," she said.

"It's Matt Dye coming down the street," Bridget told Zeb. "And whoever is with him is a big hairy man. At least I think it's a man but I'm not sure. Looks awful weird to me."

Zeb also had a sense of something foreboding whenever he was in the presence of Matt Dye. Zeb could see that his companion was a was a tall, dark black man with long dread lock hair overflowing on the top of his head. His ear lobes contained large silver ear rings and he had a large silver necklace hanging from his neck. His fingers contained large assortments of rings with all kinds of eerie symbols on them. He was wearing a large red, green and black robe. His appearance was grotesque, to say the least. He walked a few paces behind Matt.

Matt turned to this strange looking man and introduced him to Zebulon and Sallie. "This is my Obeah man, Jubert. He is a Rastafarian who I brought back with me on my last visit to Jamaica." Then turning back to face Zebulon, he added, while skinning his teeth at Sallie. "I saw you out walking and hoped you'd let me join you. You mustn't keep all this beauty to yourself, doctor."

"You're too late, Mr. Dye. We're just going in. It's too chilly out here. Good night."

"My invitation to dinner still stands," said Matt, stubbornly standing his ground. "Why not tomorrow evening? Bring the lady."

"I'll come," Zeb answered sharply. "But Miss Predino has a previous engagement. Sorry."

"Okay. Then just you, agreed Dye. See you."

Inside the apartment, Zeb told Sallie that he accepted the invitation from Matt Dye because he wanted to see if he could find out what that shady character had up his sleeve.

"By the way, Sallie, what is a Rastafarian? That went over my head."

"Me too, Jacob. I never heard that name before."

"I'll ask Tyler tomorrow. He's very knowledgeable about these things."

Then he took Sallie in his arms and kissed her long and passionately. She was soft against him and he felt that this was the closest to heaven he would ever get. He hated to let her go. Fortunately for him, Sallie must have felt the same way because she whispered in his ear, asking if he would like to spend the night. Reluctantly and without much arm twisting, he obediently followed her into the bedroom.

Bridget and Lili Tu watched jealously.

****

Next day, Zeb worked until the sun was low in the western sky. The colors were glorious. Cezanne would have loved it, he thought, admiring the rosy and copper tones. He drove to Matt's Pub and parked near the front door. "You're going in with me Bridget, no matter what anyone says," he told her. The rich brown interior was lighted by bulbs set high in the dark rafters. A spotlight focused on the tortured face of a wounded deer on a huge tapestry. Two students sat at the bar. The young man's hair hung just below his ears, and he wore a sweeping moustache like a river-boat gambler. His companion's hair was long and unruly and she wore an oversized sweater with a long full skirt that swept to her ankles. She crooned a tuneless song, one phrase repeated endlessly and picked at a tremendous hamburger between sips of beer. To Zebulon, she looked like someone in a trance. Both wore earrings but she also wore a ring through one side of her nostril. He wondered if there were any other parts of her body that she had pierced for other rings to protrude.

Today's students will do anything for a new look. And how old are they anyway, he wondered. Drinking beer? And what else?

Dye came forward, his smile tight. "Glad to see you. Glad you came. Here, this way. Zeb and Bridget followed him to a far corner where a door led to a private, paneled room. It smelled of stale smoke and warm bodies.

"We'll eat in here where we can talk," Dye said. "They'll bring us our dinner here. But first, I want you to try this cocktail. My own invention. It's pretty strong—we'd best stop at one."

Bridget watched as Zeb sipped. He looked at Matt with a smile. "It reminds me of a New Year's concoction I once had years ago. Brandy, bourbon, rum and I don't know what all went into that one— even strawberry ice cream. Thank God you didn't use ice cream in this."

"Maybe I'll give it a try some day."

Bridget grunted. "It'd be just like him."

"Good, Here comes dinner," Matt announced. It was delicious. A Paella of chicken, lobster, shrimp and mussels- deliciously seasoned with garlic and saffron, and stirred into. rice.

"This is wonderful," said Zeb. "I didn't expect anything like it in Chapel Hill."

"Well, I drive to the coast for fresh fish every week. And you can thank my excellent chef for the paella. He's something of a genius. I brought him back from Jamaica, too."

'I'll bet you did. And who else did you bring from Jamaica?' Zeb thought to himself.

"Can I put some on a dish for Bridget?" the doctor asked.

"Of course."

They emptied their plates and had black coffee. Then Dye filled their glasses with a fine liqueur and leaned toward Zeb conspiratorially. "Listen," he said. "I've got a nice little proposition for you."

"Proposition?"

"I want to make some money for you. You must know that I breed dogs on the side. And I have a champion Shar Pei that needs a good bitch. I really want that dog of Sallie Predino. Maybe you can persuade her to sell it to me."

Bridget opened her mouth in astonishment. And Zeb looked stunned by the suggestion. "Why should I do that in God's name?"

"It makes sense. I'd put good money in your pocket for your help."

"It's rotten talk. In the first place, Miss Predino won't ever sell her dog and in the second place I wouldn't help you by trying to force her. Good day."

"Then you force me to get the dog by other means."

"Now you're talking crime!" Zeb rose to his feet, towering over Dye.

Dye got up, hunching his shoulders, he leaned towards Zeb. "Simmer down. Listen." There was no geniality in his tone now. "I'm

Dr. Louis Vine, D.V.M.

just trying to make you some money. If you'll give me—"

"I wouldn't give you the right time of day if I was looking at the town clock," Zeb growled. "Leave Sallie Predino and her dog alone."

Dye's smile was mirthless. "You're behind the times, Doctor. Don't be a wimp. I'm offering you big money. Sit down and relax."

'By God, I'll never sit down in your place again," Zeb exploded. "Leave that lady and her dog alone!"

"Get out of my place!" snarled Dye.

"I'm getting out and I'll stay out. But come along with me. I'll fight you under your neon sign for a couple of minutes. If you lasted that long."

Zebulon strode angrily from the room. One look over his shoulder told him that Dye was not following him. He walked through the restaurant, noticing the same strange crowd sitting at the bar, apparently feasting on baked potatoes. They looked strangely pleased with themselves. Outside, in his car he sat quietly for a moment to allow himself to cool down. "You said all the right things," Bridget assured him. "But I'd kinda like to see you and him fight. I'd bet on you."

"You wouldn't have time to put your money down," Zeb said grimly.

Zeb usually enjoyed the drive home, past the elegant houses of professors with the flowering bushes and manicured lawns. Tonight he was too deep in thought to see anything but the young people strolling arm in arm toward the Pub. He wondered again what they found there to keep them going, sitting at the bar and humming monotonous tunes. In his little cottage, Zeb took a hot shower and went to bed. Bridget had already taken her place at the foot. Both went quietly to sleep.

He woke from a blur of dreams to feel Bridget's nose nudging him. "Zeb," she said. "Zeb, wake up. There's a snake in here."

"Snake?" He quickly reached for the lamp on the bedside table, turned it on and looked.

There it sprawled. In the middle of the floor. Long and thick and splotchy skinned, jowly-jawed, bright-eyed. A copperhead, and the biggest one he had ever seen.

"Stay on the bed, Bridget!"

Zeb reached for his shotgun, standing ready beside his bed. You might not need a gun often in Chapel Hill, but if you needed one, you needed it at once. He flung himself to the edge of the bed. The blood throbbed in his temples. The copperhead had whipped into its menacing coil. Its tongue quested, tasting the air.

With an effort, Zeb steadied his trembling hands. He pumped a shell into the breech of the gun and leveled it. The snake's coil was no more than a foot away. He touched the trigger. The explosion rang deafeningly. Zeb saw the splotched length snap out of its coil, go writhing here and there in agony. He had blown its head off. Where it had held itself, a ragged hole showed in the floorboards.

"You killed it, all right," Bridget said shakily.

Zeb's amulet heaved on his chest as he panted. "Yes. And let's get it out of here," he said.

The snake writhed less violently. Zeb reached out the muzzle of his shotgun and gingerly hooked the thing upon it. Carefully he carried it through the open door of the bedroom, on across the kitchen to the back door. He threw the abhorrent body as far as he could into the back yard. He drew a deep, grateful breath as it dropped among the trees.

"Doctor, doctor! What happened?"

Tyler Steele had raced over from the hospital, his flashlight showing him the way. He joined the doctor at the back steps, his eyes wide in his dark face.

"I heard—" he began.

"There, that's what happened," Zeb said, pointing with his gun. Tyler turned his flashlight beam upon the out flung dead length. He whistled softly.

"That's as big a copperhead as any man would want to see without the aid of liquor," he finally said.

"It was in my bedroom," Zeb explained, thankful that his voice was steady again. "How could that damned thing get in? My house is so tight that not even a cricket can break in."

"Maybe—" Tyler began, and paused. "I really don't think it was the snake's idea. It could have been put there by an Obeah man,

Dr. Louis Vine, D.V.M.

someone that believes in secret sorcery or magical rites. He believes in and practices voodoo."

"Look here. Come on into the house. We both need a drink. And please explain."

In the kitchen, Zeb poured stiff shots of bourbon and added ice and a little water. Drink in hand, Tyler went to the bedroom and studied the hole in the floor.

"You shot right through the floor and sub-flooring," he said. "I suggest that you cover that hole with something silver. Have you got a silver tray or something?"

"Sure. But why silver?" Explain all this about Obeah and voodoo."

Tyler didn't answer at once. They went to the living room and found comfortable chairs. They drank deeply. "It's most likely Obeah all right. An Obeah man can send any evil anywhere he wishes. To anybody he wants."

Zeb leaned his shotgun besides his chair. "Okay. Go ahead," he demanded.

"An Obeah man could have sent that snake, under orders."

"You believe all this," Zeb accused.

"Yes, indeed. And don't forget that monstrous man that beat up on King. Why did he get into the kennels? Have you forgotten that? An Obeah man can do anything evil he wants too. My guess is that Matt Dye ordered the Obeah man to take care of all the dirty work."

Zeb took a long drink from his glass and studied the toe of his shoe. "You expect me to believe this, don't you? Here in Chapel Hill?"

"I know it's hard to believe here. I was born where it happens every day. My people didn't believe in evil magic at first but soon they accepted it as fact. But it can scare the hell out of you."

"So you think there's an Obeah man right here in this little town. And that he sent that snake to poison me. Is that right?" Zeb looked Tyler in the eye. Tyler had always seemed such a sober, sensible person. "Do you think he'll try again? Send another snake?"

"Probably not that." Tyler shook his head gravely. He sat quietly for a moment in deep thought. "Obeah doesn't like failures and you

Talking With The Dogs

defeated his snake. He'll think of something else."

"What exactly do you mean by Obeah?"

"Some people call it voodoo. But it's worse than that. It's a religion. It's a cult that does harm to its enemies. It is a way of life in Jamaica."

"Do you really expect me to believe all this?"

"You believed the snake, didn't you?"

"It was real."

"Yes, but brought by Obeah. If you'd visit the islands and see more of this, you'd come to believe. Many famous writers have visited Jamaica, got to believe, and published their acceptance of the facts." He shook his head in his sober fashion. "You make up your mind what to believe." He finished his drink and rose. "I'd better get back to those dogs and cats."

"Wait, Tyler. Before you go, I have an important question to ask you. What or who is a Rastafarian? Matt Dye brought one back with him from Jamaica."

Tyler looked surprised but quickly responded by saying, "Well that could explain everything! I didn't know that we had a Rasta here in Chapel Hill."

"Yes, I met him and Matt out walking near Sallie's apartment. He sure was a weird looking individual with all his hair in dreadlocks. Tell me something about these characters."

"It so happens that I made a study of Rastafarians when I was in school. Their prime basic belief is that Haile Selassie, the Emperor of Ethiopia, was the living God of the black race. Rastafarians originated in Africa but was embraced by the poorer blacks in Jamaica. Their favorite colors are red, black and green which they wear quite profusely. A Rasta is a member of the largely Jamaican religious and political movement. They perform all kinds of rituals that we call voodoo and they embrace the heavy use of marijuana in their ceremonies. They believe that marijuana is sacred and approve of a mystical approach to the universe. Many believe that it is a revolutionary cult. Personally, I would advise you to stay far away from them. I'm sure Matt Dye is up to no good with one of them working for him. I am also worried about Sallie living alone. She's in danger."

Zeb, too was on his feet. "I'll call her right now and tell her of the danger and then I'll go over and protect the young lady." Then with a smile, he added, "Might turn out to be fun after all. But, seriously though, I am really worried about her."

"Doctor, I feel badly that I didn't put two and two together. I should have realized that someone was performing Voodoo in the area. A friend of mine that works for the town, mentioned to me that they were finding lots of chicken carcasses in the rivers and streams near Chapel Hill- and all of them were without their heads. That is part of the Voodoo ritual when they are trying to put a spell on someone. They sever the head of the chicken to conjure a spell on the doomed person. Be very careful, Doctor, I believe Matt Dye is serious about doing you harm. Don't walk in any dark alleys and always carry a silver knife with you to fight the evil spirits."

"Tyler, thanks for that advice. I'll be careful and thanks for coming over to help me and giving me all that information. I appreciate it. If you ever need me, I'll be right there to help you. You can depend on that. And I'll cover that hole with a silver plate until I can get it mended permanently."

"And when I get off in the morning, I'll come bury that great big snake," offered Tyler. "You haven't decided whether to believe me yet, have you? I mean about Voodoo?"

"I need some strong evidence," Zeb said.

"Well, remember the snake. And try to think if you've made any enemies here in town."

"Matter of fact," Zeb faltered. "I may have made a pretty powerful enemy this very day."

Bridget nodded her head and whispered, "Yes. You sure enough did that very thing."

After Tyler left, Zeb began to think more about this gifted Jamaican. He realized that Tyler had experience with the black magic of the islands and would be alert to any danger from the likes of an Obeah man. He realizes that Tyler is aware of demons of various kinds and he knows of charms to defeat them. Although Zeb finds it difficult to believe in the supernatural, he respects Tyler and vows he will supply him with the garlic or flour sifters or whatever else he may wish to defeat the powers of voodoo.

CHAPTER V

Tyler left, avoiding the hole in the floor. Zeb mixed himself a bourbon and water. He needed to relax. His legs still shook. He picked up a mystery novel and stretched out on his couch with Bridget at his feet.

"You saved my life," he said as he stroked Bridget's mahogany head. "I'll never forget it."

"I owed you one," Bridget responded. "You saved my life when I was a scrawny mangy puppy several years ago. Remember?"

"I surely do and I'm glad I did. It has always been my feeling that in any good relationship, or marriage, or the sometimes very close bond of dog and man, whatever is given is given freely and with love. You're worth all the trouble that you gave me to cure your mange. You turned out to be a real pal and the 'love of my life'. However, I have to confess. You weren't the first Irish setter that I ever loved. My first one lived with me for thirteen years and her name was also, Bridget McGuire. Just thinking about her reminds me of many fond memories. Would you like to hear about her? I haven't ever told anyone my inner feelings about her."

"Yes, I would like to know all I can about her. She sounds as if she was someone special."

"She was," Zebulon leaned back in his chair and began his reminiscing. "The years passed by and we were good for each other. Towns people became accustomed to seeing us together wherever I went. As she grew older, she slowed down physically somewhat, but those dark eyes never lost their shining devotion for me. Then came the dreadful night that was the beginning of the end for us. It must have been about two o'clock when I was awakened by a loud thud and a blood-chilling scream. For a moment I was too dazed to realize where I was. Then I really woke up. When I turned the lights on I saw her, my Bridget, convulsing on the floor. Her eyes were turned back; her mouth was working spasmodically; the long slender body was contorted and jerking. Somehow I managed to get my arms around her. I sat on the floor and held her for a lengthy time. Fifteen minutes of unbelievable heartache for me. For Bridget, who knows? When she stopped shaking, I gave her a sedative. Soon, with darkness all about us again, she slept. I did, too, fitfully, but constantly alert for any signs of trouble."

"The next day she was listless and quiet. I did an encephalograph (EEG) which is a test which shows abnormalities in the brain waves much as an EKG shows up an abnormality in a patient's heart. The diagnosis was Epilepsy. My neurosurgeon friend helped me all he could by prescribing drugs to control the attacks. There is no cure. From that time on she had a convulsion every four to six weeks. Usually they occurred at night. I gave her the strength of my arms, so she would not hurt herself while in convulsion. I gave her the strength of my love. How strong, how very strong, was that love. I had known it through sadness and through joy; but never had I known it as I did then, when I felt her slipping away from me."

"A year and a half after that first terrible convulsion I woke to the realization that she was having another. I had the light on in a moment. Once again I sat on the floor, holding her as closely to me as I could manage it. Five minutes went by. Ten. "It'll be over soon, girl," I murmured. With a dreadful effort her whole body became rigid. I held my breath. Then, she went limp. Quite limp, as if—as if—. Bridget, Bridget I yelled. Quickly, quickly, adrenalin. With shaking fingers I pressed in the needle. Desperately I tried artificial respiration. I don't know how long I sat there. I do remember closing those dark eyes, which would never again light up at my coming. I did not cry—then. Later, much later, just as darkness fell on her grave, the tears came."

As Zebulon put his head down, as if to hide his tears, Bridget came over to the couch and lay her head on his lap, saying, "Now, I know why I love you so much. You're so very sentimental."

He went to bed with a heavy heart, hoping to get some sleep, but every time he closed his eyes he would see that fat, menacing length of danger, its flat head weaving as it moved slowly toward him. He would hear again Bridget's voice warning—there's a snake, a snake. If only he hadn't given up sleeping pills.

At last he fell into a troubled sleep that may have lasted for two hours before the clock's alarm clattered him awake.

It was a chilly spring morning. Bridget shivered. "Pity we can't have a good breakfast at Matt's Pub," she said.

"Never mind. I'll cook some breakfast," Zeb comforted her. He pulled out a shiny skillet, found a package of bacon and a carton of eggs from the refrigerator. He worked impatiently and the bacon was limp, the eggs hard. The two ate in silence.

"I don't hear any complaints," Zebulon said. "But I know you're just being polite."

"Shouldn't I be?" Bridget asked.

After breakfast they walked through the woods to the back of the hospital. Zeb kept seeing shadows. He shook his head and told himself he was really batty this morning. The tall grass was damp with dew and Zeb tested it with every step for lurking snakes.

Safely inside the hospital everything was quiet. Zeb walked through the hall to the reception room. He went to Chip's cage with a big golden apple for his daily treat. Abruptly he stopped and caught his breath.

Chips lay on the bottom of the cage, a shockingly motionless little huddle of fur. Zeb unlatched the door. "My God! What's happened here?" he said as he reached inside.

Chips did not respond. Blood oozed from his nose and mouth, and his half-open eyes were bloodshot. Zeb caught him up. He called. "Tyler! I need you."

Tyler came running. The two hurried into an examination room followed by Bridget. Zeb studied the sad little figure of Chips and swiftly wrapped him in a soft towel. Then he quickly carried the little fellow to the surgery. "Come along, Tyler," he said. "Lib isn't here yet. You'll have to help me."

"What must I do, Doctor?"

"I'll give him some shots - we'll start an intravenous drip of saline—we don't have any monkey blood. Here- hold the oxygen mask to his face while I adjust the straps in back." Tyler understood the doctor's directions and helped him with his long, dark, steady hands.

"It's hard to find his jugular vein—blood pressure so low." Zeb's fingers explored. "Wait. Here we are."

The saline drip was adjusted, shots were administered, and oxygen mask was in place. Tyler felt the little body.

"Pulse is getting stronger, Doctor," he reported. "Your treatment is taking effect."

Chips stirred at last. Zeb again wrapped him in the warm towel. "Well put him in Intensive Care in an oxygen cage for a few days." he said. "This little fellow was beaten up! That's the only explanation for these injuries—somebody's fists did that. Who could have done such a thing? Who could have been here last night?"

Tyler plugged in a heating pad under Chip's small beaten body. "The only time I left was when I heard your shotgun go off," said Tyler. "I left the back door unlocked in my hurry. I suppose somebody could have gotten in." he paused a moment, his dark face seeming to grow darker. Then- "Maybe I should warn you, there are a kind of folks who can unlock a door whenever and wherever they want to get in."

Tyler's voice had an ominous ring. Zebulon looked into Tyler's maroon-dark eyes. "Look here, Tyler. You're an educated man. A sensible man. Do you know what you are saying?"

Well, I had good common schooling in Jamaica. And I went to a small college in Mississippi. My grades weren't bad. I guess you could say I'm educated."

"And you still believe in this supernatural stuff?"

"Seeing is believing, Doctor."

****

Morning had dawned and the staff was arriving. Lib Nelson brought Zeb his usual cup of coffee in his office. She clicked her tongue at him, like a disapproving mother.

"You look awful," she pronounced. "Like an advance agent for a new depression. No wonder—Tyler told me about the snake. I wanted to scream. I've warned you, having your house tucked in among those trees and bushes and tall grass is just asking for trouble. Snake trouble. Maybe you'll agree with me now."

"Bless you, Lib," Zeb smiled his special smile for special people and brushed nervously at his hair. "But maybe there's more to that snake story than you've heard. What if I told you that I don't expect to find any more snakes in my bedroom?"

Lib shrugged. "You can tell me anything when you look that honest," she said with an air of defeat.

"There's enough for you to worry about right here," Zeb told her. "Poor Chips got hurt sorely last night, and he needs special attention. So does that ailing cat of the Greens. Keep an eye on both of them."

Lib looked inquiringly at Zeb as if hoping for an explanation of Chip's injuries, but decided nothing was coming. However, before she left, she had to get something off her chest so in a lady-like tone of voice simply stated, "The bastard that beat up that sweet little monkey should rot in hell."

Zeb did morning rounds with Bridget at his side. When they returned to his office, Bridget lay with her chin on her paws. "Matt Dye was certainly busy last night, Zeb," she said.

"You're jumping to conclusions, Bridget."

"Maybe, but Mrs. Clement's Boxer told me that he heard some man in here last night," Bridget announced. "If you'd been listening, you'd have heard that news yourself."

"I was pretty busy back there, remember? How do you figure it was Matt Dye or one of his henchmen he heard?"

"Simple," Bridget said, grinning. "First of all, the Boxer told me there was an unusual odor that he smelled when that man was in the kennel. I'm just adding two and two and getting four. My arithmetic's good enough for that. Sometimes I wonder if you're sorry that you can understand me." Bridget looked wise and winked at Zeb.

The phone rang shrilly. Zeb picked it up. "Yes?"

"Mrs. Wiggins is on line two," came Norris Martin's voice from the front desk. "She sounds as if she's on highball number four. Will you talk to her, Doctor?"

Zeb sighed. This lady often drank herself into a stupor. And just before she reached zero, she called Dr. Zebulon. Usually it was in the middle of the night. He was grateful that this time it was a respectful hour and he wasn't awakened from a deep sleep. Once she got her favorite veterinarian on the phone, she would babble about her two little dogs to Zeb, how much she loved them, how much she needed them, how much they needed her, how she positively couldn't live another moment. Dr. Zebulon was to her like an indulgent God in heaven, who could solve all her problems, whatever they were. Only she knew what they were—Zeb and her psychiatrist understood full well that alcohol was her problem.

"Maybe I'd better talk to her," conceded Zeb. "Put her on."

"Hello, Doctor. Hello, Doctor," came a nasal chatter. "I'm so glad you're there. Doctor, I'm just at the end of my tether—can't face life any longer. You know how hard it is."

"Yes, Mrs. Wiggins," Zeb tried to put soothing syrup into his voice.

"This is it!" she squeaked. "Everything is ready, my warm bath is drawn. I've got a sharp razor."

"Now, wait," he tried to interpose.

"No, no, my mind's made up. But I can't do it until I make sure that little Snooky and little Mitzie will be looked after. I can't leave them unless I'm sure."

"I know you love your little dogs more than anything, Mrs. Wiggins." Zeb was doing his best. "But nobody could look after them the way you do. They love you. They'd die of grief if they didn't have you."

"Do you honestly think that?" Her voice wasn't so shaky, more plaintive now. "Really?"

"I really do," he assured her. "You must think of Snooky and Mitzie. Nobody could replace you. Think of them."

"Oh, Doctor, you're so understanding. And maybe you're right. I'll try for a little while longer."

Wearily, Zeb put down the phone. Then he felt that he must use it again, call his friend, Dr. Allen Sewell, the psychiatrist, who occasionally treated Mrs. Wiggins. She had taken to drinking after her husband's death the year before, had talked of killing herself and once or twice had tried it. He dialed.

"Hi, Allen," he said when Dr. Sewell's secretary finally put the psychiatrist on the line. "Let me report on our mutual friend, Mrs.

Wiggins."

He did so, in detail. "Maybe you should check on her," he finished.

"I'll do that, right away. But I must say, Zeb, you did the right thing with her. You'd make a good psychiatrist."

"Thanks, Allen, it kind of goes with my territory. But it's too late for me to change jobs. I'd rather cure animals than people. Plenty of our pets are nutty because of their nutty owners."

Dr. Sewell reminded Zeb of a story in the local newspaper only last week. "Dr. Jacob Zebulon is adding a couch in his hospital for treatment of neurotic dogs." Both doctors laughed.

"Allen," Zebulon said when the smile had disappeared from his face. "The interesting thing to me was that people took the story so seriously. The column in the newspaper is so obviously one of humor it did not seem possible people actually believed the 'couch doctor' bit but they did. Equally interesting was the fact that people were beginning to consider the possibility that their dogs had problems of one sort or another and might need psychiatric help. Of course, to me as a veterinarian it has long been apparent many dogs have quite pronounced neurotic tendencies. This seems to be a natural advancement, if one may call it so, as dog travels along life's way with his companion—man. So close is the companionship between man and dog, so deep the relationship, the dog now adapts himself to the complexities of modern days by developing neuroses. Modern dogs are to some extent victimized by the fast pace of life today. They are whirled around in automobiles and airplanes from earliest puppyhood. They do not, it is true, drink too much, smoke too much, even, as a rule, eat too much. Yet, I am sure that a dog close to a person or a family is bound to feel the tensions, the frictions, that affect them. All about us, men and women are succumbing to heart ailments, mental illnesses, or even just plain old-fashioned nerves. The dog of today is more prone to those same diseases."

"Allen, I have felt rewarded many times by helping an emotionally disturbed dog but I received a great compliment from one of my clients when she expressed her feeling to me. "You told me that when nervous dogs fell in love with a person, they fell hard. I wish people

Talking With The Dogs

could know that. They're like some people. All they need is a little more extra love and understanding. But how much, how very much, they repay you for that little more."

When Zebulon finished his discourse on neurotic dogs, Dr. Sewell remarked in a humorous tone, "Zebulon, Maybe you and I ought to go into business together. You work on the dogs and I'll work on their humans. Call me if you want me to consult with you. Thanks for calling me about Mrs. Wiggins and her problems."

Zeb began to feel better after his conversation with Dr. Sewell. He took time to ponder. Pets, he was convinced, could help their owners, even heal them. Comfort them when they were ill, at the very least. Little Marjorie Gaige, who'd broken an arm and a leg when her flying sled struck against a rock, had profited by the little waif pup her parents had adopted to cheer her. The dog had never left Marjorie's side on the bed until she was well and the two still spent most of their play time together.

It was Pythagoras who believed that the spirit of a dying man should be breathed into the mouth of a dog, the only worthy creature to preserve continuity of life. And Plato called the dog a true philosopher. So why think Mrs. Wiggins crazy? Maybe he himself was nutty, loving Bridget as he did.

A soft knock at the door and Tyler Steele walked in. He stood tall and straight at Zeb's huge oak desk. His face was heavily serious.

"Why aren't you off duty, Tyler?" Zeb asked. "In your bed? You had a hard night."

"I've just come from your house, Doctor," Tyler said. "Put a silver ash tray over that hole you made. That's a mighty pretty walk over to your house, but it could be dangerous."

"Dangerous?"

"That shaggy grass could hide more copperheads. I'd like to be sure you didn't have to make any more holes in your floor. How about sending David over to mow the grass when he comes in?"

"Sure, if we can spare him from here," agreed Zeb. "And I want to ask him what he knows about that purple-haired girl I saw at Matt's place. Have you ever seen anything like that?"

Tyler smiled wispily. "Well, recently I saw a girl with bright green hair. They say it was a fad in London before it came here. And the young people are having all parts of their bodies tattooed. What will they think of next?"

"I hope they don't tattoo themselves with splotches, like that old snake," Zeb said, his lip corners turned down.

"God, no." Tyler responded. "But nobody knows what college kids will do. When I was in school, the girls were all burning their bras."

"Right, and when I was in school, everybody was swallowing live, wiggling goldfish. That was a bit much but they did it anyway. Now go home and get some sleep."

"If I can," said Tyler. "I can't stop thinking, and thinking keeps me awake. I know that you've wondered what brought me to Chapel Hill."

"Yes, but that's no matter."

"It has suddenly become important. You see my father was thrown in jail because of something a man from this town did to him. And I came here hoping to even that score."

"And the man?"

"You guessed it. Matt Dye."

"So you know that I've been concerned about him lately."

"You're damned right."

"We'll keep on eye on him together."

****

Mid-morning, later in the week, Lib Nelson tramped in with the usual cup of coffee." You'd better look at Chips, Doctor," she said. "He's so much better that maybe he can come out of Intensive Care."

"Good. I'd like to break the neck of whoever did that to him."

"Tyler feels the same way," Lib said. "And if you'd seen the whites of his eyes when he said it, you'd have believed him."

Chips was indeed better and was returned to his own cage. Zeb and Bridget drove to a place called the Fifty Yard Line to find some lunch and decided that the food was better than Matt's.

While they were eating, a man with the longest hair and the

hairiest face that Zeb wished to see, came into the bar with his terrier dog. In a surprisingly high voice, he ordered a stein of beer and asked for a saucer. He filled the saucer with beer from his stein and placed it on the floor for the dog. Each emptied his portion. One of the bystanders ordered another stein for the hairy man and his dog. Again they drank. Each time the stein and saucer was emptied, another bystander would order another round. This continued for five or six foamy steins and brimming saucers until the little dog could barely keep on his feet. He would get up, put his nose to the saucer, and immediately fall down. Again he would try to drink and fall. Then he tried to walk to the door and stumbled over his own feet. The men in the bar loved it and cheered and applauded the dog's drunken antics.

Finally, the great ox of a man bent over, picked up his dog in those muscle-bulging arms and tenderly carried him to his car. He laid him gently down on the back seat to sleep it off. The man felt very satisfied in the fact that he drank free in all the bars that he took his dog.

The men in the bar laughed heartily but Bridget was disgusted. "How can that rotten egg of a man treat his dog that way, Zeb?"

"Don't ask me, Bridget," Zeb told her. "I've never understood people. Animals are better than folks all the way around. But the worst part about what just took place confirms a conclusion that scares me. *Dogs are at the mercy of their owners.* Fortunately, the majority of people treat their dogs as members of the family with tender loving care. However, there are some callous people who take their frustrations on their pets. I have never understood how a human being can abuse a dog, a creature so filled with affection for our species. Yet cruelty to dogs {to all animals, for that matter) is a fact of life and an obvious source of neurotic behavior."

"Some people get a dog as a status symbol, and then behind closed doors they treat the dog miserably. Other people get a dog purely and simply as a whipping boy. They have something to take out their anger on and to abuse. Such treatment causes its victims anxiety, fear and often misbehavior. I know of people that not only expose their dogs to effects of alcohol but give their pets all kinds of drugs that they themselves indulge in. I am finding that an increasing number of dogs are addicted to one thing or another. Sometimes inconsiderate owners give their dogs 'uppers' or 'downers' when they themselves participate in its use. I know of many people who give their dogs egg nog or bloody Marys during party time. Many a dog becomes a sneaky party drinker."

****

Zebulon and Bridget were glad to be back at the hospital, hoping the afternoon would prove uneventful. David Smith had cut the grass and reported no signs of snakes. What snake would be crazy enough to stay around that noisy power motor anyway, Zeb wondered. Maybe they'd stay away for good now. Zeb sat quietly in his big leather chair, a frown wrinkling his tanned forehead, trying to forget his own encounter with danger and thinking about what Tyler had told him about Matt, when the telephone rang.

"Miss Predino on the line," said Norris in her siren tones. "Are you in, Doctor?"

"Definitely. For her- anytime. Put her on."

Zeb's ears sang. What an idiot he was becoming, he thought. And Bridget in her corner, looked at him disapprovingly.

"Jacob?" came Sallie's lovely mezzo voice. "Look, I forgot to tell you something really important. I have to go to a convention of college music teachers on Friday. It's in Washington. They've put me on a panel about modern French music. So I must go, and I don't want to drive. I can't think what to do about Lili. And I don't dare think what Matt might do to her while I'm gone."

"No problem," said Zeb promptly. "She can stay with us—anytime—any time at all."

"You're so good," Sallie trilled. "You must have been a Boy Scout."

"No," he said. "Where I grew up in Brooklyn, my crowd was tough. The Boy Scouts wouldn't have us. Bring Lili over. Bridget will look after her for a few days."

"What happens to me shouldn't happen to a dog," Bridget mumbled to herself.

Zeb could only think that if he saw Lili, he would see Sallie as well. He felt a warm glow inside, and gave Bridget an extra loving pat to reassure her as she sat besides him.

By five o'clock both Zeb and Dr. Peters felt that they had done well. The reception room had filled and emptied several times. Most of the treatments had been fairly routine and both doctors were grateful. One case had brought drama. A handsome Great Dane had eaten strychnine. "That fiend must be loose on the town again," Zeb had groaned. Prompt and effective treatment saved the beautiful dog. Dr. Peters said, "I swear you could bring back a dead dog to life, Doctor."

Zeb laughed to himself. There had been a day when a young woman he knew had come screaming into the hospital. In her arms her little cocker spaniel, just hit by a car, and obviously dead. "Doctor, doctor. Bring her back to life for me. You can do it. I know you can." Bridget seemed to know what he was thinking. "You're thinking what I'm thinking, are you Zeb?"

Changing the subject, Zebulon turned to Dr. Peters and said. "I have been thinking about all the different personalities of dogs we had in our front room today. As a rule the patients in a veterinarian's waiting room act and look very much as do human patients who await the ministrations of their doctors or dentists. There is the nonchalant type. He sits quietly, either on the floor or on one of the sofa or chairs. From time to time he may favor another dog with a faint sniff. Otherwise nothing interests him. He seems to look down his aristocratic nose at anything without a pedigree. Then there is the fussy one. She clambers and climbs all over the place seeking out the perfect spot for her probably too ample rear. She thirsts until water is put before her, when she refuses to drink it. She thinks the Doberman next to her is crowding things too much and growls at him. Nothing suits her. There's the timid and shy one. By thrusting her head under the arm of the person with her she feels sure that no veterinarian in the world can get near her. There's the whiner and there's the howler. The first tells his symptoms to all who care to listen. The second is too busy making a row to care whether anyone is listening or not. You've seen them in any doctor's office. I've seen them time and time again in my waiting room. Most of them share one desire, to be somewhere else."

When Zebulon finished, Dr. Peters exclaimed, "Gosh, doctor, I'm learning a lot of things they never taught us in vet school. I really appreciate all your words of wisdom."

****

On the Friday of Sallie's trip, the evening was pleasantly cool. Zeb and Bridget drove to Sallie's apartment to drive her to the Airport and to bring Lili Tu home with them. Sallie opened the door and out flowed the lovely sounds of a Debussy Quartet, filling the air of the hall. "Beautiful," said Zeb.

The cloudy French harmonies, floating lazily from Sallie's hifi, warmed Zeb's heart and he swept Sallie into his arms. Then he held her away from him for a long hungry look at her. She stood tall and rosy in a black and white patterned skirt with a soft cropped top that seemed to float loosely over it. And she wore black snake skin pumps and a black snake's skin purse.

"Oh, God. I wish you wouldn't, "he said. "But at least it wasn't a blotchy one."

"I'm so sorry, Jacob. I didn't think about your visit from that snake. They're only just shoes to me."

He then embraced her and they kissed for a long time while Lili Tu and Bridget waited. Bridget touched her cold nose to Lili's nose and said, "Hi, beautiful."

"Don't tease," Lili urged.

With a red suitcase and small cosmetic case under his arm, Zeb escorted the three, lady and dogs, to his car. The ride to the airport was a busy one. Everyone who lived in Chapel Hill appeared to be going to Raleigh, and everyone who lived in Raleigh was coming to Chapel Hill. The Raleigh-Durham airport lay between the two in the Research Triangle. Zeb concentrated on his driving. Tailgaters thrived. Survival demanded the utmost care. There was no chance to study the scenery that bordered the highway. After depositing Sallie's luggage at the proper terminal and a quick goodbye kiss, Zeb was on his return trip with Bridget and Lili.

Zeb brooded over the wheel as he drove. "Okay, Bridget, I own up," he said at last. "This is love. I miss her already."

"And you're happy about it?"

"Hell, no. I'm miserable. I've been in love before this, three or four times, but now I feel as if somebody cut my guts out with a dull knife."

"Empty," suggested Bridget.

"That's the word for it. But don't worry—"

"Oh, I worry," said Bridget, "but I stand by you. I'm in your corner."

"Thanks," said Zeb, feeling better. "You're a pal."

"And you're a good man, the best man I ever knew."

Traffic had lessened enough now that Zeb could see something more than the road ahead bisected by its yellow lines. The sprawl of suburban buildings and the freshly leafed trees, with their greenery, enchanted him as he drove. Ahead, where the highway met a dead end side street stood a new house—lath and plaster, dark-stained and white painted, like an English country house. Strange, he had never noticed it before. Now, he saw several cars, big ones—Lexus', BMW's, Cadillac's—parked in front. Just going in was a distinguished mathematics teacher, a client of Zeb's. A quick glance at the sign told him that the place was called 'Happy Day Club'. "Must be some fancy private club," he thought.

Lili Tu noticed it and whispered to Bridget that she heard that Matt Dye owned the place.

"Well, girls," Zeb said as they neared the hospital, "I've got to go see how Mae Sutton's little Boston Bull terrier is doing with her birthing. Those little tykes sometimes have difficulty."

It had grown quite dark by now and there was a fogginess picked up by the oncoming cars' headlights—maybe pollution. Zeb was relieved to approach the entrance of the hospital, even though he caught a glimpse of Matt Dye jogging away into the distance. His ever present Obeah man, with a large colorful robe and flying dreadlocks, was following close behind him. "Dangerous twosome. Wonder why they're prowling around here at this time in the evening. I'm sure he's

Dr. Louis Vine, D.V.M.

up to no good. He's probably looking for Lili right now. I better tell Tyler he's in the vicinity. He's around here all the time lately."

It felt good to stand free of the car and stretch his legs after the long ride. But the more he watched Matt, the more concerned he got.

Everyone had gone home but Tyler. Zeb stopped at the big iron cage to greet Chips and give him his regular kiss and great big orange. "Well, thank God you're feeling better," he said as he petted Chip's little furry head. Then, "Tyler," he called through the emptiness of the hall. I've come to check on the Sutton's dog trying to whelp."

"Okay, Doctor." Tyler came from the kennels, walking fast, his tall, dark figure casting in the hall. "I looked in a moment ago. I think she's about to give birth. Better hurry."

"Let's take her into the surgery and get everything ready."

"Okay," said Tyler. He carried the little Boston into the thoroughly antiseptic room- ceramic tile covered the floor and crept half-way up the wall where clean white paint took over. Various machines stood waiting, should they be needed. An anesthesia machine to feed gas into a patient, an autoclave—looking like a small electric oven with dials for eyes—stood waiting to sterilize equipment. Even a defibrillator, if a heart should stop and need starting again. The latest in surgical equipment was prevalent throughout the room. A large surgical light concentrated its powerful beam on the table where they placed the little dog, Sara.

"You can go on about your duties now, Tyler. Thanks for your help. If I need you again, I'll yell. Then you can take Lib Nelson's place in here."

"I'll do the best I can, you know that." Tyler assured him solemnly.

Zeb studied little Sara. She was small, and many Boston terrier puppies with large heads must pass through a narrow pelvis. He sincerely hoped that this could be a natural birth. But her contractions were not very strong. After checking to be sure the cervix was open, Zeb administered a uterine stimulant to increase the contractions and the puppies began to show. The first one came normally, head first. He pulled it out, held it head down and shook vigorously. It began to cry like a baby. Zeb smiled happily. He dried it off and wrapped it in a soft cloth and laid it besides its mother. Then another came. Then, a bit of trouble- a breech. Zeb managed to rotate it and slide it out without calling Tyler and went through the whole procedure again.

Now all four of the puppies were born and little Sara had eaten all of the afterbirths. Zeb took nylon suture material and tied and trimmed the umbilical cords. He moved the new babies close to their mother and she began licking them. All the little creatures began searching for nipples, ready to feed themselves and begin the business of living.

Zeb pulled off his surgical gloves and gratefully washed his hands for the fiftieth time that day. He glanced into the mirror over the basin. His reflection gazed dimly back at him.

"Well, Dog Doctor," he addressed the image before him, "how goes it? Plenty of dogs today. In everything from pick-up trucks to a light green Cadillac. All in a good day's work for a dog doctor."

At that moment, a deafening racket came from the kennels. The whole building seemed to shake. He ran out of the surgery and into hall, his hands still dripping onto the polished floor. Cats in the cattery meowed, dogs in the kennel howled, "Help!" cried Bridget and "Help!" echoed Lili Tu from behind her in the hallway.

Zeb came running into the kennels, dimly lighted by a lamp. On the opposite side of the room was a door, and the window beside it was open to the night air.

In the window, something lurked, something darker than the outer darkness.

Zeb rushed to the window. A grotesque figure skulked there, just outside the screen. Eyes like red-hot coals glared at him. It stood high and the only thing Zeb could recognize in the darkness was a large crop of dreadlocks on its top. For a moment that seemed an eternity, Zeb gazed into its glowing red eyes, almost in reach of his hand. A rank odor streamed in, surrounding and nauseating him.

CHAPTER VI

Bridget scrambled into the room behind Zeb, uttering angry explosive growls, hair standing up on her back and fangs bared. Her boldness and ferocity didn't seem to scare the intruder at all. The face in the window writhed its lips apart, and light flashed on great white teeth. It rasped on the screen with large nails on huge hands. Large shoulders hunched up high.

Then, a rush of feet from the corridor behind. Tyler's arm pushed past Zeb, his hand held a lean blade that glittered palely. He pushed the knife at the window and the dark, snarling lace outside.

Abruptly, a blubbering whine, and the being turned around and left.

The howling of the kennel dogs hurt Zeb's ears- but the sounds softened as the creature began to retreat. "You'd better run!" yelled Tyler Steele at the departing beast and then he was at the outer door, fairly ripping it open. Tyler was outside in the night, waving his gleaming weapon. Zeb charged after him, with Bridget and Lili Tu at his heels.

They ran among the great, dark trees of the woods. The earth felt spongy after the rains; but they were not mired down. Around and among the trees, Zeb and Tyler moved. Zeb could see a great dark form, running awkwardly on his feet. It gained the belt of trees beyond the hospital grounds, and as it did so, it seemed to fade, to dissolve like a puff of dirty smoke in the foggy night. Tyler had stopped in the dark shadows, Zeb stopped beside him, breathing heavily.

"Gone, it's gone," said Tyler. "Couldn't face this knife." Still the disagreeable odor hung heavy in the night air.

Zeb felt his temples throb, but he made himself walk toward where the shape had vanished. "Careful, Doctor," Tyler warned. "It's gone for now, let's go back in."

Zeb turned and walked back to the kennels. He and Tyler went in and closed the door against the strangeness of the night. Zeb felt sweat on his face, and mopped it with the sleeve of his lab coat.

Talking With The Dogs

"What's that thing you scared it with?"

Tyler held out his hand. Zeb saw that it held a lean, pointed silver blade that looked sharp on both edges. The shaft was wrapped in thongs of dark leather. Tyler stroked it with his long brown fingers.

"How did you happen to have that," Zeb wondered. He still breathed heavily. He felt as though he had run a mile.

"I had it," said Tyler. "I've been carrying it in my belt ever since that snake was sent to you. My grandfather gave it to me, back in Jamaica."

Zeb held out his hand, but did not touch the weapon. "It has some kind of power?"

"Yes," Tyler twitched back his white coat and slid the knife into a sheath at his belt. "Silver's powerfully good against bad spirits. And this blade was treated with drops of magical oils. The Obeah man did it for me in Jamaica. Four oils—Fly Away, Stand still, Balm Balm, and Egyptian Perfume. Its magic is sworn to help the silver along. It seems to have set back our big danger." He looked grimly at the window. "Even the evil spirits of Mondongue can be stopped, they say."

"Mondongue? Isn't that the name of an African tribe?"

"I can't say to that," Tyler said wearily.

Both men were dead tired. Even the dogs in the kennels had quieted and Bridget relaxed, head between paws next to a yawning Lili Tu.

Tyler scrubbed at the tired wrinkles on his forehead. "I don't know how to explain."

Zeb nodded. "Let's just try to talk it out."

Tyler shook his head. "I don't know how to make you believe."

Bridget nudged Zeb. "You've got to believe him Zeb," she said, "You've just got to."

"I know I must believe this, Tyler," Zeb said. "Whatever that was out there, before it faded away, I saw it and it was real. I have to realize that I saw it. That it was there." He looked steadily into Tyler's dark eyes with his penetrating gray ones. "You used the word Mondongue. What is that? Is it Voodoo?"

Dr. Louis Vine, D.V.M.

"No, Voodoo is a kind of religious cult- those people are afraid of Mondongue. The less they hear about it the happier they are."

Zeb's thoughts were growing steadily fuzzier. "Well, what have you heard about it?"

Tyler gestured with both long brown hands. "People down there tremble when they mention it. They fear its evil magic. All I know is that the dog is something big in their rituals. They sacrifice dogs; sometimes they eat dogs." He paused to gather his thoughts. "Maybe they've taught some obeah man part of their magic—their familiar spirits."

The two men sat quietly, thinking.

Bridget remembered that Matt Dye had spent several years in Jamaica and wondered if Zeb had recalled it also.

"Some say they're cannibals," Tyler finally continued. "But that's only a rumor- and that's not enough for me. But we're seeing that somebody—right here in Chapel Hill, and we know who- is able to bring these evil things against us. First that snake, than this creature-or whatever it was. We've whipped him so far. But winning the first battle doesn't always win the war."

Zeb skinned his teeth in what he hoped was a smile. "It ran from that knife of yours. That silver knife that you say was anointed with the oils you mentioned. You named four oils."

"Yes, they helped it work, thank the good Lord. But what if I hadn't been here? What if you'd been here alone? Or Lili Tu?

Let's hope that never happens,"

"Look, Doctor, I was brought up to go to church, to go to school, to try and make something of myself."

Zeb nodded solemnly. "Well, you've certainly succeeded. And if you think we should have silver and those oils for protection, I'll go along with you."

Bridget pricked up her ears, the better to hear this human talk.

"It's for sure that we couldn't get those oils in the U.S. But Obeah men in Jamaica sell them," Tyler said. "You can buy them like aspirin."

Zeb began to feel better. "Can we have them mailed to us?"

"It would take too long," Tyler said. "That enemy man may strike again any time."

"Why don't you go down there early tomorrow and buy them for us? Zeb was already figuring how he could get plane tickets for Jamaica and send Tyler on his errand.

"Yes, I could do that." Tyler's brown face was furrowed in thought. "The oils are in little vials like perfume. Customs would probably think I was bringing home perfume for my lady friend." Tyler seemed to be excited about the trip and already planning which drug store to visit.

Zeb pondered long over the things Tyler had told him. Matt Dye might have learned some of the evil magic during his stay in Jamaica. But Tyler had learned at his grandfather's feet. He had remembered and could defend against it. He would be a good adversary for Matt Dye, Zeb thought. Seeing was believing—that snake sat coiling its menace under his bed. That creature almost got into the kennels. The woods still smelled of him.

****

After completing rounds in the early morning, Zeb decided to walk through last night's chase. He called to Bridget and the two left the hospital by the hospital by the back door. The spongy earth retained prints of some kind—vaguely resembling human foot prints. Zeb traced the tracks between trees, all along the mossy earth to a band of trees where it went around a giant oak.

"I think that beast or whatever you want to call it went this way," Zeb motioned to Bridget. And she put her nose to the ground, sniffing as she followed the tracks.

"By God, you're right," said Bridget. "I remember smelling that mucky, heavy odor for some distance. You don't have to be a bloodhound to follow that scent."

The two walked slowly on. Suddenly Zeb whistled. "Look at that." He said to Bridget. "That looks mighty familiar." Zeb was pointing to shoe tracks, a familiar whirl of a tread showing faintly in

Dr. Louis Vine, D.V.M.

the soft earth. The tracks met the creature's and they continued away together.

Bridget put her nose to the ground. They walked until they came to a paved road some distance behind the hospital. "I've smelled those tracks before, Zeb," she said triumphantly. "And do you know when? Always around our rose bushes in front, after Matt Dye has been walking past our clinic."

"Oh? Just what do you think of Matt Dye, Bridget?"

"Well, I can show you better than I can tell you," Bridget snorted, and she walked over to a dogwood tree and lifted one leg against it, pretending she was a male dog.

"You're too right, Bridget," Zeb said good humorously.

The two walked slowly, thoughtfully, back to the hospital.

****

Sunday came and Sallie's plane would land in the afternoon. Zeb began to worry about Bridget. "Look, old girl, you aren't really jealous of Sallie, are you?"

"Well, what do you think? She's all you think about."

"Yes, I'm in love with her. But you must know that I love you too, the same as ever. Sallie's different. Someday she and I can have little veterinarians running around the house. The patter of little feet and all that kind of mush. You must know."

"But I love you too. Dogs can have human emotions such as love and jealousy," answered Bridget.

"Of course. We love each other. There are two kinds of love. Maybe more. You mustn't worry."

Zeb knew that jealousy is one of the strongest emotions that causes dogs to react with misbehavior. Zeb realized that jealousy generally develops in dogs when they are not the center of attention. For such dogs, some of the things that can cause neurotic behavior include: a new pet, or too much attention paid to other pets in the household; a new human mate or a new baby with the dog relegated to the backyard. He knew that Bridget was suffering from this condition. He tried to be as gentle as he could with her since Sallie came into his life.

Zeb smiled to himself as he remembered tales his clients had told him about jealous pets. Mr. Hughes and his dog had lived together for years before he married. The dog took an intense dislike to the new wife. She tried every ruse, even putting intimate clothing in the dog's bed in hope of getting him used to her. Nothing worked. Whenever Mrs. Hughes came close to the dog, he tried to bite her. Zebulon finally advised the husband to get rid of the dog or the wife. And he never found out how Mr. Hughes settled the problem. It was a serious dilemma. After all, a good dog is hard to find!

Another man, a sad new husband who complained to Zeb that he had married a beautiful young woman who had owned a pet poodle for years. On the first night of their marriage, the dog had jumped onto the bed and urinated on him. If the wife and dog got into bed first, the poodle would bare his teeth and not allow the husband into the bed. But even worse was the fact that the little dog put himself between the husband and wife every time they tried to make love. "He's ruined my sex life," the husband complained. He was tired of sleeping in the guest room by himself.

Zeb stroked Bridget's beautifully shaped red head and said, "I know it's a problem. But you're a smart lady—smarter than most dogs. You'll understand."

****

Late that afternoon, Sallie's plane arrived on time and her baggage had not been lost. Everybody helped to make her arrival easy. The drive home was slow because it seemed that everyone was going somewhere. "The world's on the move. Why can't people sit still?" Zeb asked.

Sallie agreed. "Maybe they think all the fun is somewhere else."

A good many of the cars were turning in to the parking lot of the Happy Day Club.

"There goes Dan Simpson," Sallie said, "He's plodding toward the clubhouse entrance. He and his wife are separating, and I understand that he's pretty miserable."

"Maybe the Happy Day Club will give him a happy day."

Dr. Louis Vine, D.V.M.

"I've heard that Matt Dye owns it," Sallie said. "I wonder."

"Maybe he does. They say he'll do anything to earn a dime," Zeb agreed. "I've something to tell you, Sallie. That creature with the dreadlocks visited us last night. I'm calling it a creature for want of a better word. Tyler and I don't know what or who it is. We think it is an Obeah man, one that specializes in voodoo." He spent the rest of the drive telling the wide-eyed Sallie of their adventure. When he finished with his narration of last night's incident, he looked at her beautiful face and said, "We wonder what it's all about. It appears more and more to involve Lili Tu. We're going to keep a close watch on you and her all the time. I mean, all the time. In fact, I would advise you both to move into my house with Bridget and me so that we can be sure that no harm will befall ya'll."

Lili Tu had been perfectly quiet, but now she looked at Bridget with wonder in her little eyes. Bridget whispered to her, "We'll take good care of you, Lili. Don't you worry."

"Jacob, you're wonderful," Sallie said. She put her arms around him and snuggled close. "How did I ever manage without you?"

"Let's go to my house and fix drinks," Zeb said, his gray eyes filled with love.

"And I'll cook supper. I've brought shrimps and crabs from Chesapeake Bay. We'll have them stuffed. Like?"

"Great."

A stop at Southern Seasons Gourmet Shop for mushrooms and rice and some fancy tomatoes and on to Zeb's house. He left Sallie preparing the food and ran across to the hospital, where he found Dr. Peters working late. "Would you mind sleeping here tonight, Ken?" he asked.

Ken smoothed the tired wrinkle from between his brown eyes. "I did hear that Sallie was coming home tonight, Doctor."

"Never mind that. Tyler is out of town and I didn't get much sleep last night. You'll do it?"

"Sure. You know I will," agreed young Dr. Peters.

"I'll just take a look at the kennels before I leave," Zeb said. And he hurriedly walked back to the long room filled with cages, each with an outdoor run. He hoped the dogs would be quiet now and no longer fearful of what they had seen and heard last night.

"Hey, Doc," a big Airedale greeted him. "What in hell was going on in here last night? It scared the daylights out of us."

"I'm sorry about that, fellas," Zeb soothed. He rubbed at his tired eyes and wished he could give the dogs a sensible explanation of what had happened. At the moment he looked like a child who wanted to ask again and again, "Why? Why?"

"We're going to see that it won't happen again," he said. "So trust us. Dr. Peters is going to stay with you all tonight. I'm going home for some rest, now."

"Goodnight, Doc," came a chorus of voices. "You deserve a rest."

Back in his tidy little cottage with its pecan paneling and comfortable furniture, Zeb sat down in his big lounge chair. Sallie brought him a frosty drink of her own creation.

"I hope you like it, Jacob. It should chase away the tiredness of centuries."

Zeb took a sip and agreed. She must have used a bit of every liquor and liqueur in his cupboard. But it tasted heavenly.

Bridget turned her beautiful brown eyes on Lili Tu and said in a wry whisper, "Looks like they're about to forget us, Lili."

Lili Tu cautioned her with a "Shhh."

"Well, I'm glad to have your company, Lili. Because it's really sinking in. Those two are about to go off the deep end."

Zeb heard her. He turned in his chair and said, "Don't worry." Then he pulled Sallie down onto his lap and began to kiss her hungrily. To his delight, she returned his kisses just as avidly. They sat for a few moments in bliss until Sallie pulled herself away and said, "We really must have our dinner."

"I've lost my appetite for that kind of food, Sallie," Zeb said. "But if you insist."

"I do. And Bridget does, And Lili Tu does."

'The meal was delicious. but not delicious enough to keep Zeb and Sallie at the table. "Let's leave the dishes for tomorrow," they decided. And they walked arm and arm to the little bedroom with its window open to the whispering woods. Fortunately, Zeb thought, it has a strong screen wire for protection.

Bridget watched them go and almost cried. Lili Tu quieted her. "Don't forget, Bridget. We're pals. You'll have me," she said.

Zeb watched Sallie undress. As each garment fell it exposed more of Sallie's beauty- an ivory tinted body, curved in the right places, slender in the right places. His face flushed and his ears drummed. He grew warm all over. "Please hurry, Sallie," he begged. Finally, Sallie tossed aside her panty hose and crept under the sheets. Zeb took her in his arms and they made love, hungrily. The bed seemed to shake with their movements.

"I love you, Sallie."

"And I love you, Jacob."

Finally, they lay still. Then another, a quieter love-making, and sleep overtook them.

CHAPTER VII

Early Sunday morning, Bridget yawned noisily—still angry at being ousted from her place on Zeb's bed. A yawn so loud that Zeb frowned at her. "Shh." He warned. He slipped on a robe and opened the door for her to take a morning stroll. Lili Tu followed, every wrinkle on her too-big coat seeming deeper than ever.

As Bridget moved through the door, she gave Zeb her parting shot, "I'm sorry I waked you, Zeb. You must be tired. You got hardly any sleep last night."

"Hush, young lady," Zeb scolded her.

Lili Tu spoke up. "Behave yourself, Bridget. That kind of stuff's only natural for them."

Bridget almost whined. "But that was my place on the bed."

Sallie began to wake up. She sounded sleepy. "It's Sunday morning. The birds are singing, the sun's shining. Spring is the most beautiful and magical time of the year. Our town begins to blaze with greenery and with all the colors of the beautiful flowers. We're going to have a wonderful day."

"Hear that?" Lili Tu said to Bridget as she hurried her out of the door.

Zeb went to the kitchen, took down his coffee pot and began to prepare breakfast. They had bought imported coffee beans, which he ground and began to brew in the drip pot. He squeezed orange juice and filled glasses. Then he carried a tray to Sallie. It was a very special occasion. Maybe they could have scrambled eggs and country ham later.

Sallie thanked Zeb for the wake up tray and they quietly sipped coffee for a few moments. "It's Sunday. We can have a whole day together," she finally said.

"Can't do that," Zeb told her. "Sunday's just like any other day. Little animals get sick and have to be looked after. I have to run over and do morning rounds. It won't take me over an hour unless I have emergency patients."

"Maybe even snakes," added Bridget with a wry smile, as she came back into the room. Lili Tu looked disgusted.

Sallie got out of bed and slipped on a filmy pink peignoir. Her cheeks reflected its lovely color and Zeb's ears felt hot and his mouth dry.

Bridget suffered. "I'm going to get a Sallie doll and chew it up," she whispered *sotto voce*.

"You go ahead and do your rounds," Sallie said to Zeb. "I'll fix bacon and eggs."

Zeb, half dressed by now, grinned sheepishly and said, "Okay. I bet you cook bacon better than I do. And by the way, Bridget likes her bacon very crisp and she takes three spoons of sugar with cream in her coffee." Bridget seemed pleased. At last she was getting some recognition from her love-struck companion.

Zeb left, walking rapidly with Bridget at his heels.

"You've got it bad, Zeb." She accused.

"You're not to worry. I promised you," Zeb reassured her.

As they walked among the trees, Zeb sensed the familiar rank odor. It wasn't strong, but it hung there in the air. "Do you smell what I smell, Bridget?" he finally asked.

"It's there all right, Zeb," Bridget said sniffing. "I heard some funny noises in the night, too. I didn't want to bother you—you were making some funny noises of your own. Anyway, it didn't sound very close."

"Anything's too close right now. Let's not forget that," Zeb warned.

Inside the hospital, young Dr. Peters greeted them with his customary, "All is serene." There were no seriously ill animals at the moment, mostly boarding dogs and cats and two pregnant dogs who must be watched. Zeb felt a distinct relief not to be faced by a crisis when so much depended on him. He and Tyler must be constantly on the alert to protect Sallie and Lili Tu. No longer was it a doctor, client, patient relationship. He was deeply in love with this woman and he wanted to protect her for the rest of his life.

Zebulon stopped at the cage of a big Airedale and asked him if he felt okay.

"Yes, Doc. I'm fine. But something was stomping around in the woods last night. But it wasn't loud enough to get us upset."

"Yes, I know. It wasn't anything like the other night. You'll all be fine now." And Zeb left the hospital to join Sallie for breakfast.

Zeb found Sallie in the kitchen mixing an omelette with green chili peppers and avocado. "Lili and Bridget will have theirs plain, I think," she told Zeb. "We'll serve them first."

"This is delicious," Zeb said after his first mouthful. "Where did you learn to cook?"

"Oh, everywhere I've been," she said, flashing her brilliant smile.

Over a second cup of coffee, Zeb turned a very serious face towards Sallie. A deep frown stood between his bright gray eyes, and he brushed a wheat colored lock of hair from his face. "Sallie, I have something I must tell you. That monster was outside these grounds last night. He must be looking for you and Lili. I think it would be wise if you both moved in here with me and Bridget during these perilous times. We have a dangerous foe challenging us. Matt Dye plays for real and he has no scruples."

She studied him a long moment, considering what he had said. "Why, Jacob, I didn't know you were a dirty old man. It sounds like a proposition to me," she said with a broad smile on her face. "However, since I'm madly in love with you, I accept your suggestion. And Lili Tu loves you too. I saw how well you and her got along together—how well you understand each other. Look how quickly she picked up all that 'dog show technique' you've been giving her. Now I know why you are so successful with the treatment of your patients."

"Sallie, please listen." Zeb pleaded. "This is serious. As you well know, after receiving that bump on my head at the Westminster Dog Show a few months ago, I have been able to understand the vernacular of dogs. I didn't know how long this ability would last but recently, a young Irish woman, a client, gave me this four-leaved shamrock. She found it in a folk market in Ireland." He showed Sallie the talisman, hanging from a chain around his neck. "It has magic properties as long as I wear it, I can understand dog language. You don't think I'm crazy do you?"

"Jacob, you're the sanest man I've ever known. Of course I believe you." Plainly she meant what she said.

"Now listen again. Because there's more. And this may be harder to understand."

"Jacob, I love you. I'll believe anything you tell me. "Sallie leaned over and kissed him gently.

Lili Tu had sat quietly beside Bridget, listening intently to this conversation. Now she understood everything. "Bridget, you've got to get off Zeb's back," she said. "He loves you, too. He really loves all of us, I guess."

Bridget remained grumpy, but Lili Tu had more to say. "I happen to know that Sallie is jealous of you." Bridget looked at her strangely. "But she isn't always crying around about it, is she?" Lili said.

"Okay, Lili. You've convinced me to give it a go." Bridget finally said.

Zeb heard Lili Tu and was grateful. Maybe she can stop Bridget from worrying, he thought. He hated to be in the middle with two females fighting over him. But meantime there was much more to tell Sallie. Would she believe the story of an Obeah man threatening them—the idea that Matt Dye had studied Voodoo in Jamaica? She might think it was kind of cute to talk to dogs- but how cute was witchcraft or snakes? And how to convince her of all this?

"Sallie," he finally said. "There's more. Please trust me when I tell you these things. It's hard to believe. It was hard for me, until I actually saw things happen and I heard the animals in my kennel go crazy."

"Jacob darling, please. I trust your integrity and I do believe you. Go ahead, tell me everything."

"Okay then." Zeb decided. He told her about the snake under his bed. "We didn't see that snake come into the house. It didn't slither under a door. It didn't slide across the floor to seek a hiding place. It simply appeared under my bed. And Bridget heard it there."

"Well, how do you think it got there, Jacob?"

"We're pretty sure that Matt Dye had it put there with the help of evil spirits. It's an old Voodoo trick. An Obeah man can do almost anything to scare an enemy."

Talking With The Dogs

Zeb was a tall, broad-shouldered man who had grown strong from years of playing all kinds of sports. But suddenly Sallie felt motherly toward him. She took him in her arms and embraced him tenderly. "But why should he do that to us?"

"He wants Lili Tu," Zeb replied. Then he stopped to think. "He asked me to help him get her from you and he hates me for not helping him. He says he wants to breed his Shar Pei with Lili Tu. He admits Lili is an outstanding bitch—your Uncle Milt's best— her puppies would sell for thousands of dollars. And Matt's money crazy. He'll do anything for an easy buck. But he's gone too far this time."

"Jacob, I can easily believe that he could want Lili. But how could he have learned this magic? Surely not in Chapel Hill?"

"No, dear. Some time ago, Matt hid out in Jamaica for several years to let a drug charge blow over. He could have learned about Mondongue from an Obeah man. Obviously he made friends with one of them and brought him back here with him."

"Okay Jacob," Sallie said. "I've got to believe you. You look so honest." She put a softly rounded arm about his neck and gave him a gentle, loving kiss. "I've never told you some of the things about Mr. Matt Dye. He's tried several times to make dates with me. And he's pushed himself in when Lili and I've been out walking. She hates him and lets him know it. Her hair rises on her back and she shows him her fangs. She must know something that we don't."

Lili Tu nodded to Bridget. "He's a terrible man," she whispered. And Bridget agreed with her. "Yes, he sure is."

"Tyler's coming home this evening." Zeb continued to explain to Sallie. "He went to Jamaica to buy magic oils for us to rub on silver chains to counteract the evil. He routed the demon with a silver knife that his grandfather had given to him. It had been treated with these oils. Tyler knew that we would need protection when he wasn't with us. We'd need something of our own."

"It does seem like a good idea. But I don't even have a silver chain, Jacob," said Sallie.

"You do now, dear." Zeb opened a drawer and rummaged out a handful of chains. "I bought one for each of us. I even considered getting one for Henry, Tyler's cat. But Bridget says that Henry could

Dr. Louis Vine, D.V.M.

outrun any ghost. She says that he roams the hospital all hours of the day or night and instantly alerts Tyler to anything out of the ordinary. If Henry suddenly Halowe'ens his tail and his back hair stiffens, Tyler takes notice. Henry is gray like the night and can go about virtually unnoticed."

****

The afternoon wore busily on. Zebulon examined little Chips who seemed to be okay once again begging for a kiss and goodies. In the lab, he was examining specimens under the microscope when Norris announced that Mr. and Mrs. Newman were waiting in examining room one for him. "Oh, I'm so sorry her husband is along with her. He is a very belligerent and intolerable person," Zeb responded. "It seems to me that he is very jealous of the wife's affection for the poodle. Okay, I'll get up my courage and bedside manner and see them."

Mrs. Newman came in, carrying the dog. The man slouched in, slamming the door behind him. His wife put Pierre on the table. Dr. Zebulon rubbed the dog's head, conscious all the time of the perfumed hair on his topknot and of the bright red nail polish on his toenails. For a moment no one said a word. Finally he asked, "What's troubling Pierre?"

"Same old thing," growled the husband. "High living and—"

"That'll do from you," broke in his wife. "Pierre is a thoroughbred dog and you just don't understand him at all. Now, Doctor, them seems to be something wrong because he hasn't touched a bit of food the whole day and it doesn't seem—"

"Oh for Pete's sake," groaned Mathews, "let the Doc examine him and stop your yapping. Whenever I complain of being sick, she always tells me to take two aspirins. But let this little mutt miss a meal and she takes him to the doctor."

As Zeb glared at this man, he wished, as he had so often during the past year, that these people would go elsewhere for veterinary care. They weren't even Chapel Hill people, but had to drive fifteen miles to reach his hospital. He soon learned that their marital life was anything but a happy one. The man drank far too much. The woman, who had received Pierre as a gift, lavished on the appreciative dog the attention and affection that the husband thought belonged to him. The perfume on the topknot, the polish on the nails, the foam-rubber cushioned basket, the gourmet food, while they pleased the poodle mightily, only made for greater disharmony in the home. Yet Mathews always came with his wife and the dog. It may be he was afraid she'd spend too much on Pierre. Whatever the reason, there he'd stand, glowering and quarrelsome, during Zebulon's examination.

The wife spoke up. "As I was saying before I was so rudely interrupted, Pierre doesn't refuse any of my cooking, so when he doesn't eat, I know there is something seriously wrong with him. And another thing I haven't told you Doctor, he has been limping slightly."

Zebulon knew he had to take charge and end this bickering, so he picked up Pierre in his arms and announced, "I'm taking him to my laboratory so I can give Pierre a thorough examination." As he turned his back to the pair, he caught them glaring at each other.

In the laboratory room, Zeb looked at Pierre and sympathetically said, "I pity you, having to live in a house with a man like that. I don't like him. I believe he's jealous of you."

Pierre looked surprised at first, hearing dog talk coming out the doctor's mouth. But he soon recovered his composure and replied, "I'm certainly glad that you understand my predicament. He's a monster and treats my missy and me horribly. I wish I could tell her all that I know about that man, especially that carousing around he does when she's out of town."

"Now, now," Zeb said soothingly. "Tell me about how you feel?"

"If they were half smart, they would notice that I'm holding my right front paw up because it is hurting me and I feel feverish."

Zebulon checked his temperature with a thermometer and agreed with Pierre. "Yes, you have two degrees of fever. Now let me look at that paw." He lifted the swollen and tender paw and realized immediately that there was an abscess forming between his toes. With the aid of a local anesthesia, he soon had the offending splinter out. He cleansed the wound, bandaged the paw and after a shot for the

Dr. Louis Vine, D.V.M.

infection, returned Pierre to the waiting couple. He showed them the splinter that he had extracted and dispensed five days of antibiotics.

Good riddance, he thought, as they left the room. All in a day's work he rationalized and returned to his private office. He had just decided to call it a day and go home when Norris rushed into his office and said, "You have a call from England— Mrs. Dawson. She says she's terribly lonesome for Harriet—her poodle. She says that she's just got to talk to her."

"My God!" exclaimed Zeb.

"What can I do?" asked Norris.

"Bring Harriet to my office and put the lady on. I'll do my best to humor her," Zeb said wearily.

Norris rushed to the kennels, her skirt swishing about her long legs. She grabbed Harriet in her arms and whispered to her, "Your crazy lady wants to hear your sweet little voice, poor thing."

Back in the office breathless, Norris shoved Harriet into Zeb's arms.

"Pythagoras, Socrates, all you geniuses, please help me with your theories," Zeb thought, rumpling his hair in disgust as he sat by his phone. Norris hurried back to her own desk and the main telephone.

"Yes, Mrs. Dawson," Zeb said quietly to the first question he heard in the lady's rasping voice. "I can hear you as well as if you were right here in Chapel Hill."

"Oh, doctor. "You can't imagine how much I miss Harriet. How I've suffered without her! If I could hear only hear her voice."

"She's right here in my arms, Mrs. Dawson. Tell her hello and we'll see if she'll speak to you." He held the phone to Harriet's ear.

"Why should I speak to her?" groaned Harriet in obvious dismay. "If she misses me so much, why in hell did she go away?"

"Shh. That wasn't very kind," scolded Zeb in a whisper."

"Hello, Harriet!" Shrieked Mrs. Dawson into the phone. Her voice fairly shook the wires, shrill and familiar. Harriet cocked her head to one side listening. "Hello, darling! Mummy misses you so very much. Here, I'm throwing you a kiss."

"Hello yourself," answered Harriet grumpily. "Thank the lord she can't understand me," she added to Zeb. "Because I think she's a total nut. But this is my voice. I know it sounds like barking to her, but that's okay with me."

"You little angel. I've seen wonderful sights-~old castles, museums, great restaurants. But nothing can take your place, Harriet. So I'm flying home tomorrow."

Zeb decided to take charge. "Then you'll be coming for Harriet soon."

"Yes, please have her groomed for me. I can't wait. I'll be there day after tomorrow." And the lady hung up amid what sounded like sniffles.

Zeb carried Harriet back to the kennels. "Thanks, he told her. "You did a good job. You mustn't be too hard on her. She really loves you."

As he was putting the little poodle into her cage, he happened to glance at the window in the main kennel room. A wispy shadow hovered there. It disappeared as he looked, like a puff of smoke in the wind. He wondered. Was there something there or was his imagination playing tricks on him. He admitted that he had been a little jumpy ever since the snake incident.

When he got back to his office, Norris soon joined him and discreetly remarked, "What a screwball! You must have nerves of steel putting up with these characters that bring their pets to you. I don't know how you can put up with some of them."

"Now Norris, you have to be more tolerant of these people. That's my .job, to help people with their pet's physical and emotional problems which directly affect their own emotional dilemma. I wonder how many lonely people credit their pets with service past all understanding. These, the lonely ones of the world, need companionship, need affection, so very much. For one reason or another they cannot find it among their own kind. Often the dog gives it to them in full and overflowing measure. The dog, be he spaniel or terrier or just plain dog, seems to know the need of the human. Given any encouragement whatever, he dedicates the rest of his small life to one end, the pleasing of his one-person-in-the-world. You know how wonderful you feel at the end of a hard day when your dog greets you with a madly wagging tail, jumps up and tries his level best to show you how splendid you are. To a lonely person this sort of response means all the difference between emptiness and the warmth of communication."

"Gee, Dr. Zebulon, I never realized you felt that way. I promise you I'll be more charitable to these eccentric people in the future?'

"I have to admit though," Zeb conceded, "these people get to me sometimes too. But remember, most of them are well-meaning persons who love their animals and some of them are as unconventional as I am and believe that *dogs are people, too."*

Just about that time, Norris and Zebulon heard the screeching brakes of a car stopping at the front of the hospital. Peeking out from the curtain, they saw a delivery van from the University Flower Shop from uptown. When they arrived at the front door, the driver produced one of the most beautiful containers of flowers that they had ever seen.

Zebulon turned to Norris with a, "Some admirer sending you flowers, huh?" She shook her head. "Probably for one of your patients, Doctor.' She said. She was right, too. The flowers were for Flossie, a little terrier who had undergone an operation the day before. The accompanying telegram requested that the flowers be put in the patient's cage. Their wishes were followed out and Flossie seemed to brighten up when she saw the flowers.

"Not to be outdone by human hospital patients," Zebulon added, "many of our hospitalized patients receive get-well cards and we receive many telephone calls requesting the latest information on the progress of Sugarplum."

Seated in his office after Norris left, Zeb began to write a report for Lib Nelson's information. His thoughts returned to Sallie. She was on his mind so much these days. Bridget had learned to read his thoughts. He knew that Bridget was jealous and now he feared that Sallie also had become worried about his love for the beautiful dog. He knew that he must walk delicately before these two females. Although he knew well how jealous pets might react, he had yet to learn about ladies and he hoped Sallie wouldn't teach him.

Tyler should be arriving soon and their business with the oils and silver chains would keep them all occupied for a little while. He wrote

Talking With The Dogs

a note for the Jamaican and would leave it on his door, asking him to come to his cottage when he arrived home.

There was a soft knock and young Dr. Peters came into the office. "Would you like me to stay here again tonight?"

"Yes, would you stay for a while?" Zeb asked. "Tyler will be back sometimes this evening, he'll probably take over for you."

"Sure, I don't mind. Matter of fact, I need a nice quiet night with sick dogs and cats. I just had a beer at Matt's Pub and things were a bit wild over there. There was a girl with purple hair, obviously stoned. You could smell the marijuana all over the place. And another girl had bright green hair and another cuddly little item had blue. One of them danced on the tables and she had tattoos on her arms and legs. What's going on around here, anyhow?"

"I don't know. But the hair is probably the most innocent part of it."

"Right, Doctor," Ken said. He hesitated a moment. "I'm wondering what makes Matt Dye's baked potatoes so popular. It seemed to me that most of the people there were eating them."

"I hear they're pretty tasty," Zeb said with a smile. '~I'm glad you brought up that subject. I have some interesting things to tell you." He then proceeded to enlighten Ron about the serious situation with Matt Dye and his voodoo man. After he finished, he asked in a serious tone of voice, "Ken, we sure could use your help in getting some evidence on Matt Dye. Could you frequent the Pub and snoop around but be careful. Matt's a dangerous foe. Don't even use your right name and by all means, don't tell anybody that you work for me. Matt has eyes in back of his head."

"Don't worry Doctor. I've been reading detective stories all my life. If you didn't talk me into becoming a veterinarian, I probably would have been a policeman. I'll see what I can find out."

"Ken, thanks for staying late tonight. I really appreciate it. Hope everything goes all right. If not, I'll be at home. Call me if you need me."

Zeb and Bridget walked slowly through the little patch of woods to the cottage behind the hospital. He loved his house with the tobacco barn siding. It nestled so neatly among the trees that is was almost hidden from the street beyond. His nearest neighbors were the birds and the rabbits- and an occasional raccoon who came to taste his garbage. Bridget delighted in frightening the scavengers away. Now, Sallie would be waiting for him inside. As he neared his doorway, he heard a wren singing and a mocking bird in sweet imitation. And coming strongly to him behind the bird songs, soared the lush strains of Scheherazade. It's beautiful Oriental harmonies threaded their way among the trees and he hurried his steps toward the cottage. So Sallie loved his Russian music and had looked through his music collection. His hair stirred at its roots, just as this lovely music always caused it to do. But this time it was more pronounced. Maybe Sallie's presence helped.

Zeb slammed through the door and took Sallie in his arms. "You love Russian music, too."

"Of course I do," she replied. They kissed and kissed until finally, Zeb paused long enough to make a profound statement. "This is the closest to heaven I ever expect to get."

Bridget, in her corner besides Lili Tu, snorted. "There they go again, Lili."

"Hush your fuss, Bridget," Lili chided. "They have a right to enjoy the finer things in life."

After a late highball, as the evening was mellowing into night, Tyler came knocking at the door. Zeb hurried to greet him.

The dignified brown man placed four small pharmacist's vials on Zeb's pecan wood dining table. Each one held a label written in pen and ink. They read *Fly away, Stand Still, Balm Balm* and the last one, *Egyptian Perfume.* "The customs people thought they were perfume for my girl friend. It worked just like the way I thought it would."

Tyler stopped a minute and reached in his pocket again. He pulled out a paper packet. "Oh yes," he said. "I bought this for you, too." He opened the package and took out a book. It was small, thin and bound in dark gray paper. Zeb took it and looked at the cover:

John George Homan's
Pow-Pows
Or
Long Lost Friend

A collection of Mysterious and Invaluable
Arts and Remedies
Good for Man or Beast

"What is it?" Zeb asked. "Voodoo spells?"

"No, it's Pennsylvania Dutch. But you can get it in the West Indies."

"Thanks," said Zeb, and leafed through it."

There were formulas for curing colds, colic, boils, diarrhea, toothache, a whole catalogue of ills: recipes for beer making, molasses making, paper making: and among these spells with intriguing titles in boldface type: GAINING A LAWFUL SUIT, TO SPELL-BOUND A THIEF SO THAT HE CANNOT STIR, TO WIN EVERY GAME ONE ENGAGES IN, TO EXTINGUISH FIRE WITHOUT WATER, PROTECTION AGAINST ALL KINDS OF WEAPONS.

"Thanks, Tyler," said Zeb again in a conciliatory tone "Some of these things look right helpful."

"I've always liked that 'Protection against all weapons' thing myself."

"Right on."

Zeb decided to carry the book back to his office and study it between cases. And they would find time to anoint the chains early the next morning. He hadn't liked the way that Bridget had wrinkled her nose as she walked through the woods. And even his less sensitive nostrils caught a sniff of that alien smell from time to time.

Chapter VIII

After Tyler left, Sallie told Zeb that she must leave also. She loved his comfortable cottage, and most of all she loved him—but Monday was another school day and she must report back to the college. Bridget gave a sigh of relief. "Now I can have my place on the bed, again," she thought wistfully, as they all got into Zeb's car to drive to her apartment house in town.

"Final exams are coming soon," Sallie told Zeb. "Then I'll have a vacation and we can have good long times together."

"Ye Gods!" thought Bridget.

"Great," said Zeb.

The apartment looked empty and cold when they opened the door. Zeb walked to the fireplace and lit a neat pile of logs that they had left in place. The warm glow made them all feel better. "I'll leave you now, Sallie," Zeb said. "Take care. I mean you must be watchful all the time. Both of you. I want to know that you're safe. If you have any problems at all, call 911 first and then call me, no matter what time of day or night it is."

"I promise," she cooed.

Zeb thought he was hearing sinister little whispers in the walls and corners of the room. He thought he must be a little nutty these days. Paranoid? He certainly hoped not. After a lingering kiss, the two separated and Zeb left, with Bridget trotting behind him.

Mid-morning, next day, Tyler came into Zeb's office. In his hands he held two steaming cups of coffee. He took the bottles of magic oil from his pocket and placed them on Zeb's desk. Zeb pulled five silver chains from his desk drawer and laid them out besides the little bottles. There were two chains short enough for dogs and three long enough for human necks. The tall brown man carefully took an eye dropper in his hand. He opened a bottle, drew liquid from it, and let fall a single drop of Fly Away onto each chain, muttering something as he did so. He repeated this with Stand Still. A soft haze of perfume reached Zeb's nostrils. Tyler straightened the chains and repeated the entire process with Balm Balm. Then with Egyptian Perfume. The room filled with whispers, mocking voices. "We're being watched, Tyler," Zeb said.

Tyler stood quiet, in an almost holy attitude, mumbling some words.

"What was that you said, Tyler?" asked Zeb.

"They're magic words my grandfather taught me." The dark man looked almost saintly. "They're only known to a very few."

"Okay. I certainly hope they work."

"You can rest easy on that I think," Tyler assured him. "We're safe now. Just keep your chain always with you."

Zeb fastened Bridget's chain about her neck at once and put his own on over the four-leaf shamrock talisman. "We'll get Sallie's and Lili's chains to them as soon as school's out," he told Bridget.

"I hope Matt Dye behaves himself until Lili gets hers," Bridget said, looking worriedly at Zeb.

Tyler reassured Zeb. "I don't think Dye will try anything in broad daylight, or in a crowded place. Though sometimes Obeah people will try almost anything to get their way."

"I read part of the book, Long Lost Friend, that you gave me, Tyler. It looks like just what the doctor ordered," he added with a grin. "Maybe it'll even help me to cure some stubborn ailments."

Tyler found this greatly amusing. "Yes, especially diarrhea."

"Okay, have your fun. But I intend to read it through. It has some good advice on holistic treatment of disease. Although it was written many years ago, it gives good common sense elixirs for the entire body.

The day passed much as others, except for a shipment of Doberman Pinscher guard dogs from a New York City department store, Macy's. This company had long enjoyed Dr. Zebulon's surgical skills. And for years they'd sent puppies to have their ears cropped as soon as they reached eight weeks of age. It secretly pleased Zeb to know that his reputation had traveled for such long distances.

During the afternoon Mrs. Andrew brought in her little dog, Cary, for worming. Cary liked gossip better than the local paper's society editor. Today, she brought a new story about her master. When Zeb and she were alone in a back treatment room, she began. "My master's a dirty old man, Dr. Zebulon," she said. "He's having an affair with our maid. Whenever our lady is out shopping, he jumps into bed with that maid. I'll bet he's there right now."

Zeb tried to hush her.

"No listen. He even walks in his sleep, just so he can get into her room in the middle of the night. I've growled at them and tried to bite him. But they lock me out. And that's that."

"Cary, if you had two legs instead of four, you'd be a real blackmailing threat," Zeb scolded. "Wouldn't you now? You'd better watch out or they may sell you down the river."

As evening closed in and the shadows lengthened, Zeb and Bridget prepared to leave the hospital. The ususal reports had been written and orders for Dr. Peters and Tyler had been put on their desks. As he moved toward the door, little gray Henry walked in. Since Henry is gray like the night, he can go about virtually unnoticed. He roams the hospital at all hours of the day and night. He and Tyler seem to have the same type of relationship as he and Bridget had. Since Tyler and Henry usually walked together, Zeb stepped back to wait.

"I seem to be just in time, Doctor," Tyler said as he entered the office. "I've been down town most of the afternoon. I'm glad I caught you because of something that happened to me."

"Good. Tell me about it."

"I saw a beautiful young woman walking her dog. I noticed her because she looked so much like a Jamaican. And her dog was acting mighty strange-a little under the weather. So I hurried to catch up to them." Tyler hesitated a moment, standing with an embarrassed grin on his brown face. "When I got to her, she took my breath away. I swear to you she was the most beautiful woman I ever saw."

"Oh, oh," Zeb said.

"Oh, boy," Bridget thought. "Tyler too."

Tyler caught his breath. "She was tall, willowy like a model," he continued. "Her skin was the color of that brown crayon in your school coloring box and her cheek bones were high. She was very pretty. Her eyes were carved out like Nefertiti's."

"Oh, you know Nefertiti?"

"Come on, doctor," Tyler objected. "I've been to the museum."

"Okay, go on with your very interesting lady."

"I did pretty well, I think," Tyler looked pleased. "Her name is Faye and she works at the Happy Day Club."

"Did you make a date with her?" teased Zeb.

"She's too much of a lady for such fast work. What I did was tell her that I worked at your hospital and ask her why her dog looked so sick."

"Okay. I'm waiting."

"It seems that the dog is refusing food—lost her appetite—has no pep—and keeps getting weaker."

"That could be a very sick dog, Tyler," Zeb said.

"I told her that you were the best vet in the country and got her to promise to call you for an appointment. The dog is a pretty little Lhasa Apso and much too good to neglect."

Zeb remembered how early Lhasa Apsos had been used as guard dogs for Tibetan goat herds and had lived for years in the Tibetan mountains before being recognized in America as very good pets. Much dog lore came from Tibet. There was a goddess who had turned her palace guards into dogs to frighten away the enemy. Then when the fight was won, she had turned the dogs into men again. Those must have been larger dogs—maybe even Shar Peis. Americans had first found Shar Peis in China, but anything could have happened in ancient times.

"Both Lhasa Apsos and Shar Peis have Oriental backgrounds," Zeb told Tyler.

"Yes, Shar Peis used to be fighting dogs before their owners began eating them, I hear," agreed Tyler. "Too true" Bridget shuddered.

"The Communist government made it illegal to have dogs for pets," continued Tyler. "It was a crime to waste scarce food on dogs."

"Let's get back to Faye." Zeb said he wanted to hear more. His curiosity about the Happy Day Club had become a constant itch. "Are you planning to visit her there?"

"Matter of fact, yes." Tyler had suddenly become very self-conscious. The smile had vanished from his brown face. "I don't know when. She's too elegant for a lonely kennel keeper."

"Damn it all, Tyler," Zeb said angrily. He clenched his fist on the desk. "Don't downgrade yourself. You're one of the finest men I know."

"But you haven't seen her," Tyler insisted.

"That's true," Zeb agreed. "But she can't be as important as all that at the club. Maybe she's just the hat check girl."

"You could be right. But I doubt it. There's something queenly about her."

"My advice to you, Tyler," Zeb extended his forefinger toward Tyler to emphasize his point. "My advice is to go see her at the Happy Day Club."

Bridget sat listening closely to this conversation, nodding her head from time to time. "That's telling him, Zeb," she said. Tyler noticed her and said, "Your Bridget is whimpering. She must be hungry."

"You're right," Zeb answered, "We were on our way out when you and Henry came in. Good night. Ali's well here and I'll see you in the morning."

They walked out of the hospital door and into the woods behind. The path was damp and their shoes made little squeaky sounds in the grass. Zeb thought he heard an echo each time he lifted his feet. Bridget kept looking behind her. "What is it, Bridget?"

"I don't see anything, Zeb. But there are so many shadows."

"Good shadows, or bad shadows?"

"My nose tells me that some bad shadows have been here not so long ago," Bridget finally said.

Safely inside his cottage, Zeb showered to remove traces of the hospital disinfectant, shaved and changed into city-bred clothes. I-te ached to gather up Sallie and take her to a candle-lit dinner somewhere. He thought of a restaurant he knew with excellent food and soft lights. A quick telephone call to Sallie. "Dinner sounds good, Jacob," she agreed. "But what about Lili Tu?"

"We could always run her past the hospital to stay with Tyler."

"No, I'm not keen for that idea, Jacob. I have all the fixin's here for a hunter's stew. Let's eat right here."

Zeb could only answer, "Yes." Sallie would have the lights dim—the music- and she could certainly cook. She would even have a glowing fireplace. "That sounds too good to turn down," he decided.

As Bridget and Zeb neared the door to Sallie's apartment, they heard a soprano voice singing an aria from one of his favorite operas. "Who's singing?" asked Bridget.

"Who but Sallie?" declared Zeb. "I'd know her voice anywhere. But I sure didn't know she could sing like that."

Dejectedly, all Bridget could say was, "She's certainly trying all the tricks of the trade." Zeb turned to her and said, "Quiet, please."

He waited for the end of the aria before he reached for Sallie's doorbell.

"Well, well and well again," Zeb said as he pulled Sallie to him. "That was lovely. And my favorite aria."

"Strictly amateur," Sallie replied with a smile. "But I'm glad you like it."

With his arm about her waist, they walked to the big couch in front of Sallie's fireplace to sip the drinks that Sallie had ready. Zeb reached into his pocket and pulled out two silver chains. One long enough for Sallie's lovely neck and a small, shiny one that should fit Lili Tu.

"These are the magic chains, Sallie. Tyler and I anointed them this morning. Remember? They have Stand Still, Fly Away, Balm Balm and Egyptian Perfume rubbed into them- while Tyler repeated certain magic words. I couldn't possibly tell you what those words were. But he says we'll be safe as long as we wear these chains."

"It does sound medieval," stated Sallie. "But after all that's happened, I guess I'd better accept it."

"Please do."

"I promise." Sallie leaned closer. "I haven't told you all the crazy things that have happened. Almost every time I stick my nose out of the door, Matt Dye appears. He's asked me for dates several times. He's followed us on walks. He tries to join us whenever he can."

"For God's sake be careful," Zeb begged. "For my sake be on guard."

The drinks had made them hungry and they devoured the hunter's stew. It contained more vegetables than any single garden could grow—tomatoes, celery, onions, peppers, butter beans, beans, peas, corn, cabbage, potatoes and beef.

As they sipped after-dinner coffee, they sat without talking. Zeb felt no pressure to be entertaining or charming. Sallie's presence was a delight and comfort to him. He worried about Bridget when he felt her eyes upon him and realized that he must reassure her that her place in his life was secure.

The telephone rang shrilly, making both Zeb and Sallie jump. She lifted the receiver and answered quickly in her soft, musical voice. Her eyes sparkled when she heard the other voice on the line.

"Hey, Uncle Milt. How good to hear from you."

"Oh?"

"Yes, that sounds bad." She spoke only a few words after periods of listening, and her smile began to fade.

"He's right here, Uncle Milt," she finally said. "Hold on a minute and let me ask him."

Sallie turned from the phone. "Uncle Milt's prize Shar Pei bitch is having puppies. She's been in labor for a long time and can't deliver. She's growing weak."

"It sounds serious," Zeb agreed.

"Uncle Milt's vet is out of town and there is nobody closer than you except the local large animal practitioner and he works mostly on cows and horses. My uncle wonders if you could possibly be persuaded to come and save his precious dog?"

Zeb furrowed his brow and brushed a stubborn lock of hair out of his eyes. True, there were no terribly ill dogs in the hospital just now. True, Dr. Peters had won his stripes. True, Tyler could handle almost any emergency in the kennels.

"Okay. I can go. I'll have to go to the hospital, alert the staff and get my medical bag. Leave orders for Lib, Ken and Tyler. How about you?"

"I'll manage, Zeb," Sallie replied. "I'll call my secretary. She can handle things. We'll have to take Bridget and Lily with us."

"Of course," agreed Zeb "How far is it to Woodbine?

"About seventy-five miles," said Sallie. "We can make it in two hours easily."

"Pack a couple of things in case we have to stay for a while."

"Right. You'll just love Uncle Milt. He practically owns Woodbine. And wait 'til you see the house he's built for his dogs. He has over twenty five dogs in it. It's nicer than some houses people live in."

Sallie and Zeb got into the front seat of his car. Lily Tu and Bridget piled into the back and settled down for a long ride with their humans. "This could be fun, Lili. What do you think?" Bridget asked.

"It's okay," Lili said. "You won't believe Uncle Milt. His dogs have everything a human millionaire could want. He treats each dog as if they were part of his immediate family."

"Ho,ho,ho," Bridget narrowed her eyes. "Have your fun. I'll believe just so much from you."

Lili quickly answered, "Just wait and see for yourself. Seeing is believing."

Zeb drove to the hospital, quickly wrote orders for his staff. He gathered up all the medical supplies fl~at he felt he might need, plus personal things and hurried back to the car."

"Wish us luck," he said to Sallie. "And a safe trip."

CHAPTER IX

Lili Tu, all coppery-beige in her wrinkled coat, settled down close to beautiful, sleek Bridget in the back seat of Zeb's big car. Sallie slid as near to Zeb as she possibly could snuggle without hampering his driving. The night was dark, reminding Zeb of all the times he had heard 'the sky was like black velvet', and he thought how true most of those tired sayings were. As they left the lights of Chapel Hill, they could see the stars and some brighter objects that Zeb felt must be planets.

He hated to break the silence, so pleasant after the rush to get ready for the trip. "I really never enjoyed driving at night," he finally said. "But this is beautiful."

"It's the company," giggled Sallie. "How true," agreed Zeb, as he squeezed her knee affectionately.

"And these country roads aren't too bad, Jacob," she added. "There aren't so many blinding headlights to contend with."

"Right," Zeb admitted. And Sallie snuggled still closer to him. The miles sped away. They met little traffic. The road was lined with stately pine trees and a kind of tall flowering bush that burst into color as the headlights caught it. Everyone enjoyed the ride. Lili Tu and Bridget relaxed and listened. After a time, they arrived a t Woodbine.

Sallie directed Zeb through what seemed to be a maze of winding streets to a wide tree-lined avenue and a circular drive which led to her Uncle's house. It was tall, imposing, painted white, with large columns in the front and a high pitched roof. Heavy green shutters bracketed the oversize windows that looked out onto a well trimmed lawn and neatly sculptured bushes.

Zeb was stunned by the beauty and size of the place and sat for a moment in admiration. Finally he got out of the car, stretched his long legs and went to the door. Nobody answered his ring. Sallie said. "Come on, Jacob. The dog's bungalow is just there behind the house and I'm sure that's where Uncle Milt will be. She pointed next door to a house which was a miniature copy of the big one where Zeb stood.

Zeb's eyes bugged out. "That's a dog house?"

"Yes. I tried to tell you before, but I knew you wouldn't believe me. He has so much money he doesn't know what to do with it all—no children, only Rue, his wife. And 25 dogs. All Shar Peis. He and Rue treats them like children.

"Well, then," Zeb said. "Of course that's where he is. With his sick dog. Let's go."

He hurried Sallie and the two dogs out of the car. They walked to the dog's one-story dwelling quickly. It was as large as a habitation for a human family. They knocked on the front door.

"Come in," rumbled a deep baritone voice.

They opened the door and there was Sallie's uncle, a huge man over six feet tall with broad shoulders and a heavy paunch. His hair was perfectly white and his eyes dark brown. He wore slacks and a blue sport shirt with the sleeves rolled up. He sat in the middle of the floor, holding his dog, the tears flowing down his cheeks. His clothes were liberally spattered with a bloody dark green fluid—the vaginal discharge—from the helpless dog.

"Oh, God!" moaned Bridget under her breath. "The poor girl."

"Thank God you're here. You must be Dr. Zebulon. Aren't you?" Milt Porter spoke in a voice that shook with tears.

"Yes, Uncle Milt," Sallie said. "I want you to meet Jacob Zebulon. He's the greatest vet in the world. We're going to help."

They were in a large main room. The stereo was turned on, playing country music, which the dogs seemed to enjoy. There were individual spaces for each dog, indoor and outdoor runs for everybody. Every dog had their names painted on the door to their private quarters. Each run was furnished with a king-sized waterbed for the dogs to frolic and rest on. There was a room with a bathtub and all the necessities for grooming. There was a small kitchen for preparing meals and a refrigerator for perishables. One wall held a pantry where stood cans, bags of food and all kinds of goodies that a well-spoiled dog might wish was there- toys and biscuits included.

Uncle Milt arose and lovingly placed his pregnant, Ming Toy, on a table covered by clean sheets and soft towels. The dog trembled and was obviously in great pain. Zeb saw at once that he must act quickly to help her.

"Where can I scrub, Mr. Porter?" he asked.

Milt pointed him to a corner room where a plump, kindly looking woman waited smiling warmly. Her brown hair was streaked becomingly with gray and she appeared to wear no makeup. She extended a hand to Zeb which wore the largest diamond ring Zeb had ever seen.

"I'm Sallie's Aunt Rue," she said. "I hope we have everything you need. There's antiseptic soap and sterile towels. And I have new surgical gloves for you."

"You seem to have thought of everything, Mrs. Porter," Zeb assured her. "If I think of anything else, I'll ask for it."

The scrubbing over, he began an internal examination of the ailing dog. One finger in her vagina told him that this was to be a difficult one—a breech presentation. He could feel the tail and knew that the rear end of the puppy had blocked the pelvic canal. He attempted to grab the hind legs of the puppy. If only he could reposition the puppy, he could pull it out- a posterior delivery. The baby puppy wouldn't budge. He tried to use its tail as a guiding lever and pulled very gently. The tip of the tail came off in his hand. But the puppy didn't move.

"Mr. Porter, we're in trouble." Zeb turned a serious face to the big man. "This has to be a Caesarian operation to save the mother and her puppies. There's no other way. The longer we wait, the more danger there is." A worry frown showed between his gray eyes. "Can we use your vet's hospital?"

"The nearest one is forty miles away," Milt said. All at once he brightened. "We can beat that. We'll use the operating room at Woodbine Memorial. Hold on."

Milt went to the phone and dialed. Zeb didn't hear the name of the person on the other end. But Milt spoke with authority. He told his story, and his request when he made it, sounded more like an order. "I'm bringing an emergency Caesarian in at once, and my own surgeon." A few seconds of quiet. Then he turned to Zeb and asked if he would need assistants. "We could use a nurse and an anesthesiologist. Thanks."

Talking With The Dogs

Milt then explained in more detail. "This is my prize dog. Ming Toy. She's in real trouble giving birth. I have my own veterinary surgeon with me. He's Dr. Zebulon from Chapel Hill, a highly regarded man. He'll be able to fill you in when we get there." He hung up.

"Your friend certainly does throw his weight around," Bridget whispered to Lili.

"You don't know him yet, Bridget. He's a wonderful man." Lili was on the defensive at once.

"That was the director of the hospital." Milt explained to Zeb, with a smile on his face. "I've helped them out from time to time, whenever they need money, and he was glad to help me."

"He'd better!" said Sallie. "I hear tell that you practically built that hospital"

"Well, he knows that I'll get him anything he needs if I possibly can," replied Milt.

As Milt prepared to take Ming Toy in his arms, Zeb stopped him and asked, "Can we take Bridget and Lili Tu to the people hospital with us.'?"

"No. They can stay here."

"I've got to tell you something. Somebody has tried to kidnap Lili Tu several times. He's crazy enough that he'll stop at nothing. I'd hate to have them here alone."

Milt thought a moment. "We can make them safe. My caretaker lives on the place—right next door. He's a fine figure of a fightin' man. He trained guard dogs in the war. He came from Jersey City where you learn to defend yourself and whatever belongs to you. Matter of fact, he wears a gun all the time. Name, Dante Forriatti. No wrong guy could get near him. I'll tell him to stay here at the dog bungalow."

"Sounds good," Zeb agreed. "Make sure he understands."

"Rue will get the word to him. Let's go." He picked up Ming Toy lovingly. Her wrinkles seemed to have dug deeper, her coat looked far too big for her. She had endured much pain. Her little triangular eyes had almost disappeared into their slits. Milt held her close and whispered comforting words in her ear during the short ride to the hospital. She seemed to trust him and tried to endure for a little longer.

It was early morning when they arrived at the hospital. A handsome, middle-aged man with even features and graying hair met them at the door.

"I'm Dr. Winthrop, Chief of Surgery. I'll assist you in any way I can." He pulled a red haired nurse, in stiffly starched white uniform toward him. "This is Nurse Lipkin. She is here to help you too."

They entered one of the operating rooms. Zeb looked about him. It looked much the same as his own O R except that everything was larger. The operating table held its overhead light beam aimed at the patient. Everything was stark white and clean. Two other men and another nurse followed the party into the room. "May these other physicians observe?" asked Dr. Winthrop.

"Of course," said Zeb.

Again the scrubbing procedure. Nurse Lipkin scrubbed and robed Sallie who had come close to Zeb and whispered, "Will you let me help too?"

Everyone in the necessary green gathered around Zeb. He knew he must warn Sallie about what she might see.

"You're welcome to help, if you really want to, Sallie. But it will be messy. And there's plenty of jokes about the med students fainting at their first surgery."

"I'll be good," Sallie promised.

"Don't worry, Doctor," said Nurse Lipkin. "I'll brief her." Scrubbed and ready, Zeb stood looking at the ailing patient. A pre-anesthetic was injected by one of the doctors. Then when Ming Toy was on her back, he instructed Nurse Lipkin to prep the dog. "Clip the hair, then shave the entire abdomen with the electric clippers. Bathe away all the debris with disinfectant and apply an iodine solution."

Another nurse stepped in to help and she and Sallie draped curtains around the table. Ming Toy had now dropped into a deep sleep.

An IV drip was put in place. An anesthetist had been called in to insert an intra-tracheal tube for the gas anesthesia and to watch the vital signs—respiration, pulse, color. Zeb—mask in place and hands gloved—took the scalpel in hand. Skillfully, he opened the abdomen, exposing the large womb.

"How adroit," whispered one of the watching doctors. "So little bleeding."

Soon Zeb had made an opening into the womb and was able to lift out a puppy snugly encased in afterbirth. He removed the membrane and handed the slippery little slug to the nurse. She took it in a towel and began to rub briskly.

"Let me have it," pleaded Sallie"

It was the puppy with the shortened tail. The nurse gently handed it to Sallie who tried to rub as the nurse had done. "Rub it harder," Zeb said over his shoulder. The nurse leaned over and showed her how to rub briskly. Sallie tried again. Finally she heard a gratifying cry. It sounded almost like a human baby.

There were six—dripping, oozing puppies. All held by their hind legs, head down, until the severe rubbing could start their breathing. A puppy had arrived almost every five or ten minutes—almost an hour of hard work—keeping Nurse Lipkin and Sallie busy—spanking, rubbing and wrapping in towels. Everyone was tired. They studied the little puppy who had lost the tip of his tail and smiled. "I'll never forget that little fellow," Zeb said.

With all the puppies safely delivered, Zeb could turn his full attention to Ming Toy. He carefully sutured the layers of the womb and the peritoneum, muscle and skin. Suture material was wrapped around the stump of each puppy's umbilical cord. Now Ming Toy was beginning to show signs of waking up and must be wrapped warmly for her trip home.

Zeb peeled off his gloves and gown and stretched a hand to Dr. Winthrop and Nurse Lipkin. "You were wonderful. I want to thank you both."

"You did a great job there, Doctor," said Dr. Winthrop. "That was extremely delicate work. You have fine surgeon's hands to have done that—the blood vessels were so close together. So little bleeding resulted. You could have been a real doctor."

"I thought I was."

Everyone laughed. "Indeed you are! A very good one at that," agreed Dr. Winthrop.

"Thanks again, Doctor. I couldn't have done it without your help. And thank you Nurse Lipkin. And Dr. Cole, you did a fine job as anesthetist."

Uncle Milt lovingly placed the tiny puppies in a basket to carry them home. He looked every bit the proud father. Ming Toy was placed carefully on the back seat of the car, warmly wrapped in soft blankets.

Back at the dog's lodging, Ming Toy was put to bed in the alcove marked with her name. Zeb put the puppies to her breast. She was awake enough to notice and began to lick them. The puppies began to search for nipples and tried to feed.

"Now she knows they're her puppies and doing what comes naturally," Zeb said.

Everybody was hungry. Aunt Rue had prepared sausage and eggs with hot biscuits and honey. The coffee was Uncle Milt's specialty. He roasted and ground the beans himself and now sat waiting to hear his guest's reaction. "Delicious coffee," Zeb remarked. Milt smiled winningly. "It's our own blend," he said.

"It's time we got back to our own pastures. I hope everything is going well at my own hospital."

"At least Lili and Bridget were safe," said Sallie. "Thanks to Mr. Forriatti."

Zeb handed Milt Porter a box of antibiotic pills. "To protect her against any infection," he said. "Give her one twice a day for five days. And call me if anything worries you."

Uncle Milt announced that he was naming the short tailed pup, Zeb, after the doctor who brought him safely into this world. He reached his hand to Zeb. As they gripped, Zeb felt a thick wad of bills.

"No. You don't owe me a thing, Mr. Porter," he said. "This was for Sallie and Lili Tu."

Throughout the entire operation, Milt Porter was quite impressed with the expertise of Dr. Zebulon and since Sallie was about to leave, he bluntly told her she would do well to marry the good doctor. Zeb, a bachelor of 47 years, has begun to think of this as a jolly good idea himself.

"Ummm," mumbles Bridget. "There he goes again."

Lili Tu gave Bridget a look of utter disgust. Her tiny triangular eyes grew even smaller. "Get off Sallie's back," she said. "Won't you ever understand humans?"

The four climbed into the big car and settled down for the long ride back to Chapel Hill.

CHAPTER X

The sun shone brightly and the heat was rising when Zeb pulled his big car into the hospital driveway. As usual, Dr. Zebulon always felt a sense of pride and accomplishment when he drove up to his hospital. His long days and many hours of hard work were worth the extreme pleasure that he received from helping people and their pets. As for the hospital itself, Zeb continually updated the facilities to give his patients the most modern equipment available. A row of miniture bright red fire hydrants lined the driveway, and they were continually being used for the enjoyment of the patients. Rose bushes adorned the front of the hospital for the delight of the people who owned the dogs.

"I hope Dr. Peters has everything under control," Zeb said. "I could do with a breather after that hard night's work."

Bridget looked at him with melting brown eyes. "Nobody can take your place, Zeb," she said. "Doc Peters does the best he can, though."

Zeb had taken Sallie home to her apartment. Rings under her big blue eyes told him how tired she was, and he had urged her to get some rest.

Bridget spoke again of her worries. "Let's hope that Matt Dye keeps his cotton pickin' hands off of Lili Tu for a while, Zeb. I really hate that man."

"He probably knows that we're on to his game now," Zeb added.

When they opened the hospital door they sensed a fever in the atmosphere. Norris rushed to meet Zeb. "We have a very sick dog here, Doctor. Nurse Nelson and Tyler are trying to help her until you can take over."

A beautiful woman, with skin and eyes the color of good brandy, rose from the reception room chairs and ran to Zeb. "I'm Faye Howell, Doctor. It's my dog that's so sick. Will you please save her?"

Zeb remembered Tyler's telling him of 'a lady with skin like a brown crayon'. Her name had been Faye, he thought. Could this be Tyler's lady?

"I'll do my best, Miss Howell," he promised and went hurriedly to the examination room.

Nurse Lib Nelson came to him, holding her gloved hands away from her sides. "I've given this little dog an internal examination and done the lab work. Her uterus is very swollen and the lab work shows a problem. Her appetite is gone and she was vomiting bile. I've started an intravenous drip."

"Good work, Lib." He studied the results of the tests. "My God, the white blood count is so high—her uterus must be about ready to rupture—so high! She has an infection of the uterus. I'd better open her up at once. Tyler—go sit with Faye while we do the surgery. Lib and Dr. Peters will help me."

Once inside the abdomen, Zeb saw a womb that looked like a balloon about to burst. Another day would have been too late. He performed a complete hysterectomy on the little dog. Nurse Lib fed dog's blood into the IV drip. "Lucky we had plenty of blood. And lucky we don't have to match dog's blood." Zeb thought as he worked.

Zeb's relief was so great when he had finished and knew the surgery was a success that his knees felt rubbery. He had done this procedure many times. But every time he had considered it a battle with death and was shaken when it was over. He lifted the ailing dog in kindly arms and placed her in a fleshly scrubbed cage, wrapped snugly in a warm blanket. And the three—Ken, Lib and Zeb stood for a moment looking at the little dog.

"Thank God that's over," Zeb said at last. "She couldn't have waited another day."

He went, on trembling legs, into his office and poured a cup of strong coffee. He sank into his big chair and rang Norris. "Ask Tyler to bring Faye Howell to my office, please."

Faye sat down, gripping a cup of Zeb's coffee in her slender hands. "Thank you, Doctor. Hattie is all I have. I probably love her too much. Matt Dye had advised me to use another vet in town—but she just got worse—his treatment hadn't helped at all. I hope Matt won't be angry that I came here."

"He can't possibly mind," Zeb soothed her. "We got the uterus out just before it would rupture. Tyler can drive you home now. You can see Hattie tomorrow. We'll see how she feels."

Tyler drove Faye back to the Happy Day Club where she worked. She asked that he not come in. "Matt is terribly jealous," she explained. "He's my boss. And he doesn't like me dating."

"B-but—"

"I know it's not a date—but I'd rather not have to explain. Please?"

"Okay, then. But I want to see you again."

****

Zeb stopped at Hattie's cage the next morning. "Sorry I didn't know your name yesterday. Bridget told me later. And your lady, Faye, too. How are you feeling today, Hattie?"

"Truth is, I'm pretty sore." Hattie looked at him quizzically. "Bridget told me that we can talk to each other, and I'm sure glad Doc."

"Yes. It's nice isn't it? Of course you're sore—that's to be expected. I'll give you medicine for pain. Is there anything else?"

"Yeah, I'm worried about my human—Faye. Do you happen to know Matt Dye?"

"Unfortunately, I do know him."

"He's my missy's boss, you see. And he wanted her to take me back to his vet but his treatment wasn't doing any good and I was getting worse by the hour.

"Oh, he surely wouldn't mind that she brought you here."

"If you really knew Matt Dye, you wouldn't say that. He'd mind very much. And he'd probably do something about it!"

"Please don't worry. Tyler can handle almost anything and anybody. You just work at getting well." Zeb patted her head and went on to the next patient.

Zeb went into the hall from the examination room and almost ran headlong into Tyler. "Doctor, I've just had a call about Faye. I've got to go get her. She's been beaten up. One of the girls who works with her called me. Gotta run!"

Bridget, listening, said to Zeb. "Hattie told me some things. She says Matt is crazy jealous of Faye and won't let her look at anyone else. There's something mighty strange going on there—you can bet your bottom dollar on that."

"You may be right, Bridget."

It was not long before Tyler was back at the hospital. With him came Faye Howell, trying to hide a badly bruised face and swollen eye.

"Matt Dye did this, Doctor," Tyler said angrily. "I wish I could get him alone for a few minutes—I know a few dirty holds—just right for the likes of him." His mahogany colored eyes stood out from a face turned gray with anger.

"I had to get her out of there," Tyler said.

"Of course," Zeb agreed.

"If you don't mind, she can stay with me in my cottage for a while."

"Sure, if there's room."

"I'll make room for her," Tyler answered. "I've got some things to tell you about the Happy Day Club."

It was several hours before things quieted down and Zeb could spend time with Tyler. He still was puffed with anger and needed Zeb's listening ear.

"I got to the club, Doctor, and found it very strange. The reception room was filled with beautiful girls—dressed in fancy negligees—it was afternoon, remember. Their faces were all made up not well-almost as if their fingers had slipped when putting it on. And their eyes looked blank—they were staring at spots—they were so full of dope they were floating off the ground. Can you explain that?"

"Is Faye on drugs?"

"No. She hates them. And Matt was in love with her. He didn't want her hooked, I guess."

"What kind of place is it? A private club? Or is it a massage parlor? Or worse? Or what, Tyler?"

"You name it! Where do the drugs come from? And why do they keep those girls doped?"

"Okay. Another question. If the club's for sex, does Faye take men upstairs, too?"

"No. Faye told me that Matt kept her for himself. He said that he'd kill any other man who touched her."

"How did he get her in the first place?"

"He met her when he was hiding out in Jamaica a few years ago. He really fell for her. She says he learned of things while he was there. Not only dope. A kind of magic that she doesn't understand, called Voodoo. We know about that of course."

"Yes. That's what we figured." Zeb ruffled his tawny hair savagely. "He probably made contacts for drug buys while he was there too."

Tyler looked as if he'd been hit by an inspiration. "Remember all those characters in Matt's Pub. Girls with their sing-song tunes, and kids with purple or green hair. They could have been hard rock types. But there were some really tough looking cookies there too. Remember?"

"That's right," Zeb said. "We asked David Smith to do a little research there for us."

"Yeah. He flunked that. Those kids were ordering Special Baked Potatoes. He tried to order one, but they asked him to show them twenty-five dollars before they'd serve it to him. He fanned out on that."

"Okay. We'll have to send him back with the money."

"Good enough. But right now I'm concerned about Faye. I think I've fallen in love with her the way you've done with Miss Predino."

Bridget gave out a loud groan. 'Can't they forget Sallie?' she thought.

"Is Bridget sick, Doctor?" Tyler asked. "She sounds as if she's in pain."

"No. She's all right I think," Zeb said. "Just trying to get comfortable on the hard floor probably." To himself, he thought that she must be in one of her jealous moods again.

Tyler left.

"If you've ever wanted to help me, now's the time," Zeb told Bridget when they were alone. "We're in real trouble now. We have two things that Matt badly wants—Faye and Lili Tu both. Hattie

Talking With The Dogs

might tell you things she'd never tell me. Do you think you could probe a little as she's getting better?"

"Sure," responded Bridget happily. Her big brown eyes were filled with love as she looked at him. "Maybe I can make him forget Sallie," she thought wistfully.

The day wore on. More patients and their owners to see. More problems to solve for both.

Mr. Hawkins came in, complaining that his dog wouldn't let him make love to his new wife. "Every time I try to get into bed with my wife, Bonzo pushes between us," he said. "I've heard about this before and I always thought it was funny. But, believe you me, doctor—it ain't! And besides I'm tired of sleeping in the guest room."

Zeb scolded the dog. "Maybe you should give Bonzo away, Mr. Hawkins."

"Not that, please. Not that." The dog whispered. "I promise to be good. I hate that dame, but I'll be good. I don't want to get shipped out."

Zeb looked confidently at Hawkins and said, "Why not give him one more chance. I have a feeling he's going to turn over a new leaf from now on."

The harassed gentleman nodded. "I'd like to. I love Bonzo, too and I'd hate to lose him but he has to learn the facts of life. I'll try once more."

"If he misbehaves, tap him on the nose with a piece of crackly paper. He'll hate that."

"Okay, and thanks," Mr. Hawkins said as he left. Bonzo, following, gave Zeb a grateful look over his shoulder.

A gentle darkness had settled in and the trees looked fragile and beautiful against a rosy sunset when Tyler knocked on Zeb's office door. He asked if he might come in for more talk. So much had happened.

"Sure, Tyler," invited Zebulon. "Come on in."

Tyler poured coffee. His long brown fingers gripped the cup and it trembled in his hand. He was filled with suppressed anger and excitement. He began by saying, "As I told you before, Doctor, I came here to Chapel Hill to avenge my father's misfortune to have

Dr. Louis Vine, D.V.M.

been a fall guy for Matt Dye. He went to prison because he was framed by Matt Dye. Now I have another reason for revenge. What he did to Faye is a coward's way of punishing a woman."

Zeb suddenly interrupted. "Tyler, I know how you feel. However, if you want my help to get this scoundrel, you have to promise me one thing and I respect you enough to know that you would never go against your given word. You must agree that you will never take matters in your own hands. You must consult me or the police first. Do you give me your word Tyler?"

Tyler thought for a moment and then lowered his head. "Doctor, you must be a mind reader. I wanted to go over there and fight Matt Dye to the last breath in my body."

"Yes, I know how you feel because I probably would have felt the same as you if someone had done that to my father and the woman I love. However, I beg you not to take matters in your own hands. We have the law on our side and I promise you from the bottom of my heart that we are going to get that son of a bitch. He's not worth the powder to blow him up and I don't want you to get into trouble yourself. You are worth more than one hundred Matt Dye's. And what's more important, you are my friend." With that statement, Zeb rose, looked Tyler straight in his eyes and shook hands in a warm way that only two close friends can understand.

"Thanks for those kind words, Doctor. I promise to cooperate with you and not do anything that would make you ashamed of me."

Tyler, looking straight at Zeb, continued. "I'm trying to understand all that I saw at the Happy Day Club."

Zeb settled down in his easy chair to listen. He turned his burning gray eyes on Tyler.

"The young woman, Suzanne, who'd called me about Faye answered the door," Tyler began. "She put her finger to her lips and pulled me inside." He stopped a moment to think. "Then we went into the main room where girls sat around in negligees. They were stoned—some were singing, some were staring. They didn't pay much attention to me. Then Suzanne brought out Faye. She looked terrible—so bruised- so hurt. I wanted to hold her. Suzanne and I wrapped her in her big fur coat and put a silk scarf around her head. And I got her out to my car quickly. You saw her."

Zeb listened intently, ruffling his hair from time to time until one strand stood up like a Kewpie lock. "You're sure that Matt Dye owns that place?"

"Everybody says that. And, by the way, I just saw him hanging around in the woods out back. And he had that Obeah man with him. That's hardly the best spot for jogging, is it?"

"Hmmph. You're right—it's strange." Zeb thought for a moment. "We just can't go off half-cocked on this thing. You keep Faye under constant watch. We'll try to find out more about Dye with the help of David and Hattie. And we'll double our watch over Lili Tu."

After Tyler left, Zeb spoke to Bridget. "Have you gotten anything out of Hattie yet?"

"Yeah, I'll tell you this-she's worried to death about her human. She says Matt Dye brought Faye from Jamaica because he was in love with her. He was so crazy jealous he wouldn't let anybody even look at her. He tried to keep her shut away in the club house. So he gave her Hattie to make her happy—he didn't want her to be too lonesome. She was his mistress, Hattie said."

"That makes sense," said Zeb. "Did Hattie mention drugs?"

"He gives the girls that work at the Club something—she's not sure what. He gave some to Hattie once—but it made her so sick that Faye threatened to leave him."

"Okay, go on."

"Well, the Club isn't what you might think. Men come there and go upstairs with the girls. Hattie never went along—but she says she has a pretty good idea what goes on there."

"Good, Bridget. This is important. Thank you."

"Now don't you think we'd better tell the police, Zeb?" Bridget asked anxiously. "Hattie is afraid for Faye—she knows he had beaten her and other women at the club. And she was afraid he might not stop with that."

"Wait a minute, Bridget," Zeb said quietly. "What would the police think of us if we told them that a little dog had told us all of this?"

"Oh, God," groaned Bridget. "Sometimes I forget that not all humans are as smart as you are."

"However," Zeb interjected, "It's time I went to see Chief Ira Carter of the Police Department since it could get violent from here on out. I'm going to tell him everything I know about Matt Dye and let him take it from there. We already have Matt Dye on assault and battery charges on Faye. We're just getting started on opening a can of worms for him. And he is the lowest form of a worm that I know of."

CHAPTER XI

Zeb had read Matt well. Henry, Tyler's loyal gray cat, came nosing his way into Zeb's office late in the afternoon. He searched out Bridget and stood talking to her while Zeb looked on curiously. Henry was a great friend of Bridget and kept her informed of any irregularities in the hospital.

"Henry's brought you a message from King, Zeb," Bridget finally told him. "King's stayed here so long he kinda thinks he owns the kennels, you know. He says there's some trouble brewing down there."

"Okay, let's go see," Zeb answered.

The long hall to the kennels led past the treatment rooms and Zeb could sense nervousness among his patients. "What's been going on, I wonder," he thought, as he pushed his long legs faster.

"Gorry, I'm glad to see you, Doc," said King as the doctor and Bridget came in at the door. "There's been a crazy man hanging around out here."

"Tell me about it," Zeb asked.

"He's gotta be drunk, or stoned or something. He can hardly walk straight." King furrowed his brow at Zeb. "He looked in at the screened window first—but I think Tyler was sitting in that room. So he came down here." King stopped a moment to search for the right words. "He was mumblin' somethin' under his breath all the time. He came to my outside run and tried to bend those bars."

It would take a mighty strong man to do that," Zeb said.

"Yeah. He couldn't do it. He pulled wire cutters out of his pocket." King grinned at Zeb. "Well, you aren't so crazy as to put wires on cages that cut that easy. So he couldn't do that. Then the language!"

"Weren't you getting scared?" Bridget asked him.

"Yeah, you might say that," King agreed. "You wouldn't believe the language. He practically foamed at the mouth. He grunted and heaved and swore and carried on like crazy. But he couldn't make those bars move. So I tried to scare him away. I growled a little. I couldn't tell whether he was scared or not, but he did give up. He mumbled that he was going to get better tools and left."

"Let's go and have a talk with Tyler," Zeb announced. "Maybe he still has some of those magic oils." He turned to leave King's cage and seek out his dark kennel man.

Bridget wondered aloud as she followed him. "We've used up all the chains. What can we use for silver in King's cage?"

"I've a collection of old silver coins," Zeb said. "Maybe Tyler can use those."

Tyler, helpful as usual, agreed to try. "Nothing's impossible. Let's anoint a few coins with my oils and put them along the far edge of the cages. That ought to foil Matt for a while."

Tyler solemnly repeated the anointing process with a handful of silver coins and Zeb carried some of them to King's cage. Bridget tagged along.

"Jesus wept and tore his valuable sealskin jacket!" King quoted. "What makes you think that'll keep the big stiff away?"

"Don't scoff," Bridget scolded. "To err is human, all right. But these humans know what they're doing."

"Humph," King mumbled. But he subsided and waited to hear what crazy idea these humans would come up with next.

Zeb tried to imagine what kind of weapon Matt Dye would produce today. Dye's scaly mind obviously knew no limits. He'd better gather Sallie and Lili Tu in, under his protection. He hurried back to his office and picked up his phone. He dialed Sallie's number and she answered at once. "Sallie pack a few things," he said. "I want to bring you over here where we can watch over you. You may have to stay several days." He didn't want to frighten her but he must convince her. "Please get ready. We'll be right over to pick you both up. And bring Lili's show equipment, too. It's not long now before the show in Ralcigh."

"Why all this sudden drama?"

"There's too much to explain on the phone. I'll come for you in a little while." Zeb hung up and hurried to find Dr. Peters and put him in charge of the hospital. Then he warned Tyler to keep a close watch.

He passed Norris' desk as he left by way of the reception room.

"Send all patients to Dr. Peters for an hour or so until I get back. Tell them I had an emergency case."

He waited for Bridget to jump into the front seat of the car with him, then started the motor. The sky began to darken as they sped down Franklin Street, the main drag in town. Inky black storm clouds bunched in the southwest sky. "That's where most of our heavy rains come from, Bridget," Zeb said. "I hope it can hold off until we get back home."

"A lot of thunder and lightning might keep Matt at home," hoped Bridget.

"There's his place now. Look at all the cars." Zeb gave a quick glance at the parking lot. "Weather hasn't kept people away from the Pub."

The parking lot was filled. Every kind of car. Little sports cars and pickup trucks. A van with modern finger paintings all over its sides. Cars with tinted windows, so that nobody could see who might be riding inside. Bridget wondered if the white powder had brought them all there. Certainly they couldn't be admirers of Matt. Bridget still thought of him as that 'weird man.'

"Well, old girl," said Zeb. "All I can say is that I hope the Pub keeps him too busy to think about us."

Sallie met them at her door. She had packed a suitcase and filled a brown grocery bag with cans of Lili's favorite goodies. Her big blue eyes twinkled when she said, "I hope your imagination's been working overtime about Matt, Jacob."

"No chance," he said defiantly. "No chance. You and Lili will be much safer with the rest of us at my place. Let's go."

The rain came down like daggers from the blackened sky. Sometimes it seemed to be a solid sheet, so that Zeb could barely see the road. He warned that he wouldn't talk. It took all his concentration to follow the fading yellow line that marked the middle of the road. The rain almost obliterated it. And the lights of oncoming cars danced on the windshield and rear vision mirror. He had forgotten to turn it to the dark side and strongly regretted the lapse. Sallie crossed her fingers and kept as quiet as possible. Bridget and Lili kept silent. They didn't even look at one another.

With relief, Zeb turned the big car into its parking space at his cottage and stated, "Well, this certainly ought to keep Matt at home tonight." Bridget added, "That's just wishful thinking."

Bridget looked at Lili and shook her head. She thought there had been a familiar shadow among the distant trees. And she sensed an odor, a rank smell that was becoming evident too often, of late. Lili nodded in agreement. Her tiny eyes could see for long distances. "Yes," she whispered to Bridget. "I think you're right."

"I'll run between the raindrops," Sallie said. And she raced to the front door.

"I'm not that good," laughed Zeb. He picked up her suitcase and the bag of groceries and nodded to Lili and Bridget to come with him.

Once inside, Zeb looked in every corner of the house, under the bed, in closets—everywhere—to be sure that nothing was lurking there. He stowed Lili's food away and put Sallie's suitcase within easy reach.

"I'm going back to the hospital. Bridget will stay with you," Zeb said. "If anything strange happens, call me at once. I'll leave the house-to-hospital line open. Understand?"

"Sure she understands Zeb," Bridget spoke up with a slight hint of sarcasm. "And even if she didn't, I know all about it. So don't worry. I'll take good care of your precious doll."

"Thanks Bridget, I knew I could depend on you. I'll come home as soon as possible."

He opened the door and looked out. "Thank God the rain has slowed down."

"Glad to hear it," said Sallie. "I'll fix us some supper. I hope there's something in the refrigerator."

"I'm sure you'll find something, dear. There are some pizzas in the freezer. Help yourself." He kissed her and went back to duty. He touched the shamrock talisman as he went through the door and thought gratefully of its help to him in his veterinary practice.

Zeb's wish that the bad weather would keep his patients away was to no avail. It had become a cliche that nothing could keep the owner of a sick dog away from the doctor. "And rightly so," Zeb had said many times.

Talking With The Dogs

A young woman was seated in the reception. She held a mixed-breed town dog on a leash beside her. She was what Zeb had always thought of as a looker. Her hair was cut close to her shapely head and curled softly in golden waves and her eyes were as blue as a forget-me-not. She said that her name was Sandra Jenkins and that her dog was Toodles.

"Bring the lady into room one, please Norris," Zeb said.

As the doctor bent to pick up the little dog to place her on the examining table, his eyes fixed upon the young woman's blouse. It was flesh colored lace cut very low and it seemed to be completely transparent. What will these college students think of next? Zeb thought. At the same time, Miss Jenkins leaned over to give Toodles a comforting pat on the head and her breasts nearly jumped out of her blouse. Zeb felt his cheeks bum. He daren't meet the lady's eyes, nor could he take his eyes from her bosom. Helplessly, he stammered, "You have a mighty pretty blouse." He remembered that in vet school, the professors had warned them that there would be days like this. However, they advised the students that chastity should always be the order of the day.

"You aren't the first guy she's done that too," Toodles said to Zeb in a whisper.

Sandra Jenkins only smiled coyly and said, "Thank you."

Zeb treated Toodles' sore throat and bade Miss Jenkins a relieved goodbye as quickly as he could. He returned to the reception room to find it empty and went to his office.

As he opened the office door, the private line from his cottage began to ring. He picked it up quickly.

"Jacob, Jacob! We have a fire," came Sallie's frightened voice.

Zeb dropped the phone after saying he'll be right there, yelled to Tyler about the fire, rushed to the door and out of the hospital, through the woods and to his cottage. He saw fire tumbling out of the wall next to his bookcase in the living room. Sallie held boxes of soda in their hands, sprinkling the blaze. It wasn't quenching it. Tyler came running into the room with a fire extinguisher in his hands and quickly went to work until he had the fire under control. David Smith had soon followed with another fire extinguisher and together they soon had the flames completely out.

As Tyler fought the blaze, he could be heard muttering words of unexplainable origin. It sounded like jibberish but Tyler looked very serious while he was uttering these words. Finally, he said, "That was no ordinary fire or my Jamaican words wouldn't have worked."

"Well, thank God that it did work," Sallie exclaimed fervently. "You made a believer out of me."

"And you all were here, practically in the flames. Thank God none of you were hurt," said Zeb. He threw his muscular arms about Bridget's neck and hugged her. She grunted "Ugh."

Sallie turned flashing blue eyes on Zeb. "You really love Bridget more than me, don't you? More than anyone else in the world! She spoke angrily and a tear tumbled down her cheek. If she had been a foot-stamper, the building would have rocked with it. "That's disgusting Jacob. You didn't even think about me—or Lili Tu, either, for that matter." Her cheeks flushed crimson. Sallie straightened her shoulders and drew a deep breath as she always did when confronted by her personal dilemma, jealousy.

Zeb was shocked into silence. He suddenly realized his misguided reaction by embracing Bridget before Sallie. His mouth dropped open as he searched for words to say and none came. He realized that he would never understand a jealous woman. Finally he pulled her close. She angrily resisted, but his powerful arms held. He put his lips to hers and gave her a hungry kiss.

"Just a minute, Sallie," he finally said. "You and Bridget have got to understand me. I love you both- but in different ways. There's no way to compare those two loves."

Sallie gave him a long and solemn look. Bridget looked at him with questions in her big brown eyes. "Think a minute," Zeb continued. "We're in a mess of trouble right now with Matt Dye. And we've all got to pull together."

All at once, Sallie felt laughter bubbling up inside. How foolish to be jealous of a dog! And she couldn't help but laugh at herself. "Zeb, you're right as usual. I'm a slow learner. But I'm going to do better."

Bridget looked up at Zeb and nodded in agreement.

As he held Sallie in his arms, he looked around the smoldering ruins of his house. Fortunately, everyone had reacted quickly and with Tyler's and David Smith's readily available help, the destruction was held to a minimum. However, he winced with a pained sigh as he noticed the sorry condition of his favorite easy chair, the price he had to pay for tangling with the lowdown people in this world who don't even show respect for dogs as well as people.

CHAPTER XII

Sallie met Zeb's eyes and felt strangely guilty. She put a round white arm about his neck and pulled him close.

"Please try to forget how foolish I've been, Jacob," she whispered. "Let's sit down and have a quiet talk. Do you realize how little we really know about each other? I mean, I'd like to know what sort of little boy you were. The real story of why you chose veterinary medicine? You know what I mean. Let's talk. Tell me about yourself."

Zeb's gray eyes softened into a smile. "That's my Sallie. You too. I could know a lot more about you."

Bridget studied them warily. "They better not forget me," she muttered.

"I grew up in Brooklyn. You know that, Sallie," Zeb began. "I always had pets. I loved animals more than most kids. One day I saw a little stray dog hit by a car and nobody cared whether he lived or died. That, I think, was the moment when I decided to be a vet. And to take care of animals."

"What happened?" Sallie asked.

"The little mutt pleaded with huge brown eyes for someone to help him. But a big fat policeman raised a gun in his hairy hand and shot the pitiful animal between the eyes. I cried a whole day."

"You're still that boy—only a lot bigger now, Jacob. And I love you for it."

"When I came to Chapel Hill to practice, I got off to a bad start. Dr. Noland sent me out into the country to treat a very sick mule with colic. A crowd of people happened to be picnicking in the field where the mule lay. He had been thrashing around on the ground for several hours due to his severe intestinal pain. I looked him over and realized that he was dying. I spoke to the owner and explained that I thought that the mule had a twisted bowel or a ruptured gut. I told him that I didn't think there was anything that could save him. He told me to get him out of his misery. I gave the mule the necessary injection into the jugular vein. He walled up his eyes and died. The crowd of picnickers

Talking With The Dogs

stared at me. They almost pointed accusing fingers and I could almost hear them thinking murderer. Humiliation overwhelmed me. I got into my car and back to the hospital to hear Dr. Noland's reassuring words as fast as I could go."

"Had you done wrong?"

"Not at all," Zeb said. "I'd done the only humane thing possible."

"Doctor," the elderly Dr. Noland said in a very compassionate voice, "there will be many times in your future practice when you will have to make Solomon-like decisions between life and death of an animal. You have to do what is best for the animal- not for the wailing owner."

"How true those words were. I have been faced with similar decisions hundred of times since then. Euthanasia—the providing of a quiet and easy death to end the suffering of a loved one, human or otherwise—has long been debated. I am constantly asked, "What would you do if he were your dog, Dr. Zebulon?" The question haunts me, as do the faces of the doomed dogs and the tragedy in the eyes of those who love their pets and must make the decision. To those who have decreed a quiet and easy death rather than a life of suffering when such suffering is inevitable, let me say that if he were my dog I would do the same. God knows I can say no more than that."

"I firmly believe that any animal who is diseased beyond all hope, and to whom there is no adequate relief from suffering, should be allowed out of his misery. The two questions I ask myself are: Is the animal undergoing undue suffering that cannot be relieved? And is the animal enjoying life? If the answers are obviously unfavorable, then I wholeheartedly advise euthanasia."

"However, some people make these decisions hastily, or cold-bloodedly, with the thought, *You can always buy another dog to take his place.* How wrong they are. Each dog is an entity in himself, just as each man is. No one has the right to wipe a dog out if he has the slimmest chance of living without pain. At least such people should be honest enough to admit that the misery they are so anxious to get rid of is theirs and not the dog's."

"It is heartbreaking to see these people, and there are more of them than you would suppose, thrust a sick animal at me and tell me to put him out of his misery. The dog, with care and proper treatment, may have many years of good living before him. Is it the animal or the human who wants surcease from misery? So long as life exists is it not dearer by far than death, to a dog no less than to a man?"

"Any way you look at it it is a solemn question, to take or not to take a life. Yet a lot of men and women play God in this way with no thought except to rid themselves of an animal that has become a burden to them. Others, to whom a dog is loyal and loving, suffer dreadfully when confronted by such a decision. These are the people who have the special kinship with their dogs. Always such people will do everything in their power, and that of their veterinarian, to save the life of the dog. After all, an animal can lead a good existence with perhaps one leg amputated; with the sight gone from an eye or the hearing from an ear; with a cranky heart; or even with a toothless jaw. I know this is so. I have treated them. What such a dog requires is a little more love, more care, more thoughtfulness than the average healthy dog needs. And that is just what the run-of-the-mill dog owner does not have in his power to give."

"And while we're talking about euthanasia," Zeb continued, "I still have nightmares about a foolish thing I did many years ago when I was young intern right out of veterinary school. It still haunts me. This man and woman came to the clinic where I was working and asked me to put their young dog to sleep. I tried to talk them out of it but they insisted. So I did it, as quickly, as painlessly as I knew how."

"The second the little dog lay still, all life ended, the man and woman went into hysterics and tried to wrench the dog from one another. The man finally explained to me their outrageous actions. He said that they were getting a divorce and neither of them would give up the dog to the other person since they both loved the dog very much. The sacrifice to a selfish love lay motionless between the two of them. I shall never forget those two deranged people. In all my years of practice, I have never put a healthy dog to sleep ever again."

As Zeb finished, he took Sallie's hand and brought it to his mouth and kissed it tenderly.

Sallie sat listening to all these expressions of compassion from this man and then with pride and a few tears in her eyes, said, "Now I know why I love you so much. You are the kindest man I have ever known." With that statement, she lunged for Zeb, grabbed him and engulfed him with warm, passionate kisses.

"Thank you, Sallie. I needed that."

"It sounds a little like my public performances, Jacob," Sallie said. "I always wanted to be a concert pianist. But the first time I played to a large audience, my legs shook so hard that I could hardly keep my feet on the pedals. It was torture. So I went to teaching. An old friend used to say, Those who can, do. Those who can't, teach."

"Tain't so! I've heard you play. Remember?"

After dinner, Zeb returned to the hospital for late rounds. He carried an orange for Chips. "Hi, old buddy," he said to the little monkey. "You're looking your old self again, thank the Lord."

Everything was quiet in surgery. Tyler and Dr. Peters apparently had things under control. So back home he went. He was anxious to appease Sallie's hurt feelings and get back in her good graces again. As he entered the devastation caused by the fire in the living room, he noticed Sallie hard at work, attempting to sanitize the mess in the house.

"Not to worry," Zeb announced to her. "I'm having a cleaning crew here early in the morning to get this mess straightened out."

"I have a great idea. We both need a few hours of relaxation so why don't we go to the Club in the morning while they clean the house. We can play some tennis and have a spot of lunch. How does that sound to you, my dear?"

Sallie quickly responded. "It sounds like just what the doctor ordered-peace and quiet- for a while anyway. And even though I've heard you're a good tennis player, I'll give you a good game. I played tennis on my college team so you better be on your best game if you expect to beat me."

Zebulon beamed a broad smile and showed excitement in his eyes by the challenge from the lady he loved. He took her hand and led her to the bedroom.

****

Dr. Louis Vine, D.V.M.

The next morning, as they were playing tennis, Zebulon could hardly concentrate on the game as he watched the athletic and graceful body of Sallie glide about the court, hitting powerfully guided forehand and backhand shots right back at him.

Wow, he thought to himself. She knows what she's doing. She's been on a tennis court before. Maybe I'll get her on the golf course where she might not be so skillful.

While they played, Bridget and Lili Tu sat quietly in one corner of the court watching the contest between the two lovers.

Bridget slyly said to Lili Tu, "Women will do anything to catch a man. They know all the tricks of the trade. I hate to admit it but Sallie is quite good at tennis. The old doctor is getting quite a workout and all the competition he can handle. Just watching them run around is making me tired."

After the game, the four of them went on to the patio to have lunch, the two dogs sitting under the table.

Sallie looked all around the club's grounds and saw the rolling fairways of the golf course. "This is so heavenly," she said. "Just seeing you relax for a few hours does nay heart good. I love to be with you. That golf course looks very beckoning. I'd love to play golf with you sometimes. That's my best sport. Tennis is my secondary achievement."

Wow, Zebulon thought again. If she's better in golf than tennis, I'd have my hands full trying to beat her. I better practice more often.

"Jacob," Sallie began, "I'm so glad that you have influence with the directors of the Chapel Hill Country Club so that they allow you to bring Bridget and her friend on the grounds."

Zebulon responded with a proud smile," Sallie, it's not what you know, it's who you know. Ted Seagroves, the president of the club is a good friend of mine and he gave Bridget McGuire honorary membership into the club. I told you that this is a dog's town."

As they were finishing lunch, Sallie looked at Zebulon and with an inquisitive look on her face, asked, "Jacob, there is another thing I want to find out about you. How come you picked Chapel Hill to settle in and give all your patients your exceptional skill at curing them?"

"You're so kind, Sallie, to say that. I just try to do my best. As for picking Chapel Hill, I think it was fate that brought me to this "Southern Part of Heaven", as the Chamber of Commerce so wisely named it. I had heard that it was a small university town where animals ruled supreme and plentiful. This town was the answer to a veterinarian's prayer. It was utopia from an animal doctor's viewpoint."

"I wish I could say it was intelligence, skill, and ability that got me a job in this divine place-but it wasn't. It was just plain luck. I was in the right place at the right time. You see, intelligence and good looks does pay off."

Sallie smiled while saying, "Jacob, I've always known that modesty was one of your virtues."

He grinned at her and said, "That was the second best thing that ever happened to me. Falling in love with you was definitely the best."

Sallie quickly answered, "Jacob, I bet you tell that to all the girls." She giggled and grabbed at his hand under the table.

Bridget groaned with disappointment, while murmuring to LiliTu, "How mushy and gooey can they get?"

"Getting back to Chapel Hill," Zebulon said while eyeing Bridget in a negative way. "This town is really a dog haven. Most dogs are treated with love and respect. They are a part of our lives. It has always been my feeling that in any good relationship there is no thought of indebtedness. Whether it is friendship, or marriage, or the sometimes very close bond of dog and man, whatever is given freely is given with love."

"I've overheard a lot of clients say, "It costs me just as much for that dog as it does to raise one of my children." Usually she lets that penetrate, then adds, "But he's worth it." Then all the heads in the waiting room will nod in agreement. The dog isn't always a pedigreed beauty either. His value in cold hard cash simply doesn't enter into the picture at all. All this bears out my thoughts about love and care freely given. In return the dog's love-filled eyes as he turns them on his owner is pay enough. All friendship is a two-way street, as I see it."

Sally looked at Zebulon and said, "Jacob, the more I know you, the more I am intrigued at your close liaison with animals. You bond so well with all of God's creatures."

CHAPTER XIII

David Smith reported to work the next afternoon to find a message that Dr. Zebulon wished to see him. He knocked on Zeb's office door and was told to come in.

"David, I'd like you to do something for us, if you will. It smacks a bit of danger," Zeb warned. "Maybe that'll intrigue you. I hope it won't scare you off."

"I could stand a little change, Doctor," David replied.

"Here's the scoop," Zeb began stealthily. "We'd like you to go back to Matt's Pub. We think there's something crooked about those Special Potatoes of Matt's. You sensed something funny the first time you were there." Zeb's expression became more serious. "We want to give you the twenty-five dollars for a Special and we'd like you to go and order one."

"It might take a little doing."

"We know that," Zeb assured him. "If I were you, I'd take some friends along. Maybe some guys who go there from time to time."

"Yeah. Some of the fraternity crowd go over there. And I'm good friends with some of them."

"Fine. Order a potato. You'll have to work the money into the waiter's hand so that nobody notices. Okay?" Zeb watched David closely.

"I ought to be able to do it. I don't think they know me from Adam. I've always gone there with other students." David assured Zeb. He seemed to be trying to assure himself as well. "Matt couldn't know anything about me, where I work, or anything else, I don't guess."

"As you eat the potato, search for something hidden in it. Probably a capsule. Hide it in your pocket and bring it back to me. Do you think you can do that?"

"I'll give it the best asparagus in the store."

"That means yes?" asked Zeb.

"That means certainly!" David answered "I'll get my friends and go over there about suppertime."

I can see the jail yawning for Matt, thought Zeb. Aloud he said, "Take care. Don't let anybody suspect anything. Hear?" And Zeb sent David away.

Bridget nosed the door open and came to Zeb. "I've been out looking around, Zeb. Matt was out in front. He's drunk as a lord, just stumbling around. He was scowling and mumbling, Zeb. He means trouble."

"I'll see about that," Zeb snorted. He rose from his desk, strode down the hall, out the front door and down the slope to the walk in front of the hospital. His long strides took him to where Matt stood, swaying slightly on feet planted wide on the walk.

Zeb looked into eyes like bits of blue glass. "Get out of here, Matt," he ordered. "I don't want you near my hospital!"

"This street is public property," snarled Matt.

"Not for you," retorted Zeb.

"You can't make me leave," said Matt. He shook a clenched fist in Zeb's face.

"Try something and I'll knock you on your ass. And you know I can do it," Zeb shoved his face close to Matt's. "I've whipped you with everything you've tried so far!"

"I'll go find that little bitch, Suzanne and make her pay for what she did to me. Then I'll come for Faye and take her away from you."

Matt took a step closer to Zeb and looked him squarely in the eye. "I'm giving you the old cliche, Zeb," he snarled. "This town isn't big enough for the both of us."

"Right. When are you leaving?" grated Zeb.

Matt turned on his heel and started unsteadily away down the street.

Bridget's old friend Eric, the Kerry Blue terrier, had quietly joined the group. And with Matt's departure, Bridget walked gingerly toward him.

"How much did you see, Eric?" she asked.

"Enough to wonder what this is all about," Eric told her.

"I'm going on in, Bridget," Zeb called.

"Be there in a minute, Zeb," Bridget answered, and turned back to Eric.

Talking With The Dogs

"Hey, that's pretty neat, talking to your human. I wish I could converse with my man. I'd tell him that he's messing with the wrong person when he does work for Matt Dye. Bridget, fill me in on all the details."

"I'll try to tell you as fast as I can," Bridget promised. She talked rapidly telling Eric as much as she knew about how Matt Dye treats humans and animals alike. When she finished, she asked, "Do you understand now?"

"Yeah, I think so," Eric said. "Enough to try to help you anyhow."

"Well, thanks Eric. And good luck," Bridget answered and hurried inside to report to Zeb.

Bridget nosed the office door open and joined Zeb. "That was Eric out there. You know him. He's been in here a lot of times with his owner, Dr. Pender, when he's been hurt, which is quite a lot 'cause he has an Irish temper and gets in lots of fights."

"Sure, and sometimes he comes alone," Zeb said. "He's a big Kerry Blue and I bet he can handle himself in a fight."

"Well, he's allowed to run free. Knows this town from one end to the other," Bridget explained.

"Yes. Go on," prompted Zeb.

"His human's a doctor. He treats the ladies at the Happy Day Club sometimes. Eric says they're going out there today. Eric likes to go with the doctor because the ladies give him treats. So he said he'd go along today and see if he could find out anything for us."

"How much did you tell him?"

"Enough," said Bridget. "I filled him in pretty good."

"We've got to get Suzanne out of that place," Zeb vowed. "The way Matt talked-he probably knows she helped us get Faye."

"Eric thinks Matt has spies everywhere. Suzanne is a sweet little thing, Eric says. Not long from the country. She is just one of Matt's girls in the club who is hooked on drugs. She is helpless against a man as dangerous as Matt Dye. The girls do anything that Matt commands them to do" Bridget frowned in thought.

Zeb lifted his phone. "Norris, please get word to Tyler that I would like to see him and Faye in my office immediately. Please."

Dr. Peters and Lib Nelson had done their jobs well and Zeb

finished his visit to the surgical patients without incident. When he returned to his office, Faye was waiting for him.

"I need your help, Faye," Zeb said at once. "We've got to get Suzanne out of the Happy Day Club. Matt threatened that he's going to get even with her. We've got to beat him to it."

Faye nodded in worried agreement.

"Call Suzanne—here, on my phone. Tell her I'll be there in my car in front of the club in exactly fifteen minutes. When she sees my car, she must dash out and get in with me. She must bring nothing with her—no clothes—no handbag—nothing she doesn't have on her or in her pockets—nothing. Please hurry. I'm on my way."

Bridget got into step behind Zeb. "I'd better come along, too. I can help you keep a lookout."

"Okay," agreed Zeb. "Matt could be going out there any time." Faye lifted the telephone and repeated Zeb's instructions word for word to Suzanne. Zeb and Bridget were out in front door and speeding away in his car before she had finished. As they pulled up in front of the Happy Day Club, the front door flew open and out ran Suzanne, coatless, her blonde hair flying in the breeze. Zeb flung open the car door.

"Get in, fast!" he ordered.

They were barely a block from the club when Bridget called from the rear seat, "There goes Matt! You were right, Zeb. We hardly made it."

Close behind Matt's car, they saw another carrying Eric and his human, Dr. Pender. The big black Cadillac was traveling in the wake of Matt's little sport car. "Good for Eric," said Bridget. "He'll be able to hear what happens when Matt finds out Suzanne's gone."

Zeb braked his car at the hospital. "Get out and follow me quickly," he told Suzanne.

The young woman's face was chalk white with fear and her big blue eyes stood out from her face. "I'm right behind you," she said. Her legs shook. She ran unsteadily to the hospital and inside.

Zeb held the door for Suzanne and Bridget. The three hurried through the crowded reception room, to the hall behind and on into the safety of Zeb's office. Faye and Tyler sat waiting, impatiently balancing coffee cups in nervous hands.

"Thank God you made it," Tyler said.

"Matt's probably there by now. And he won't find Suzanne. He'll be madder than ever and won't stop at anything to get her back. So what do we do next, Tyler?"

"He'll find me, he'll find me," whimpered Suzanne.

"We won't let him find you, Suzanne," Zeb assured her. He turned to Tyler. "Will our magic be enough this time?"

"We'll keep trying," said Tyler. "We've whipped him every time so far."

"You can't know what all he might do," Suzanne said, tears pouring down her painted cheeks.

Faye put an arm around her. "Trust them, Suzanne," she said. "They do wonders."

"What can I do? Where can I hide from him?" begged Suzanne.

"We're here to help you. But you must tell me something," Zeb said. "And you must tell me the truth. Are you on drugs?"

"Yes." Suzanne trembled. "He made me take them. He made all of us."

"Do you want to quit?" Zeb asked.

"I don't know if I could," Suzanne replied. She clung to Faye.

"We'd all help you," assured Faye. "Others have quit. Malay quit all the time but I know it's difficult. "Thank God Matt didn't get me hooked on drugs." She nodded her head solemnly. "I'm clean and I'll help you get clean."

"And we'll see that you're safe from Matt," Zeb promised.

"Okay. I'll try," Suzanne finally decided.

"Good," Zeb said. He took up his phone and dialed his friend Dr. Sewell at the Rehabilitation Center. Zeb explained Suzanne's problem. Dr. Sewell listened and said, "Okay, Zeb. Bring her over. But we'll have to report the case. You know that."

Zeb felt great relief that Dr. Sewell was at the Rehabilitation Center and not at the office where he met private patients. "It's okay, Allen. Do what's necessary. But I could wish that you might delay reporting it for a couple of days."

"I'll try."

"I can't send her in my car, Allen," Zeb said. "Matt Dye might be watching. "Could you send for her?"

"Certainly," replied Dr. Sewell.

An hour later, Zeb put Suzanne into a little red van in front of the hospital. Tyler climbed in after her. "I'll go with Suzanne, to help sign her in," he said.

"Good. And Tyler, will you and Faye please come into my office after you get back?" Zeb sighed with relief. Now he could return to the ailing animals who were waiting for his care.

He was staring into the throat of a handsome Golden Retriever when he heard an outburst of screams and laughter from the reception room.

"Watch Jimbo a minute," Zeb said to Mrs. Caraco, who was a new client and looked stunned by the sounds she heard. "I'd better go see what's happening out there."

"Yes, Doctor," Mrs. Caraco answered, her eyes wide.

Zeb saw at once that tiny Mrs. Jordan, all 85 pounds of her, had once again run into trouble with her Newfoundland, Rebel. But this time, instead of licking the faces of the waiting clients, the 200 pound dog was giving Mrs. Jordan a ride around the room. He had somehow tangled his leash in such a way as to catch his little human in it and she was riding him like a bucking bronco. Zeb could only guess how it might have happened. He strode over to the huge dog and took the collar in his strong hands. "Rebel, stand!" he ordered in a strong voice.

The dog quieted.

Zeb took Mrs. Jordan's shaking hand and led her to the front door. "I'll help you," he comforted her. "And after this, I'll treat Rebel at your home." He hoped he had sounded kind.

Zeb returned to the examination room to give Jimbo a shot of penicillin for his infected throat. "Ugh, that hurts," the patient complained.

"It will make you well," Zeb told him.

Mrs. Caraco, who had stayed with Jimbo, smiled and said, "You're so kind, Doctor. I wish Jimbo could understand you." Jimbo winked at Zeb.

Talking With The Dogs

Office hours were barely over when a timid scratching came on his back door in his office. "Come in," Zeb called as he opened the door.

"Boy, have I had an afternoon," Eric said as he pushed his way into the room. "Bridget told me that you want to hear about it."

"She was right," replied Zeb. "We'd both like to hear. Come and sit next to Bridget."

The handsome Kerry Blue said, "Hi, Bridget," and settled down next to her. "My human and I got to the Club right after Matt Dye. We went in while the door was still shaking from Matt's heavy hands. He acted as if he had lost his mind. He was staggering and he kept muttering to himself. It sounded like he was saying, "I'll get Faye! I'll take care of that little bitch!"

"Yes," Zeb agreed. "We thought he was off his rocker when we saw him out in front of the hospital."

"Well, he still acted nuts," Eric said. "He went up to a redheaded girl who was sitting in a big ottoman. She acted stoned—was kind of crooning a song. He said to her, "Thistle. Go get Suzanne and tell her I want her. Now!"

Thistle looked at him as if she didn't understand. "Wh-what, Mr. Dye?"

"I said, go get Suzanne. Now! Get her before I take a punch out of you."

Thistle nodded kinda tiredly and looked down the hallway. "Suzanne ain't here," she told him."

"Of course she's here. Her car's out front!"

"She didn't go in her car," Rosemarie added. She was a tall thin girl who was sitting on a cushion nearby. "She went with somebody else." Rosemarie, as well as all the girls were very nervous. They were all scared of Matt.

"You tell a good story," Zeb said to Eric.

"I may not tell it exactly. But I tried hard because Bridget told me how important it was." Eric crinkled his brow. "Then Matt began shouting at the girls. 'Where did she go?' he yelled. 'Who did she go with? You'd better tell me everything!'"

"Thistle began to blubber. Tears poured out and smeared on her makeup. 'I don't know him, Mr. Dye,' she said."

Dr. Louis Vine, D.V.M.

"Then Matt looked around the room at all the girls. 'Somebody knows him. Somebody knows him!' he yelled. 'Out with it. Fast!'"

"He must have frightened the girls badly," said Zeb.

"You can bet your bottom dollar on that. It made Rosemarie speak up. She said, 'I think it was a vet. A friend of Faye's.'"

"Then Matt turned and rushed out of the room. I could hear his tires squealing as he roared out of the parking lot. I had to wait for my human doctor to finish checking all the girls out before we could leave. So I don't know where he went, or anything else."

"Thanks, Eric. You did a fine job," Zeb said.

There was yet another knock on the office door. Eric left as Tyler and Faye came in. Zeb welcomed them.

"Everything's A-Okay with Suzanne, Doctor," Tyler said. "Dr. Sewell knows the dangers and is going to keep a close watch over her. He'll work out a health-building schedule for her, he said. Lots of fluids. And all kinds of vitamins and amino acids that's been depleted by the cocaine. He doesn't expect any problems, since she wants the treatment and promised to be very cooperative."

"Good. Dr. Sewell's a good man," Zeb remarked. "Now. I want Faye to cue us in about Suzanne. She seemed to be a naive little girl."

"Yes, doctor," said Faye. "Suzanne came from a little town near here. She started as just one of the girls. But men liked her looks—she was so beautiful—and she has sex appeal you wouldn't believe."

"I believe it," Zeb affirmed, remembering Suzanne's slender waist, her rounded hips and full breasts.

"Well, Matt got interested in drugs when he stayed in Jamaica some years back. He decided to sell the stuff. His only love is money—he'll do anything to make a dime."

"Did he ever try to use you at the Club?" Zeb bluntly asked Faye.

"Oddly enough, Doctor," Faye answered. "He really loved me. He couldn't bear for another man to touch me, or to give me drugs, either."

"So maybe he's not as bad as we think he is?" Zeb looked doubtful as he said it. "Okay, I'm just kidding. Go on."

"Well, Matt opened the Happy Day Club as the kind of house you thought. Then he started the Saturday night drug parties and really began making lots of money." Faye hesitated a moment to gather her thoughts. "They are a strange sort of party, exotic in a way. He figured it would attract men from all around."

"And because of the way Suzanne attracted men, he chose her to be the hostess. She almost had to be poured into the slinky dress he had designed for her. It really accented those curves." Faye looked at Zeb with embarrassed eyes. "Then he had her taught a small dance—more of a wiggle really. Then he was ready."

"Where did he get his customers?" Zeb asked.

"He sent invitations to his richest clients. They would arrive on Saturday night. Suzanne would greet them and seat them in cushioned chairs in a semicircle in the especially prepared reception room. Everyone was handed a crystal glass of imported champagne. Suzanne then shimmered her way to the first guest. She held in her hand a crystal tray that held a mound of white powdery cocaine in its center. Suzanne would stop before the first man and do her little dance. Then she would take her forefinger, which was almost hidden under a huge emerald ring, and dip it into the guest's champagne, then into the pile of cocaine. Then she would lick her lips sexily, and peer into his eyes. Then, with a smile, she would put the finger into the guest's mouth. Next, she would repeat the entire procedure, placing the champagne-wet cocaine in her mouth. After five or six guests were served, Suzanne was enjoying the evening, having a delightful time."

"How did this make Matt money?" Asked Zeb.

"Well, this foreplay cost plenty. And after this some of the men pulled out packets of cocaine they'd bought from Matt. They'd make lines and sniff their stuff—some through rolled up hundred dollar bills. They were the show-offs. Other just used soda straws."

"My God!" said Zeb. "Modern Arabian Nights. Naturally Suzanne got hooked. But did all the other girls get the night off?"

"No," Faye smiled. "Some men always went upstairs with the girls. Up there they can free-base or get anything else their little heart desired."

"Matt knows he's got Suzanne hooked, now," Zeb said. "So we've got our hands full to keep her safe from him."

"I know she'll be all right with Dr. Sewell," Faye asserted. "He's a fine man."

"Shouldn't we call in the police?" asked Tyler.

Zeb answered by saying, "I've already spoken to Chief Carter and filled him in on all Matt Dye's exploits and enterprises. He's having him checked out now with the F.B.I."

****

It was late evening. The day had been so full that Zeb had stayed at the hospital longer than he should. He could feel every bone and muscle in his body. Though Dr. Peters had shared the load, there had been plenty of sick dogs and cats to keep both of them busy. Then the trouble with Matt had intruded. Zeb was exhausted. He wondered how so much could happen in a single day. Thank God I can leave soon, he thought. Then a knock at his office door interrupted his thoughts.

"Come in," Zeb called in what he hoped was a friendly voice. He rubbed at the tired lines between his gray eyes, and brushed a stray lock of tawny hair from his face.

The door opened and David Smith came in. "Gee, I know it's late, Doctor," he said. "If it's too late for you, I'll report tomorrow."

Zeb sensed the excitement in David's voice and knew that he couldn't wait until tomorrow. "No David," he said. "Come on in. Let's talk about it now."

David spoke eagerly. "I think I've got something, Doctor," Even his freckles seemed to shine.

David pulled a little wad of paper from his pants pocket and carefully placed it on the desk. He opened it and lifted out a gelatine capsule filled with white powder.

Zeb felt a surge of triumph. "Well, if it isn't Sweet'n Low sugar, you may be right."

"Should we taste it?" David asked.

Bridget came from her corner and peered at the capsule. "Can you open it, Zeb?" she asked.

David's mouth dropped open. "I never heard Bridget make such funny noises before," he said, grinning.

Zeb quickly answered, "She's probably tired and hungry." Then he turned to Bridget, for David's sake, and said, "We'll be going soon, old girl."

Bridget winked a sly wink.

"I'll taste it," Zeb said. He carefully pried the capsule open and took a trifle of white powder on his finger. He put it into his mouth and felt a slight numbing sensation. "It tastes bitter," he announced. "And it has a numbing effect on my tongue even though it was just a small pinch. But it's there, for sure."

"Does that prove it's cocaine, then?" David asked.

"It's two of it's properties," Zeb affirmed.

David then spoke up in a very positive manner. "Dr. Zebulon, I also found out some very important information for you. Matt Dye is very smart. He never goes near any of the drugs himself. In the Pub, there is only one waiter who handles the sale of the potatoes. And he is very careful in selling the stuff. He won't sell it to you unless he knows you. The only reason I was able to purchase one is the fact that one of my buddies was a regular customer of his and he spoke up for me."

"And another interesting event on campus occurs when an ice cream truck cruises around. Some students really get happy. Besides ice cream, you can purchase some of the white powder for an extra twenty-five dollars. The truck is driven by one of Matt's henchmen."

"Shouldn't we report it?" David asked. "I don't know how many Special potatoes they served tonight. But there were plenty."

"I think it's too soon." Zeb replied. "We've got to be sure of ourselves before we take Matt Dye on. However, I am going to give Chief Carter this capsule for analysis."

"I guess that's wise." David agreed.

"We're going to set this in concrete, David," Zeb said. He reached into a drawer and got a sheet of his hospital stationery. At the top of the page he wrote the date and the hour. Then, with David's help, he put down the facts.

I bought a Special Baked Potato from a waiter named Harold at Matt's Pub on this date. While eating it, I found a capsule filled with a white powder, which I took to be cocaine. Dr. Zebulon and I have placed the capsule in a locked file with this statement for release to the proper authorities at the proper time.

They both signed: David Smith and Jacob Zebulon.

"I know Ira Carter, the Chief of Police, pretty well," said Zeb. "He's a great guy. He raises hunting dogs and I've treated them. I know he'll help us out with this when the time is right. David, you've been a great help. And I appreciate it. We'll think about what to do next. But go on home now. I'll see you tomorrow."

After he left, Bridget expressed her concerns to Zeb. "There's still the problem explaining to the police that we heard all about this mess from dogs."

"We'll worry about that part when we come to it," Zeb answered.

Zeb was almost too weary to write his reports. But it must be done for Tyler and Dr. Peters. He finished as quickly as he could and called to Bridget. "Come on, beautiful. I hope Sallie has something good to eat waiting for us. Thank God you all got out of that nasty fire without getting hurt."

Bridget said sleepily, "Boy, were we lucky. And I have to agree with you, OUR Sallie is a very good cook."

Zeb laughed for the first time that evening.

Sallie greeted the two weary friends with a brandy for Zeb and warm beef broth for Bridget. The house smelled of a spicy Minestrone and Zeb sank thankfully into his slightly burned big leather chair. He felt happy and relaxed. He felt at home and of course, that's where he was—at home.

CHAPTER XIV

The minestrone was delicious, fragrant with a hint of ham and beef, spiced with herbs. It was Sallie's mother original recipe. Zeb enjoyed it to the last spoonful. Lili and Bridget ate brimming bowls of the soup and complimented the cook by licking her hands.

"That's better than the stuff Zeb buys for us, Lili Tu," Bridget said. "Sallie' s really good."

"I once had a patient who was a vegetarian, Bridget," Zeb remarked. "And here you are, eating all those vegetables and licking your chops over them. Are you about to become one?"

Bridget raised her soulful brown eyes to Zeb's gray ones and said, "I don't expect my humans to be consistent—why do they ask it of me?"

"Okay. You can have both meat and vegetables from now on," Zeb said. "How about you, Lili? Are you for that?"

"If this is a dog's life, I'm all for it. I love people food." Lili replied, giving Zeb an undershot look from her slits of eyes.

Bridget and Zeb laughed appreciatively. "We make a pretty good family, I think." Zeb stated.

But it was a tired family. And they decided that it was time to get some rest. Zeb put on fire-truck red pajamas.

"I'll not be able to sleep with that in the room," Sallie teased, looking at the brilliant color.

"You wouldn't sleep anyway," Bridget said and grinned.

"Oh, oh, oh, children," Zeb scolded.

They turned out the lights and prepared, yawning, to lie down. All at once, the air outside was filled with a tinny, shrieking, bird-like sound. The air vibrated with it. Zeb ran to the door, opened it and looked out just in time to see a flock of strange looking birds flying away. They reminded him of a kind of primitive bird he'd read about in encyclopedias and books about pre-history, the dinosaurs and other strange creatures. But they moved away so quickly that he could only glimpse them. He went back to his bed.

He kissed Sallie lovingly and folded her in his arms.

Again he heard the screeching. He got to his feet and ran to the door. If he could move fast enough, maybe he would see what the creatures were. But as he opened the door, they retreated. He saw plumelike tail feathers vanishing and heard the rat-tat-tat of their song as they faded in the distance.

But, almost in his ears, he heard the tinny, scratching voice of one of the birds. He looked up. Sitting on the edge of the roof was a lone creature. He must have been the leader. He cocked his head at Zeb impishly. He was about the size of a hawk, partly scaly like a lizard and partly fluffy. His long tail was sheathed in plumes, as were his wings. He stretched out a long scaly neck and gazed down at Zeb with an eerie look of mischief. It was truly a bewildering sight. Zeb had never seen any bird like it ever before.

Zeb swung an arm at the creature. It dodged and swiped at Zeb's face with a vicious claw. Then it turned and flew away after the others.

Zeb again went to his bed. He fell into a restless sleep. When morning came, Zeb felt wearier than he had been the night before. He climbed into his clothes, shaved listlessly and walked to the hospital. Bridget tailed along behind him. "I can barely move, Zeb. I feel like an old lady today," she said.

They entered the hospital into semi-darkness. Tyler sat at the desk with Henry asleep next to his notepad. "Morning, doctor," Tyler said. "You look like the advance agent for judgement day."

"I feel like it too," Zeb replied. He told Tyler about the birds of last night.

"That sounds like more of Matt's funny business," Tyler said. "We can't forget him. He still wants Lili Tu. And now we've got Faye and Suzanne. That's really bothering him."

"They haven't told us everything they know yet," Zeb said. "But we have found out that the Happy Day is no ordinary club."

"Faye has told me some things," Tyler mentioned. "And when she gets her nerve up, she'll tell me more. Don't you worry. I'm sure of that."

"And Suzanne," Zeb said thoughtfully. "Dr. Sewell will keep her safe from Matt. She's probably got plenty she can tell us. How she came to be addicted—Faye has told us some things-now Suzanne must talk too."

"Yes," Tyler agreed.

Zeb took morning rounds slower than usual. None of the dogs were in critical condition. He looked in on a strychnine case that Dr. Peters had been treating and thought that the little dog was going to make it "God, I'd like to get my hands on the fellow who gave that poison to that little dog," Zeb thought. "I'd get him to the sheriff mighty fast."

Finally, Zeb and Bridget arrived at the kennels. Zeb stopped to speak to King and to see if the anointed silver coins were in place. "Morning', Doc," King greeted him.

"Has anything happened here since we saw you last?"

"That crazy man was out in the yard last night, but he didn't try to get in. He was talking to himself. I think he was saying,' She'll be needing a fix. I'll get her then. She'll have to come to me.' I didn't know what he was talking about."

"It's okay, King. I think I know," Zeb said. He and Bridget went back down the hall to his office. He took off his lab coat and went to find Dr. Peters.

"Ken, I'm going out for a little fresh air," Zeb informed the hard working young doctor. "I hardly got any sleep last night and maybe a little walk will pick me up."

"You certainly look peaked, doctor," Ken answered. "I'll look after things for you. There won't be any clients for a little while, anyway."

"Thanks," He and faithful Bridget left. The morning air lifted his spirits. Flowering trees lined the road. "Crepe Myrtle is beautiful," Zeb thought. "The rose man should be here soon to look after my bushes. They were healthy last year—he certainly has a green thumb."

They had descended the slope and left the hospital behind. And they were nearly to the top of the hill when they heard the scream of brakes.

They raced towards the sound. A hit and run driver again. The green BMW was roaring away down the hill, leaving a big Shar Pei tumbling head over heels behind it. Zeb ran across the street to the injured dog, dodging between oncoming cars. Bridget kept besides him. They reached the dog. It was a handsome male Shar Pei. He was conscious but apparently in great pain and bleeding freely from the mouth. Zeb bent over him to see what help he could give.

"I'm afraid I'll need to have this fellow at the hospital, Bridget."

"You can't carry him," Bridget replied. "I'll bet he weighs sixty or seventy pounds. More than I do," her brow furrowed in worry.

"You stay and watch over him, Bridget and I'll hurry back for my car. We'll get him to the hospital as fast as we can." Zeb turned and ran back in the direction from which he'd come.

Bridget spoke to the injured dog. "What's your name, my friend?" she asked.

The big dog had been moaning softly. He stopped for a moment and looked at Bridget. "Jimmy Wang," he replied. Pain had dug the wrinkles in his face even deeper and his little eyes seemed smaller.

"Try to relax," Bridget said in a comforting tone. "My human is the best vet in the world. He'll be back here in a minute and he'll look after you."

"Thank you," Jimmy Wang murmured.

"I see him coming now. He must have run all the way back to the hospital. Here he is."

Zeb jumped out of the car, medical bag in hand. He bent over Jimmy Wang to give him a quick examination. First, he gave him an injection for pain and a steroid into the muscle to prevent shock. Then he felt him over very carefully for broken bones. He found none. He lifted him to his feet and found that he was able to stand up. When he felt that is was safe to lift him, he picked him up in his arms, thanking the Lord for all the tennis, golf and other sports he'd played. It was at times like this that he appreciated his well-developed muscles.

"Now, my boy," he said to the wounded dog. "We'll soon be at my hospital where I can look after you properly."

He placed Jimmy Wang gently on the back seat. Bridget seated herself beside him. "I'll be with you all the time, Jimmy Wang" she assured him. "I wish I knew more about you. You don't even wear a collar."

"Don't ask," Jimmy Wang moaned. "Just call me a stray."

"No," protested Bridget. "You look like a highly pedigreed dog to me."

"But I don't want to go back where I came from. I ran away in the first place. A dog can take just so much," Jimmy Wang said.

"Please tell me," Bridget insisted. "Where did you come from?"

"I've told you too much already," Jimmy Wang protested. "No dog wants to turn against his human—but I've had it with mine. I beg you, don't send me back to that man!"

"Well, you sure look like a pure-blood to me," Bridget insisted. "I don't know why you weren't wearing a collar. But I know you're well-built enough to be a champion."

"Yeah. But that's because he fed me some drugs called 'uppers' to make me strut my stuff better at the shows." Jimmy Wang admitted. "How would you like that?"

"Ish! That's terrible," agreed Bridget. "That sounds like something that old Matt Dye would do."

"He isn't old, but if you mean nasty, you're right," Jimmy Wang said. "Do you know him?" There was relief in his voice as he sensed that he had a friend in Bridget. "I'll give you my story on a silver platter. I've been best in show many times. Matt makes money on me when I'm at stud and he treats me like a king. But if I haven't won and I'm not at stud—then he's mean to me and beats me sometimes." Jimmy Wang stopped for a breath of air. He seemed to feel his pain again.

"I can believe anything about that man," Bridget said.

"Yeah. When I'm making money for him he loves me, when I'm not he throws me out in the back yard and forgets about me. All he cares about is money."

Suddenly Zeb spoke up from the front seat. "And that's a true word for Matt Dye."

"Oh, oh," groaned the big dog. "It sounds as if your human understood what we were saying."

"You're right. My human isn't just a great vet," Bridget said proudly. "He can talk to dogs in our own vernacular."

"My God!" Jimmy Wang sounded frightened. "If I'd known that, I wouldn't have said all those things."

Dr. Louis Vine, D.V.M.

"Relax. If there's one sure thing, it's that you can trust Zeb." Bridget sounded stuffy. But Jimmy Wang seemed to believe her, so she felt vindicated.

Zeb spoke up again. "Jimmy Wang, you're the only one who knows I've heard this conversation. So let's just say that you're a stray. Okay?"

"Thank you, doctor," Jimmy Wang said gracefully.

"However—there's a but to this. If Matt Dye finds out I have you, and he can identify you—the law says I must give you to him. Truth is, it's against the law for me to hold another person's dog."

"Oh, ye Gods!" exclaimed Jimmy Wang. "He's sure to find out. He can talk to spirits. And gangsters. And all kinds of evil people."

They arrived at the hospital and Tyler helped Zeb get the big dog into surgery. Zeb examined him carefully. It seemed a miracle that Jimmy Wang did not have serious internal injuries after being tumbled by that speeding car. The blood from his mouth was caused by a cut gum as a result of his head hitting the pavement. He must be watched carefully. Luckily he'd been treated for shock at the scene of the accident. Zeb placed him in a fresh cage in the room next to the surgery where he could be kept under close observation. Lib would be alerted to give him special attention after the saline drip had finished going into his blood stream.

"Now you must rest," Zeb said. "We'll keep your pain deadened so that you can sleep through the night. Okay?"

"I'll be all right, I'm sure. I feel better already," Jimmy Wang said drowsily as the medication began to take effect.

Zeb went to check the board for his next appointment.

Later in the day, Zeb was back in surgery. Mrs. Penny's Dalmatian had managed to break his leg. Zeb was busily setting the bone when he overheard Bridget and Jimmy in the room next door.

"Maybe Zeb will let you come home with us. If he does, you'll meet the prettiest girl Shar Pei you've ever seen," Bridget assured him. "She belongs to my human's girl friend. And they're staying at our house for a few days."

"Oh? How come?"

"Well. You see Jimmy Wang, we heard that Matt Dye wanted to

Talking With The Dogs

steal Lili Tu. She's Sallie's beautiful Shar Pei," Bridget explained.

"Hey! I've heard something about that." Jimmy Wang sounded excited. "Matt tried to steal a beautiful bitch for my mate. He wanted me to make champion pups for him."

Bridget nodded. "That's got to be Lili Tu. He tried everything to get hold of her," she said easily. "And so far he's failed."

"Matt's evil spirits'll help him," Jimmy Wang said. "Your doctor better watch out."

"Tyler's magic can stop him," Bridget said proudly.

"Don't be so sure," Jimmy Wang insisted. "Matt's spirits can do anything. Matt's down at the shore now buying drugs. That's why I decided it was a good time to get away from him but that car that hit me changed everything. But when he gets back, you'd better look out!"

"What's all this about drugs and the shore?" Bridget asked, mystified.

"When Matt buys fish for the Pub, his dealers stuff some of them with drugs—cocaine, or whatever he's ordered. They put capsules with the white powder into the fish's mouths and bring them back so that Matt can sell them to whoever will pay the price. He makes most of his money that way. Us dogs are just a sideline—a hobby."

"What about the Happy Day Club?"

"Oh, drugs are the main thing there too. Women and drugs," Jimmy Wang said unhappily. "He makes lots of money there too. Matt keeps the girls hooked on the drugs so they'll stay and work for him."

Zeb was almost finished treating the ailing Dalmatian. He hoped he didn't miss any important information filtering in from the next room. But the bone was set and the leg in a cast. He and Lib Nelson put the dog into a cage to let him rest.

Bridget and Jimmy Wang became quiet at once and watched the doctor finish administering to the Dalmatian. Lib Nelson left the room.

"I wonder if he got hit by a car too?" asked Jimmy Wang.

"No, he had a hard fall," Zeb told him. Jimmy Looked at Zeb with wonder. He still found it hard to believe that the doctor really understood what he said. "Amazing," he muttered.

Zeb then added, "I assure you Jimmy Wang that we are going to get Matt Dye in spite of all his evil spirits, voodoo spells and henchmen. He's going to spend lots of years behind bars breaking big rocks into smaller ones. I guarantee you that."

"I certainly hope you do. I've seen him do some mighty bad things. He deserves whatever he gets, the worse the better. And I'll help you all that I can. Just say the word and especially now that you and I can talk to each other," Jimmy said with a smile on his face.

CHAPTER XV

The next day began very early for Zeb. After turning and twisting in the bed for an hour, he decided that he was simply wasting time that might be spent at the hospital. He got out of the bed and dressed quietly, hoping not to disturb Sallie. But she heard him moving about.

"Wait a minute, dear," she said. "I'll make you coffee and toast."

"I'm not hungry, my love," Zeb protested. "Just nervous and worried about Jimmy Wang over there at the hospital."

"At least a cup of coffee," Sallie begged. "Please."

Zeb sat down for a moment and gulped the hot coffee as quickly as he could. Anything could have happened during the night and he couldn't rest easy until he saw that everything was safe. Of course, Tyler was utterly trustworthy and capable. But he was so much in love with Faye—maybe his concentration would lapse. Zeb hoped he wasn't being silly. Then he hoped he was.

"I'll call you in a little while," Zeb said to Sallie as he left the house.

The reception room was quiet in its semi-darkness. Chips puckered up for a kiss and after that accepted a red apple with a chirp of thanks. Zeb went back to the surgery to look in at Jimmy Wang and the Dalmatian. Bridget followed him.

The Dalmatian was sleeping. Jimmy Wang stretched and yawned as Zeb opened his cage door. "Good morning, Doctor," he said. "And hi, Bridget."

"Good morning, yourself," Zeb said. "How do you feel?"

"Pretty good, thanks to you," Jimmy Wang replied.

"Okay. If you're still saying that later today, you can go to my house and stay with Sailie and Lili Tu."

"That'd be great, Doc," Jimmy said with a smile on his face, in anticipation of meeting Lili Tu.

The Dalmatian did not move in his deep slumber. Zeb decided to leave him until later in the day, and went back to the kennels to see the boarding guests.

"Hi, Doc," King greeted him in his gruff voice. "I'm glad to see you."

"Has something happened?" Zeb asked him.

"No, but I think somethin's up," King said. "That crazy man was out here in the middle of the night blathering to himself. He'd been out of town, he said, and you pulled a fast one on him." King fixed Zeb with a knowing eye. "He said his spirits had told on you."

"Sure," Zeb answered. "But don't worry. He can't get at you in here."

"Yeah. Those silver coins must be working." King turned a worried face to Zeb. "But can he hurt you? He threatened to get the law on you." King was plainly nervous. "When David Smith takes me for a run this afternoon, I want to find out all I can about that man. Okay?"

"Sure. Do what you can," said Zeb.

Back in his office, Zeb found Lib Nelson waiting for him with fresh coffee. "You look as if you've about used up that candle you've burning at both ends, Doctor."

"You're too right, Lib," Zeb answered. "I never thought this job could result in so many sidelines." He sighed. "I'll need your help and every one else's these next few weeks."

"You'll have it," Lib said. "It's that bad, eh?"

"Lib, it's worse than that," He told her about Faye and Tyler. "They've fallen deeply in love and Matt Dye is furious. He constantly pokes about, watching for Faye. And if matters weren't bad enough, that injured Shar Pei in the other room is one that belongs to Matt Dye that Bridget and I found on the street after he was hit by a car. I wish you'd keep your eyes open for anything unusual going on around here."

"Don't worry! I'll notice that man," Lib vowed. "My hair stands up like a fright wig every time I see him. I'll notice him all right." Lib grinned her teeth in a smile that was not a smile. Norris Martin might have called it a grimace.

"You've seen some of the things that've happened here in the hospital," said Zeb. "Just imagine what would happen if Faye left this place." He stopped for a moment to think. "And now there's Suzanne. She worked for Matt too."

"Doctor, don't get hold of anything you can't turn loose," Lib cautioned.

"I'm not turning loose of what I've got hold of," Zeb assured her. "Dr. Sewell will help all he can. He has plenty of security guards over there."

"He's a good man, Doctor," Lib agreed. "I think you can depend on him." She left the office to get on with her work.

Norris Martin came into the office. She shook her long pale hair back from her face and brushed at her blue eyes as if a hair had gotten into them. She was always aware of the way she moved and wore short skirts to accent the shapeliness of her long legs. "Mr. Home is here to see you, doctor," she said. "He says his dog isn't sick, but he really needs your advice about something."

"That's okay," Zeb replied. "Put him in room one, I'll be right there."

"Doctor, I'm desperate," Mr. Horne greeted Zeb nervously. "Jason isn't really sick. I wouldn't call it that. But there's certainly something wrong."

"All right, tell me about it," Zeb said. This had begun to sound like a day when he needed a consulting room with a couch. Jason, the Golden Retriever, sat sedately at Mr. Home's feet and looked delightfully normal. Surely, this handsome dog didn't need a psychiatrist.

"You see, I've been divorced—two years now. Soon after I got divorced, I purchased Jason and the two of us have been inseparable since then. However, I became lonesome for a lady's companionship so I've had some dates. But none of these worked out for me until lately." He hesitated a minute as if embarrassed. "I've finally found a woman I could really love," he finished.

"Splendid," applauded Zeb.

"Not so splendid," said Home. "Every time I try to bring her into the house, Jason pushes himself in the way. I've tried two or three times and he just won't let her get near me." Mr. Home said sorrowfully. "And he's usually so good."

"I know what you mean. I am having the same problem with my dog Bridget," Zeb confessed. "Our dogs becomes so possessive of us they do not want anyone else to get close to us. Jason has had you all to himself for two years. He loves you dearly. He needs you."

"He'll still have me," said Home.

"Half of you, maybe," Zeb replied. "Let me take Jason to my examining room and check him out carefully. There might be an underlying cause to all this."

He led Jason out of the office. He wanted time to be alone with the patient so he could have a man to man discussion with the misbehaving dog. Zeb said a silent thanks to his shamrock that let him hear what dogs spoke. When they were alone except for Bridget sitting in the corner of the room, Zeb began the inquiry.

"Okay, Jason, what's this all about? Why don't you like the new lady?"

"She's okay, I guess but I don't like the way she bosses him around. He follows her around with a moonstruck look on his face. One word from her and he jumps to attention."

Zebulon answered in a very somber tone "It sounds to me as if old man Home has been bit by the love bug. That's how men act when they fall in love with a woman. But I want to emphasize to you and Bridget over there, that it is a different kind of love that we have for our woman and our dog. We love you both from the bottom of our hearts but it's just not the same. We can't love two women at the same time but we can love a dog and a woman. Remember, there is no contest between the two of them. You can have both for the rest of your lives. Jealousy should never enter into such an arrangement. The three of you can live together happily ever after."

"OK, Doc, since you put it that way, I'll give it a try. What do I have to do?"

"Jason, first thing you do is try and get friendly with the lady. Otherwise, you might get shipped out. Love is a powerful incentive. Be nice to the lady. Accept her as a permanent fixture. She might be around for a long time to come. If she is attentive to you, show her your appreciation by warming up to her. You cagey canines know how to put on the insecure act. After all, she might be a genuinely nice and loving lady. Give her a chance, will ya?"

"All right, I'll give it a try. I love my human so much, I would

Talking With The Dogs

hate to be sent away to a new home with strangers. I can take a hint. Shape up or ship out. Is that it?"

"You take the words right out of my mouth," Zeb answered.

Bridget entered into the conversation by saying, "You men are all alike. You all fall for a pretty face while Jason and I can give our undying love and loyalty."

Zeb quickly responded. "Who asked for your opinion Bridget?" And with a smile on his face, he led Jason out of the room.

He addressed Mr. Horne with a victorious attitude by saying, "I believe everything is going to work out for your complete satisfaction and happiness. You have to impress on your young lady to show Jason lots of tender loving care and he will respond to her attention. She should feed him and take him for walks. I have a feeling that Jason is a very understanding and intelligent dog and will respond to the occasion. Won't you, Jason?" Zeb bent down and patted the dog as he muttered these words, winking in a secretive manner that only Jason perceived.

"You say you've tried this before?" asked Mr. Home.

"Yes." Zeb grinned. "And that man has ten children now. It worked fine."

"Thanks a million, doctor," Home said. Apparently he believed Zeb. "You'll be invited to our wedding."

The man and dog went triumphantly out of the hospital.

After they left, Zeb's thoughts went to Suzanne. "I must check on her." He picked up his phone and dialed the Rehabilitation Center. When Dr. Sewell came on the line, Zeb asked, "How's Suzanne, Allen?"

"She's trying to cooperate with us, Zeb," Dr. Sewell replied.

"Good, that's half the battle."

"Yes. She's a beautiful girl. I think she realizes how important it is to get back into the mainstream of life."

"The drugs were forced on her, Allen," Zeb said. "Will that fact help with the cure?"

"I don't know. We're trying to rebuild her health and get her body metabolism back to normal again," Sewell went on to explain. "Good nutrition does much, you know."

"Right, Allen."

"And a natural sleep pattern is necessary too," Dr. Sewell amplified. "The drugs have disturbed that. So we're trying to develop her own natural pattern."

"Allen, I want to ask a favor. Matt Dye has threatened to take Suzanne. I don't know if you can discourage that," Zeb stated. "How tight is your security?"

"We try."

"I have a suggestion," Zeb said.

"Okay," replied Sewell. "What is it?"

"I have a boarder, name of King. He's a splendid Airedale who knows Matt Dye and his tricks." Zeb hesitated. "If we could send him to stay with Suzanne..."

"Sorry, Zeb. Stop there," Sewell interrupted. "The Board of Health would never allow it."

"How well equipped are you to handle people like Matt Dye and his henchmen?"

"I have excellent security guards. Officer Goad checks everybody at the door. And I can assign another officer to keep watch at Suzanne's door."

"Well, that sounds good," Zeb said. "I didn't know you could do that."

"We all are very fond of Suzanne and want to help her out of the snakepit she fell into. We'll do everything we can for her, Zeb, don't worry."

"Thanks," Zeb said as he put down the phone and turned back to Norris. "Any more patients out there?" When she replied in the negative, he packed his gear and motioned to Bridget to follow him.

Evening came and with it a heavy rain. Zeb and Bridget trudged through the spongy woods to the cottage, both huddled under Zeb's big umbrella. Sallie had prepared dinner—a chicken stuffed with rice and corn, then roasted in a rock-salt jacket.

"It's just tremendous, Sallie," Zeb said, eating eagerly. "I'll never be able to give you up. Never."

"What if I couldn't cook" Sallie asked, her blue eyes impudent.

"Not even then." He leaned over and gave her a long and persistent kiss. "You've got it all."

Sallie thought to herself, "well I have a bruised lip to prove it."

"Bridget and I have a surprise for you two," Zeb announced. "Jimmy Wang is well enough to leave the hospital. I've decided to bring him over here to stay with you in the cottage. Okay?"

"Okay, Jacob," said Sallie. "But I don't know how long I'll be here."

"We won't worry about that now. I'll bring him over in the morning."

Lili Tu lifted her chin high and looked at Zeb through her narrow slits of eyes. "Can I trust you, Zeb," she asked. "I remember that Matt Dye wanted Jimmy Wang and me to breed little puppies for him. You aren't partners in that, I hope."

"As a joke, Lili Tu," Zeb scolded her. "That just isn't funny. A man has to be pretty bad for his own dog to hate him- but Jimmy Wang does a mighty good job of doing just that."

Bridget broke in. "Lili Tu, if you could see that poor dog, you wouldn't even think such things. He hates Dye like poison and wants to get free of him." Bridget sounded thoroughly disgusted. "If you two fell in love, okay—but he sure wouldn't do anything just to please that old crook."

"Sorry," Lili Tu said. "Sometimes jokes don't turn out to be jokes, I guess."

"There's a lot more to this," Zeb informed everybody. "Jimmy Wang didn't wear a collar, so officially we don't know who he is or where he came from. He's just a stray who got hurt, out in front of this hospital. We brought him inside to care for him. Remember that."

"Isn't it against the law to keep a stray without reporting it, Jacob? Sallie asked.

"Yes, after a time. But Jimmy Wang is still under treatment."

Bridget and Lili Tu walked to their corner where there were soft blankets waiting for them and curled up to go to sleep. Sallie and Zeb looked longingly at their bed.

"It's late, Jacob."

"Yes," agreed Zeb. "I hope those strange birds have climbed back into the brain that spawned them."

Sallie looked deeply into Zeb's gray eyes. "I'm knocking on wood," she said as she turned down the covers on the bed.

CHAPTER XVI

As usual, Zeb arrived at the hospital when it was barely daylight. He found Faye sitting at the desk in the reception room with little gray Henry curled up besides her on the telephone directory. Zeb stopped a moment to give Chips a piece of orange and his morning kiss, then went to greet Faye.

"Good morning, my dear," he said. "You're here bright and early."

"Tyler's afraid for me to be alone in his cottage,"' Faye answered. She looked tired. The brown skin was pulled tight over her high cheekbones.

"Have you been here all night, then?" Zeb asked.

"Yes, I have." Faye replied. She yawned. "I stretched out for a while on the couch in your office. I hope you don't mind."

"Of course not," Zeb said. Just then Tyler came into the reception room.

"Good morning, doctor," he greeted Zeb with a cheerful but worried voice. "I hope you don't mind that Faye stayed over here. I heard Matt Dye outside last night."

"You too?" Zeb said. "I thought there was something wrong over here."

"I could hear him mumbling to himself. I think he was drunk," Tyler said. "He was saying over and over again that his spirits had told him that you have Jimmy Wang."

"Thanks, Tyler," Zeb said. "Suzanne, Faye, and now Jimmy Wang. I'm afraid Matt will go berserk."

"We'll take care of him, doctor." Tyler assured Zeb. "And that's no idle promise."

"I'm going to check on Jimmy Wang right now," Zeb said. "If he's well enough, I'll take him over to my cottage today. He can stay with Sallie and Lili Tu.

"How safe will they be over there?" Tyler wondered.

"You know about our direct line. Sallie will call at the slightest hint of trouble," Zeb answered. "I've considered letting Bridget stay with them. But I really need her here."

"I can get there faster than anybody, Zeb," Bridget said. "I can help you in both places."

"So right," agreed Zeb as the two entered the surgery recovery room. "You've still got all that youthful speed."

Jimmy Wang was wide awake and greeted Zeb happily. "Hi, Doc. I'm sure glad to see you. I'm starved. When do they eat in your place?"

"That makes my day, Jimmy," Zeb said, a smile spreading his lips. "You're really improved if you're hungry."

"Yeah, I guess I am. I'm a little sore all over but it's a lot better than living with that monster of a man, Matt Dye."

Zeb gave Jimmy a small dish of minced chicken and egg. Jimmy set to with an eagerness that delighted Zeb and Bridget. "I should've brought you a cup of coffee, Jimmy," Bridget teased.

"Just leave me alone to enjoy," Jimmy Wang replied.

"Later on, we're going to my house in the woods," Zeb told Jimmy. "Sallie and Lili Tu will look after you there."

"You'll love Lili Tu!" said Bridget.

The three walked slowly through the woods. The trees held an early morning mist that smelled of rich earth and tender leaves. Zeb relished the walk between the hospital and his cottage. When he could linger among the trees and enjoy the earthy smells, he was his happiest.

Sallie opened the door. Lili Tu gave Jimmy Wang a long look and decided that he was all right. "Come on in, Jimmy Wang," she said. "We've been expecting you."

Sallie gave Jimmy a loving pat on the head. "You look as if you could stand some nourishment. I'll get you something."

"He just had something, Sallie," Zeb said. "Keep it fairly light today. Maybe several small meals until he feels whole again."

Zeb took Sallie in his arms and held her tightly. She almost felt her ribs creak in his grasp. He kissed her again and again. "God, I wish I didn't have to go," he whispered in her ear.

****

Patients had begun to fill the reception room. Zebulon had often thought about all the different type of people who frequented his hospital. Doctors; lawyers; perhaps not Indian chiefs but their equivalents in this modern world, the executives; farmers; laborers; many professors; housewives; cooks; nurses: name the occupation or profession and he was sure he had some representative from it listed in his files.

Norris expertly divided the clients between Ken Peters and Zeb. But his was a long list because many clients refused to see anyone else.

Mrs. Lutton came into the examination room, cuddling a beautiful Pekinese to her softly rounded bosom. She was a plumpish middle-aged lady with tightly curled auburn hair. She had been a client of Zeb's for several years and she always seemed to own little Pekinese dogs.

"This is Annie, doctor," Mrs. Lutton began. "I've brought her to you because she has become a nervous wreck lately."

"How do you mean?" Zeb asked. "Is she unusually hyper? Or is she frightened of particular things? Tell me more about it, please, Mrs. Lutton.

"I really can't explain it, doctor." Mrs. Lutton looked at the doctor as if she wished he could put words in her mouth. "She seems to be afraid of my living room. When I call her so I can hold her in my lap, she stops at the door and whines."

Zeb thought of his four- leafed shamrock and silently thanked the Irish girl who had given it to him. He could do with a few minutes alone with Annie. "Let me take Annie to a private examination room, please, Mrs. Lutton."

"Yes, doctor," Mrs. Lutton agreed. "Anything you say. Anything you think might help."

Annie settled comfortably into Zeb's arms. When he placed her on the examination table, she began to speak. "Doctor," she began, "Word has gotten around that you can speak to dogs."

"That's right, Annie."

"Well, I'm sure glad. My human doesn't understand me at all." Annie nodded her head sadly. "My mate, Woodrow, recently died and she's had him stuffed."

"I've heard of people doing that," Zeb said.

"Yes, doctor," Annie said grimly. "But to make matters worse, she stood him up on the mantelpiece in the living room. He just stands there and leers at me. I can't go in there with him staring at me like that."

"I can understand that," Zeb said. "But try and get used to it. Why—I had one client who had six of her dogs cremated when they died. And she kept them in urns, side by side, on the mantelpiece."

"Ye Gods. You're right. That's even crazier," Annie agreed. "But they were in urns. Nobody had to look into their dead eyes all day long. No way, Doctor. I just won't go into that room with Woodrow looking at me like that. My nerves can't take it. Woodrow and I were good buddies. Can't you talk the old biddy into removing my pal from the mantelpiece?"

"I'll try, Annie."

When they arrived back in the examination room with Mrs. Lutton, Zeb turned to her and asked, "Is there anything newly arrived in the living room that might possibly be scaring Annie so that she won't enter the room? Think carefully. It's very important."

With Mrs. Lutton in deep thought for a few minutes, her face suddenly showed a look of surprise and she blurted out, "The only thing new in that room is poor Woodrow, my last dog, who passed away recently. I had a taxidermist fix him so we can remember him for the rest of our lives. He was such a wonderful part of our family."

"I believe that Woodrow is the cause of all of Annie's nervousness, Mrs. Lutton. She is probably scared of his appearance in the living room. I would advise you to remove him to a nice spot in the closet where you can always look at him from time to time."

"I'll do whatever you say to get Annie healthy again. I love her so very much. But it's hard to believe that the sight of poor Woodrow would frighten her. They were inseparable playmates. However, I'll take him down as soon as I get home. Thank you, Doctor. You're so smart. You can figure anything out."

Talking With The Dogs

As they were leaving the office, Zeb and Annie looked at each other and exchanged nods with smiles on their faces.

It was growing late and visions of steak and kidney pie were dancing before Zeb's eyes. "I wonder if Sallie has ever baked one," he thought. Bridget, for her part, had dreamed up a nicely browned T-bone steak. But reports must be written, ailing dogs must have one more look-see before Zeb could leave. All at once, there came a staccato knock at his door.

Norris came into the office. With a perplexed look on her face, she asked, "You have a surprise visitor, doctor. It's the police chief. He doesn't have a pet with him. Shall I send him here to your office?"

"Sure. He's an old friend." Zeb cared for all of Ira Carter's hunting dogs. And when a poisoner had been loose in Chapel Hill, Zeb saved the life of one of Ira's most valuable hounds. The Chief was young and eager to do an excellent job for the town. He had studied modern crime detection and had adopted many of the newest methods.

"Come right in, Ira." Zeb greeted him. Ira seemed embarrassed. His dark hair, neatly cut, was a perfect fit for his handsome face. And his feet found the path to the guest's chair besides Zeb's desk with difficulty. He wore a neat blue uniform and visored cap. "Before we get down to business, Doctor, please tell me one thing. As I drove up to your hospital just now, a delivery truck from the florist was delivering a large bouquet of exquisite flowers. Was it for you or one of your patients?"

With a smile on his face, Zeb answered, "Not to be outdone by human hospital patients, many of our hospitalized dogs and cats receive get-well cards, telephone calls and some even receive flowers."

All that Chief Carter could respond to this statement was, "Now, I've seen everything!" And both men laughed.

"Getting back to business," Ira Carter began "I hate having to do this, but Matt Dye has filed a complaint against you. He says that you're holding his dog a prisoner here."

"Huh!" Zeb said. "I don't even know Matt Dye's dog. He's never brought him to me for treatment—I don't remember ever seeing him."

Dr. Louis Vine, D.V.M.

"Have you any strays here?" Ira Carter sounded almost apologetic. His brown eyes avoided meeting Zeb's brilliant gray ones.

"Yes. There was an accident out on the main road." Zeb said. "I brought the injured animal inside and treated him." "No identification?" "Nothing."

"I have a description of Dye's dog here, Zeb," Ira said. "Let me read it to you."

"Sure. Go ahead."

"It's a large, gray, male Shar Pei—whatever that is. Says it weighs about seventy pounds. Has a wrinkled coat and little tiny eyes." "Sounds like a Shar Pei all right, Ira."

"Have you seen such a dog, Zeb?" Ira asked, still too embarrassed to look Zeb in the eyes.

"Sounds pretty much like any Shar Pei, Andy. The one I have here is kinda like that."

"Okay, then, Doctor." Suddenly the Chief began to use an official tone as if this were a duty call. "I'll bring Dye over to look at him. And if he claims the dog, I'll have to take him away from you."

"That's the law all right," Zeb conceded. "I'll have to let you take him, if he swears it's his." Zeb looked Ira squarely in the eye. "But if I ever hear that he mistreats that good dog, I'll have the Animal Protective Society of Chapel Hill after him-and fast! It's my personal theory that the dog was running away from him when he got hit by that car. Matt Dye is a mean man. We both know that."

Chief Carter could hardly have been gone an hour before he was back with a glowering Matt Dye. "Will you please show Mr. Dye the dog that you found hit by a car outside your hospital, Dr. Zebulon."

Ira's official tone made Zeb feel that he must respond in the same manner. "Yes, certainly, Chief," he said. "The dog is at my house. Will you be good enough to follow me?"

Matt skinned his teeth angrily. "So you were hiding him, eh?" he snarled. "You must've intended to keep him!"

"Nobody keeps him until we find out whose he is," Ira announced in a firm voice. "It's up to you to identify him if you take him away."

The three walked through the woods. Matt was uptight and barely spoke. He walked heavily. Bridget followed behind. Birds were

Talking With The Dogs

singing and the trees whispered in the breeze. Zeb wished his life might be as peaceful as the life of those trees. As they approached the cottage, Sallie's beautiful lyric soprano floated out to them, singing melodies from The Sound of Music. Zeb's heart raced, as it always did, at the sound of her voice.

The three men entered the house with Bridget leading the way. Sallie quietly greeted them. Lili Tu and Jimmy Wang retired to a corner to watch frora a safe distance. Bridget joined them. She whispered, "Don't be afraid."

Zeb pointed to the three dogs. "Here are my canine friends. Do you know any of them, Mr. Dye?"

The chief watched Matt closely. Matt's hard little eyes glinted in triumph. "That's my dog, all right," Dye snapped. Chief Carter couldn't be sure which dog he looked at, his scowl was so deep. "That's Jimmy Wang. Come here, Jimmy."

Lili Tu whispered to Jimmy Wang. "Stay here. I'll try to fool him." She moved forward. Bridget whispered. "He's bound to know you're a lady," But, for an instant Matt looked confused. Then he appeared to notice the difference. Zeb thought to himself, "What a difference!"

"By God. You thought you could fool me did you?" Matt said furiously. "Well, try again. That's my dog sitting there!" He sounded almost like an animal, himself. "Come here, Jimmy Wang. Get on your feet."

"So. He's your dog, is he?" Chief Carter asked.

"By God, yes, he's my dog." Matt yelled, the veins stood out on his neck. "I don't know what you've done to him to make him act like that," Matt clinched a fist. "He used to come to me when I called him."

"We've given him some loving care," Zeb said. "You might try that, Matt."

The Chief of Police asked the dog to come. "Go with him, Jimmy Wang," urged Zeb. Lili Tu saw tears in the big dog's eyes and said, "We'll see you again one day, Jimmy. We love you."

Jimmy turned to Lili Tu and Bridget and said, "I'll be back. I shall return. I'll get here one way or another, I promise you." And with that, the saddened Jimmy Wang finally walked to Matt and left Zeb's cottage with the chief and the despised Matt Dye.

Zeb eased himself into his big comfortable chair and said, "That was about the hardest thing I ever had to do."

Sallie threw her arms around him and kissed him. "I know. I know," she whispered in his ear and tenderly kissed the ear with a warmth that he had never experienced before.

A short time later, the tall, broad-shouldered figure of Ira Carter suddenly appeared in the cottage doorway. "I had to come back to apologize, Zeb," he said. "I hated to see that scumbag get back that dog almost as much as you did. But the law tells me what to do. And I do it."

Sallie's stepped to the bar. "Maybe one of Zeb's bourbon and sodas will make you both feel better," she said.

"Thanks, but I'm on duty," the chief answered.

"I'm on duty, too," said Zeb. "Is there some coffee in the pot?" Sallie poured and the three sat down to sip Zeb's special Columbian brew. "Delicious," said Ira happily. "This certainly beats the stuff that Dye serves at the Pub."

"I haven't been in his place for a while, Ira. We had some words and we almost fought the last time I was there."

"I go in now and then. We watch his place closely," Ira said. "But we haven't caught him yet. He's very clever and careful but he'll slip up one of these days and we'll throw the book at him."

"There are rumors," Zeb stated nonchalantly.

"They're just rumors until we get some solid evidence."

"I might be able to help you with that," Zeb said. "Could you send in an undercover man?"

"We're working on it," Ira replied. "I've contacted the narcotics division of the FBI."

"If I might make a suggestion," Zeb offered. "A fellow who could pass for a college student might work."

Bridget nudged Zeb. "Why don't you tell him about David Smith?"

"I hear that Matt's special baked potatoes are the source of cocaine for the young people," Zeb said.

"That's still in the rumor stage," Ira answered.

"I would also advise you to keep a careful eye on the Happy Day Club. I'll soon have a lot of personal evidence about that place."

"As a matter of fact, we've had several complaints about that place recently. If it's true, a place like that shouldn't be in a nice college town like this."

"I'll be able to tell you something soon," Zeb said. "I know a good many young students."

"Right. And I'll be happy to hear anything that's good solid evidence."

The Chief rose to his feet. "Thanks for the coffee. But duty calls."

"And you must answer," Zeb said. "I know. And I must get back to the hospital, too."

CHAPTER XVII

Zeb spent such busy days at the hospital that he almost forgot to think about Matt. Not so, Suzanne. And not so, Tyler and Faye. Zeb found time to call Dr. Sewell every day and got some good reports. Suzanne was beginning to feel better under her program of good nutrition, but had not yet recovered a healthy sleep pattern. Dr. Sewell felt greatly encouraged by her cooperation and her willingness to accept the unpleasant effects of withdrawal.

One sunny afternoon, when the sky was as blue as Sallie's eyes and the air was sleepily warm, Matt Dye came in at the door of the Chapel Hill Rehabilitation Center. He approached Dr. Sewell with a sheaf of papers.

"I'm glad you're here, Doctor," he said. "I'm the legal guardian of a young woman you are holding in your hospital."

Matt was dressed in a rumpled business suit, shirt collar open at the neck, a red necktie hanging loosely. His slipon shoes had been stylish ten years before. Matt had probably worn jeans and pullovers most of those last ten years.

Dr. Sewell led Matt into his office and reached out a hand for the papers. "Let's have a look," he said.

A superficial glance told the doctor that these were forgeries. He looked up into Matt's narrowed eyes and simply stated, "There's no official seal."

"I was told it wasn't needed," Matt answered back.

"For me it is," said Dr. Sewell and handed the papers back to Matt. He turned to a burly guard, standing at the door. "Show this gentleman the way out, please."

Matt glared furiously. "Okay, Doctor," he said. "You win this one. But I'll be back." He turned and stamped away. The security guard saw him out the door and strode back to Sewell's office.

"That's the man we were warned about, Timmons. I've assigned Boggs to special duty for Suzanne—to watch over her all the time. We'll assign relief later."

Talking With The Dogs

"Good," responded Timmons. "I don't like that man, no how. He muttered all kinds of threats against you Doctor and this rehab center."

"Please give Boggs a full description of Dye and an account of what just happened," the doctor said. "That guy'll probably be back with some dirty tricks or other."

When his office emptied, Dr. Sewell dialed Zeb and told him in great detail everything that had happened.

"Thanks, Allen," Zeb said gratefully. "This may be just the beginning."

Zeb felt that Matt's desperation might lead to anything. Matt had been involved with dope smugglers, drug users, and various types of criminals. And there was still the constant threat of obeah magic. Zeb thought- a many-faceted, dangerous man. His wish to breed dogs for a few thousand of dollars was only a small sideline. The risk of faulty puppies that would sell for only a few hundred dollars was always there. A champion full-grown dog worth ten thousand dollars was what he longed for—and what he was willing to steal for. So he targeted Lili Tu for himself long ago. Big money justified anything. And a cured Suzanne would only be a hindrance to him.

"I understand that you have faith in your man Boggs," Zeb said.

"But please explain everything to him. Matt's mighty unpredictable." "Will do," Sewell promised.

Zeb left his office to see his next patient. Mrs. Sinclair waited for him in the examining room with Topper, a little terrier of mixed breed. She greeted Zeb nervously.

"Dr. Zebulon, I don't understand Topper at all," she said. "He won't eat dog food."

"He looks healthy," Zeb remarked. "What do you feed him?"

"He loves tomatoes. Fresh, or canned, any old way. He likes carrots, broccoli, watermelon." She looked at Zeb to see if he believed her. "He just loves fresh fruit, I can feed him cantaloupe by the hour."

"Yes?" Zeb prompted her.

"He was begging for a peach with sugar just before we came here." She still looked at Zeb wonderingly. "I can't make him eat meat. He'll gobble alfalfa meal-but not steak."

"I've heard of vegetarian dogs, Mrs. Sinclair," Zeb said.

"But is his diet adequate? How about his bones? His muscle?"

Zeb put Topper on the examination table and gave him a thorough check, rubbing his hands down the back to test the bone contour, looking in his mouth for the color of his gums and condition of teeth—everything. "He seems to be in fine shape," Zeb finally announced. "If that food's good enough for people, it must be good enough for a dog. Give him a variety. His trouble is that he thinks he's a people!"

Mrs. Sinclair left happily, as did Topper. "Thanks, Doctor," the little dog whispered. "I was afraid you'd take my goodies away from me."

"No, sireee!" said Zeb.

Office hours were over and velvety dusk was settling down in the west. Zeb felt that he had done his duty at the hospital. He walked back to the kennel to speak to King for a moment. "Is everything okay back here?" he asked. Zeb still felt a prickling of his nerves when he came back to the boarding cages.

"Yeah, Doc," King replied. "That crazy man hasn't been here today. But I don't trust him, do you?" King looked intently into Zeb's eyes.

"No, King, I don't," Zeb said. "But I know where he was this afternoon. He just couldn't be in two places at once."

"Thank God! The longer he stays away from me the better I like it"

"Well, goodnight," Zeb said. "Tyler will be in charge the rest of the night."

Zeb returned to his office to write his reports and orders for the staff. Then home for what he hoped would be a quiet evening.

After a dinner of deviled crabs, music with Sallie and some lively conversation, the little family was getting ready to go to bed when the phone rang. Zeb picked up the instrument.

"Zeb! It's Allen Sewell," said an excited voice. "There's been some trouble. Could you come over?"

"Is Suzanne all right?" Zeb asked urgently.

"Yes," Dr. Sewell said. "But come over. We must talk."

"I'll be there right away." Zeb agreed.

Zeb gave Sallie a woebegone look and said, "Here I go again, Sallie." He quickly ran a comb through his hair and hurried into a T shirt and slacks. "That was an SOS from Allen Sewell."

"You poor guy," Sallie murmured. "You're going to be sorry that Matt Dye was ever born before we're through with him."

"I've been sorry ever since I met him," Zeb said. "You stay and look after Sallie, please Bridget," he added as he moved quickly to the front door.

He arrived at the Rehab Center to find the parking area filled with police cars, blue lights winking. He found a slot for his car and pulled into it smoothly and quickly.

Zeb was met at the front door by Boggs. "Evening, doctor," the blue-uniformed man said. "Good to see you. We had a little trouble here."

Allen Sewell hurried to greet Zeb. "Thanks for coming over, Zeb," he said as he reached out to shake hands. "Suzanne got a big scare tonight." He hesitated a moment. "Shall I tell you about it here, or would you like to hear it from her?"

"Let her tell me, Allen," Zeb said. "The closer to the horse's mouth the better, I think."

"So right," agreed Dr. Sewell.

They strolled into a large bedroom, painted white with lacy curtains and Venetian blinds at the window. There was a potted azalea blooming pinkly beside the bed. And propped up on three fluffy pillows lay Suzanne. Dr. Sewell turned on the switch. She looked pinched and wan in the bright light.

"Hello, Doctor," she said to Zeb." I'm glad you came."

"Of course I came, Suzanne," Zeb comforted her. "When Dr. Sewell told me that something had frightened you, nothing could have kept me away."

"It's Matt, Doctor," Suzanne began to sob. A box of Kleenex sat on a little bedside table, and she pulled a tissue from it to mop her eyes. "I knew he'd find me—no matter where I went. He can always find me. His spirits will help him."

"We'll stop him," Zeb promised vehemently. "We know too much about him and his crazy magic."

"I know things, too, Doctor," Suzanne said. "But it hasn't stopped him yet."

"Please trust us. And now, tell me about tonight. What happened here?"

"Well," Suzanne began in an unsteady voice. "I haven't been sleeping well for a long time. One of the things that Dr. Sewell is trying to do for me is to get me sleeping better."

"Yes, I know," Zeb said.

"It must have been about midnight. I'd been reading a romance novel. They usually help me to sleep." Suzanne looked up at Zeb whimsically, hoping he would think she was making a joke.

"But it didn't. Is that right?" Zeb prompted her.

"Yes. I was lying still with my eyes closed, trying to pretend I was asleep when I heard a funny scratching at the window."

"I see bars at those windows." Zeb said.

"That's right. And that glass is thick—I think it's double. I don't think anybody could break in through it. But somebody was hitting at it, and it sounded as if there was sawing at the bars too. I don't know for sure. All I know is that somebody was there." She looked frightened and even paler than betbre.

"So I began to scream. I screamed so loud it hurt my ears! Mr. Boggs was outside my door and he came in fast!"

"Good," said Zeb.

"He went to the window and saw two men running away."

Dr. Sewell interrupted Suzanne and spoke. "Boggs heard the rumpus and went out the front door after them. He chased them for about a block, but they got into a car down the way and got out of here."

"Sounds as if they made a good try, Allen," Zeb said. "Matt's probably enlisted some of his henchmen to help him. But we know what to look out for now. If Officer Boggs will stay on guard and you can assign somebody else to relieve him, I think we can whip Dye at this game."

"At least for a while," agreed Allen Sewell.

"I don't think it will have to be for too long. We're getting ready to close in on him—with the help of the law." Zeb said. "I wish I could tell you more. I can before long and then I'll fill you in."

He comforted Suzanne once more before leaving. "Keep your chin up, little girl. We're going to take good care of you."

And he bade the group goodnight. Now maybe he could go to bed and get some sleep. He crossed his fingers and knocked on the wooden bedside table, the only wood in reach. All went well for a few hours when the shrill sound of the telephone awakened him from a deep sleep. He shook his head to knock the cobwebs out and looked at the clock. Four thirty. Then he thought about Suzanne and quickly picked the phone up. A woman's voice came over the phone line. "Is that you Dr. Zebulon? This is Mrs. Murphy and I might have an emergency." Reluctantly he answered. "Yes, this is Dr. Zebulon. What is your problem?"

"To be frank with you, I don't have a problem yet but my little Boopsie is pregnant and she is looking frantic like she is about to have puppies. I'm calling you to make sure that you are home in case Boopsie gets in trouble and I need you. I hope that I didn't wake you up."

"Oh no," Zeb replied sarcastically. "I had to get up to answer the phone, anyway." Oh why didn't I become a botanist like my father, he thought as his head hit the pillow.

****

Zeb enjoyed a handful of peaceful days. He had a family now—Sallie, Lili Tu and Bridget. They created a home atmosphere that pleased him mightily. He could almost forget the threat of Matt Dye. Almost. Tyler kept Faye under watchful eye all the time—she had begun to stay with him during his nights at the hospital, helping him through his late chores. Dr. Sewell had reported no new threats to Suzanne. And Zeb kept the line open between the hospital and his cottage, so that Sallie felt near to him.

Occasionally, Bridget and Lili Tu engaged in violent combat. They raced widely about the cottage, leaping recklessly in the air and

Dr. Louis Vine, D.V.M.

wrestling with each other amid fierce growls and sounds that could frighten a casual observer.

Sallie got worried during one of these outbursts and excitedly asked, "Zeb, won't they hurt each other?"

"No, sweetheart. They're just having some playful fun and they're showing off for our benefit. They want to show us how ferocious they can be."

Whenever the encounter reached an indication of impending disaster, Zebulon slipped a video of animal life into the VCR to calm them. Watching a variety of animals on the TV screen seemed to fascinate both dogs.

****

Summer had brought its lush green leafing between the hospital and the cottage. The grass was deep and spongy. Bridget kept a constant watch, "There could be snakes hiding there," she warned. And she insisted on walking ahead whenever they were in the woods.

After a quiet and restful night, Zeb awoke to the aroma of coffee and the sizzle of frying bacon. She's up first, he thought. "Good morning, beautiful," Zeb called to her. "I'm just opening my eyes. I'll be right out." The smell of that coffee could wake the dead, he thought.

"You must have a good breakfast, Jacob," Sallie greeted him. "I've got to go to the college and I might not be back for lunch. I'll do my best—but you never can tell."

"You're not to worry about me, Sallie. Bridget and I can scrounge something if we get hungry."

Sallie had prepared a ham and cheese omelette, laced with green chili peppers- a favorite of Zeb's. He ate with relish and put a few bites down for Bridget.

Zeb made rounds and found his ailing patients doing well. One little poodle, named Snookie by her doting human, spoke to him appreciatively. "Doc, you've certainly fixed me up. My human nearly ruined me with that rice diet. But now I feel pretty good again."

Talking With The Dogs

Zeb reached over and petted Snookie. "Your human was on a rice diet for obesity and high blood pressure. She thought that anything that's good for a human should be good for you."

"How wrong she was!" laughed Snookie. "I lost so much weight, I was just skin and bones. Thanks for straightening her out, Doc. You saved my life."

"She knows better now, Snookie," Zeb promised. "You won't have that trouble again." He rubbed his amulet thankfully. He loved this business of talking to his patients. At that moment he stubbed his toe on a six foot bathtub that Mrs. Griffin had insisted upon leaving for her retriever, Griffy. "He just won't be happy without his own bathtub," the lady had insisted. "On these hot summer days, he likes to get into the tub and lie in the cool water."

"Damn!" Zeb muttered under his breath.

Zeb stopped at the board to check for his next appointment when his ears were assailed by someone yelling at Norris Martin. "Help! Quick! Get some help, please. My dog has been hit by a car."

Tyler Steele came hurriedly into the emergency treatment room carrying a limp, bleeding dog in his arms. Zeb immediately began treatment by giving injections for pain and shock while Tyler held an oxygen mask over the muzzle of the injured dog. He called Lib Nelson to him and ordered her to prepare for transfusions and afterwards, X-rays.

All of this took time. After he finished he went to the reception room to meet the owner. He found a tall, very pale man, apparently coming out of a faint. His dark hair made his face look extremely gray and when Zeb shook his hand it felt clammy. "How is Moonshine?" the man managed. "My name is Sam Jones and I brought him in to you."

"I think he'll be fine, Mr. Jones," Zeb comforted the man. "However, I'd like to keep him for a few days, for observation and treatment. Although we don't see any problems right now, we like to be very careful with accident victims."

"Thank you, doctor," Jones said. "My dog's name is Moonshine and I love him. I served in Viet Nam and saw some of my buddies

Dr. Louis Vine, D.V.M.

blown to bits. But seeing my dog hurt was something else. It just got to me."

"I can understand that," Zeb agreed, giving Bridget a fond look.

"I'll be on my way, now" Jones said. "And I'll call you tomorrow to see how things are."

After he left, Zeb announced to Bridget that he was hungry. He began to walk to the kennels. "I'd like to tell King hello and then let's go home for a spot of lunch."

Bridget pushed herself down the hall ahead of Zeb. She had grown to enjoy these daily visits to the crusty old Airedale. Her gentle nature somehow offset his rough personality. "Hey, King." Bridget said as she and Zeb came to his cage.

"Anything happen out here lately?" Zeb asked.

"Not much," King replied. "Those coins you put out seem to have slowed that crazy guy down a lot."

"Good," Zeb said.

"But I smelled that same old odor when we came in this morning, King," insisted Bridget. "Maybe he didn't get close enough to the hospital for you to notice."

"You may be right," said King. "That bum has caused me enough trouble anyway."

"We'll be seeing you, King" Zeb said and they both left.

Mulling over the situation, Zeb wondered if he dare feel safe now. They had defeated all of Dye's obeah magic. He had sent strange spirits indeed and maybe he'd used up everything he knew. Zeb wondered if he dared to hope.

"Come on, Bridget," Zeb said aloud. "Let's go home and get some chow."

They pushed their way through the tall, damp grass-watching everywhere they put their feet. The woods could be teeming with snakes. Song birds followed them through the woods and no ugly spirits seemed to be near. As they approached the cabin, Zeb saw that Sallie's car was gone. "Sallie and Lili Tu are still gone, I guess," he said to Bridget.

Zeb pulled his key from his pocket as he came to the front door. "You won't be needing that," Bridget growled.

Talking With The Dogs

Zeb looked at the door. It had been battered, the lock was broken and hanging loose. The wood around the lock was splintered. "My God! Zeb exclaimed. "What's going on here?"

He pushed his way into the living room. The place was a shambles. Furniture was turned upside down. A lamp had been pulled out from the wall and lay splintered on the floor. His favorite overstuffed chair was ripped and torn.

"Here's blood," said Bridget, as she sniffed along the floor at the door to the kitchen. "It smells like Lili Tu."

"I thought Lili would go with Sallie," Zeb dejectedly remarked. "I certainly hadn't expected her to be here alone."

"Alone or not, Zeb," Bridget said with a deep frown. "I know Lili is a fighter. Her breed used to be trained to fight in old China. And it's in her blood."

"You're right, Bridget," Zeb looked mystified for a moment. "And her anointed chain would've repelled any obeah magic. Matt must have given up on his magic and gotten help from some of his hoods."

Zeb began straightening up the room. "Don't touch anything, Zeb," warned Bridget. "That's evidence for the police."

"I'm not sure that I want to talk to the police about it yet," Zeb said. "Let's go find Tyler."

Zeb heard Sallie's little car driving up to the cottage. He stood still waiting for her to come into the house. "My God!" she said. "Lili Tu! Lili Tu! Where are you?"

"Why wasn't Lili Tu with you?" Zeb asked in an irritated voice. "It seems she's been kidnaped."

"I should have taken her with me, Jacob," Sallie was in tears. "But it was almost time for lunch when I left, and I thought you'd be right over. I only meant to be gone a little while but I got caught up in administrative duties."

"It didn't take Matt very long."

"I thought her silver chain would protect her," Sallie said.

"So apparently did Matt," Zeb said angrily. "So he must have brought plain old American criminals to do the job."

"What can we do?" Sallie cried. "Will Chief Carter help us?" Tyler came at once. His first glance at the ruined living room told him all he needed to know. "That's the way Matt Dye's hoodlums work. They've got Lili Tu, that's for sure."

"We've got to get her back," Zeb vowed.

"We'll go over there." Tyler said in a calm but firm voice. "We'll go over there and I'll smell her out," Bridget added.

"Tyler, you know martial arts. And I'm not a bad boxer. And Bridget can bite!" Zeb looked grim "We ought to be able to handle this without the police."

"Let's go," Tyler said. His lips narrowed into a grim angry smile. "Can I go too?" pleaded Sallie, her blue eyes beseeching. "No indeed," said Zeb.

"It won't be a fit place for ladies," added Tyler.

CHAPTER XVIII

Zeb and Tyler looked at each other, their faces set in angry lines. Tyler said, "I have a blackjack at my house. I'd like to stop by and get it."

"Okay," Zeb pulled open a drawer in a heavy maple bureau. "Here's a roll of dimes I was going to take to the bank. It could make my fist pretty deadly."

Tyler skinned his teeth. "We probably won't need any help like that, but it might make us feel better. Let's go."

Anger boiled in their throats as they ran through the patch of woods. Bridget raced behind them. If the birds were singing, they didn't notice. If there were snakes in the grass, they scattered before the hurrying feet. And the three thought only of the wretched men who had stolen Lili Tu. Zeb started the motor of his big Buick and Bridget settled herself comfortably in the back seat in double quick time. Bridget had formed her own plan of attack. She hated Matt Dye—his weirdness- for these long weeks and longed to sink her strong sharp teeth into his skin. Tyler sat grimly quiet.

When they entered the parking lot of Matt's Pub, they could see that the lunch crowd was beginning to leave. Zeb found a space under the big sign that invited everybody in. Hastily setting the parking gear and the brake, Zeb jumped out of the car. "Come on!" he called. Tyler and Bridget quickly joined him.

"Easy does it," Zeb warned as he opened the door for his companions. "Stiff upper lip."

Bridget knew that she must keep low, the customers mustn't notice her. But when she sniffed Lili Tu's scent, she forgot everything and thought only of rescuing her dear friend. "Zeb," she whispered. "She's here. I smell Lili Tu. Follow me." She put her nose to the floor and placing her feet delicately, she moved toward the back of the restaurant.

"That's the kitchen, Bridget," Zeb said.

"No," Bridget whispered. "I'm going to that corner, I think. Isn't that Matt's office?"

"Right," Zeb agreed. "Be careful."

Tyler walked quietly in their rear. He could see their reflections in the long polished mirror behind the bar. But the customers were busy picking at large baked potatoes and nobody seemed to notice the three of them.

Bridget came to a halt before a heavy polished door of dark wood. "This is it, Zeb," she said.

Zeb lifted his arm and rapped on the door. Nothing happened. Zeb waited. He knocked again. Nothing. Then he slammed his fist against the panel, slammed again. The door creaked inward. There stood a big, heavily built man in smudged jeans and a striped pullover. "Hello! What's with you?" he growled at Zeb.

"I'm looking for Matt Dye," said Zeb defiantly. "On business." He shoved his feet against the door to keep it open.

"Take care of that man, Bubba," called Matt Dye from inside.

"A pleasure," said the big man. Zeb flung his shoulder against the door and was inside with the man, Tyler and Bridget at his heels. "Oh, oh," grunted the big man, and clutched at Zeb, who dodged sidelong and came against a wall.

"I smell her, I smell her," blurted Bridget, heading for a door at the rear corner of the room.

Matt Dye had risen behind his desk. He held a small blue automatic pistol.

"Take care of him," he ordered Bubba again. "And I'll look after his buddy. Put up your hands, dark boy."

The man called Bubba lumbered after Zeb. His outstretched hands looked as big as baseball gloves. Tyler shoved past him and lunged suddenly at Matt Dye.

"How'd you like your ribs stove in?" Bubba inquired, as he moved threateningly on Zeb.

Zeb's left fist jabbed straight to Bubba's mouth, and his right drove solidly for the jaw. Bubba blinked, only blinked. He gripped the smaller man by the shoulders.

Zeb went for the heavy belly, right and left and right again. He heard Bubba wheeze, and Zeb pulled loose from that biting grip. His sleeve tore as he won free.

Talking With The Dogs

"You son of a bitch," mouthed Bubba, swinging ponderously. Zeb bobbed inside, belaboring that gross belly again, then coming up with a hard right under the jaw. Bubba swore again, raked at Zeb's face with clawing fingers. A nail gashed Zeb's cheek but Zeb scored to the mouth again, and blood sprang out on Bubba's face.

Zeb pounded to his head and body. Head again. Bubba floundered awkwardly, launching a blow that struck Zeb high on the brow. His head began to hum, but he kept hitting.

All of a sudden Bubba went down backward and sat on the floor. His arms crossed in front of his face.

Zeb panted. His knuckles ached. "Don't get up," he warned. He looked at his bruised hand and rubbed it gently. *I hope it won't ruin my Sunday morning golf game*, he thought.

"I won't get up," mumbled Bubba.

Bridget walked over. "I'll keep an eye on him for you, Zeb," she said.

Zeb could see Matt Dye, also on the floor, face down, limp and motionless. Tyler stood over him with the automatic in his hand. "What happened?" Zeb asked.

"I grabbed his gun with one hand and judo-chopped him with it," said Tyler. "He's out cold. I was tempted for a split second to pull the trigger, remembering what he did to my father."

"I'm so very glad that you controlled your temper. Killing him would have ruined your life," Zeb calmly counseled.

Zeb looked toward the corner where Bridget had sniffed Lili. "Yes, she's in there, Zeb," Bridget assured him. He wrenched at the door and it came open in his hand. The grateful Lili Tu walked stiffly out of the little room. It had been a tiny bathroom, too small for her to stretch to full length. Now she relaxed with real pleasure.

"Oh, thanks Zeb!" she said. "I thought I was a goner!"

Bridget walked over and licked her ear. "We missed you, Lili. We couldn't rest until we found you."

Lili Tu looked at the fallen men on the floor and said happily, "You sure gave them what they deserved. They were very mean to me, yelling and kicking at me."

"Now hurry, all of you. Let's get out of this den of iniquity." Zeb said. He went out into the restaurant. Customers were sitting at the bar. He realized that he had seen some of them before. There sat the girl with the purple hair still humming tunelessly. She wore a pierced ring through her nostril. Some of the young men looked familiar also, especially the ones with earrings in their ear lobes. He spotted a fashionably dressed young woman and wondered why on earth she had come to the Pub. She certainly seemed out of place there. To each their own, I guess, he thought as he left the restaurant.

They pulled their weary bodies into Zeb's big car and closed the doors, thankful to be able to leave Matt's place.

Bridget and Lili Tu settled down in the back seat. "Gee, I'm glad to have you back, Lili," Bridget said.

"Gosh, yes. I'm sure glad you found me," Lili sighed. "But how did you figure out where I was?"

"How could we miss, with that old Matt Dye around?" Bridget asked. "You'll never know how much pure hell that weird guy has caused us."

"Well, he's at the head of my hate list," Lili said grimly.

The car purred smoothly down the main street. Chapel Hill was a beautiful southern college town which had retained it's unique atmosphere even though it had become an international educational center where students from around the world attended. It was very cosmopolitan indeed. Students were seen strolling along the avenue in all types of attire, from shorts and bikini tops to suits with shirts and ties. When Zeb looked at all the young people, it gave him a feeling of being young again and reliving his own college days.

Summer had gone its more or less merry way. Autumn brought its usual quickening of life in a college town. Once more students were literally everywhere. The trees along Franklin Street, Rosemary Street, Cameron Avenue-and every side street and lane-began to blaze with color. Most people think spring is the magic time in Chapel Hill. That may be so, but when the orange and red and yellow, with every shade in between, flame in all directions, then indeed is the town clothed in beauty.

As they drove to his hospital, he noticed all the neatly trimmed lawns and the fresh colors of the trees which were a comfort to him after his recent encounter with Matt Dye. He wondered why the neighbors didn't suspect Matt and how they could walk calmly down the street so closely to his Pub. He hoped to stop all that soon.

He drove directly to his cottage and Lili Tu scrambled out on her wobbly legs. Sallie heard her coming and opened the front door. She stooped down and gave Lili a hug and a loving kiss. "Oh, Lili. I'll never leave you alone again," she swore. "I didn't dream that anything could happen that fast."

"Thank God we've got her back," Zeb said. "And we're going to keep her."

Tyler handed Zeb the gun that Matt had threatened them with. "I kept this as a souvenir, Doctor. I thought maybe that you could let Chief Carter check it out to see if it's legally licensed. If not, that would be one more crime to charge that evil man."

Tyler told everybody goodbye and went to see if Faye was all right.

Sallie jumped up after hugging Lili and wrapped her arms around Zeb and embraced him very warmly, grateful for bringing Lili Tu back to her.

Sallie then announced. "I have more good news for you. We have an important visitor inside the house."

"Who is it?" Zeb asked impatiently.

"You'll have to come inside and find out for yourself," Sallie answered.

When everyone entered the front door, they were greeted by a tail wagging Shar Pei by the name of Jimmy Wang. Sallie explained, "I heard scratching on the door a little while ago and when I opened the door, there he was. He and I were so happy to see each other that I let him lick my face in between my kissing him. And that's not all, Jacob. Jimmy brought you a present. I put it in the refrigerator because it smelled so bad. When he walked in the house, he was carrying a fish in his mouth. I figured it was important so I wrapped it in plastic and it's waiting for your inspection."

Zebulon suspected the origin of the fish so he asked, "What gives, Jimmy? Is it what I think it is?"

"Yes it is," the Shar Pei happily replied. "The fish fell off the table while Matt's henchmen were about to remove a capsule from its mouth. The men neglected to pick it up so I grabbed it when they weren't looking and took it outside to my kennel. I dug a hole and put the fish inside, covering it up with dirt so no one would find it until I could escape from that horrible man. I guess that's why it smells so badly. But if it will help put that bum behind bars, it will be worth all the trouble."

"Yes, it will be," Zebulon explained. "That's why Matt goes to the coast every week, ostensibly, to bring back fresh fish for his pub. But actually, he is bringing back drugs stuffed in capsules in the fish's mouth, the same white powder that he puts in the stuffed baked potato for resale to all who desire it and its resultant effects. That's how Matt smuggles drugs into Chapel Hill for his various enterprises. Good work, Jimmy. Now we have more evidence to nail that guy."

"But, tell me, how in the world did you ever get away?" Zeb asked.

"I climbed a six foot fence to escape. It took me a few days before I could learn how to climb to the top and get over it. Please don't let that man take me back with him. He was very mean when he took me home last time. He kicked me and yelled and screamed at me blaming me for the escape of Faye and Suzanne. He's a maniac. Please don't send me back. I want to say here with all of you folks," while giving a side glance at Lili Tu.

"Don't worry Jimmy," Zeb announced. "We'll never let you go back to that man again. I've been reading psychiatric journals about men like Matt Dye. I'll bet when he was a child, he was mean to animals. It has been proved that children who torture animals are likely to grow into criminal adults. Parents should teach their children at an early age to be kind to animals as well as people."

Zeb strode purposefully and straight to his telephone. "I've got to talk to Chief Ira Carter about this entire mess we're in," he said. "Sallie, would you fix us sandwiches and coffee if I can persuade the Chief to come over?"

Talking With The Dogs

"You know I will, Jacob," Sallie assured him. She threw her arms around Zeb and hugged him to her. She could feel his heart pounding.

Within the hour, Ira Carter was knocking at the cottage door. His dark hair curled around his face and beads of perspiration sat on the bridge of his straight nose. "Hi, Zeb," he said. "I must say you sounded right excited."

"Things've been happening, Ira," Zeb said as he shook hands. "I'd be happy to hear anything you've got to tell me, Zeb," as he seated himself in the comfortable chair that Sallie offered him. "But before you continue, that male dog over there looks very familiar to me, just like the one that Matt Dye took out of this house a few days ago."

"As a matter of fact, it is the same Jimmy Wang that belongs to Matt. He appeared at this door a few hours ago on his own accord. Obviously, he escaped from the clutches of that monster of a man." He couldn't possibly tell the chief that Jimmy told them so. "That's one of the problems that we have to discuss with you. We've been so busy that we missed lunch. Sallie made sandwiches. Will you join us while I fill you in on a very bizarre and interesting story?"

"From Sallie's fair hands? Who could refuse?" Smiled Ira. "Luckily, I'd stopped to buy some of Zeb's favorite sour rye bread," Sallie said as she handed Ira a plate and passed the tray heaped with ham and cheese sandwiches. "For a little while I'd been afraid it would cost me Lili Tu."

"What's this all about?" Ira asked. His square jaw sagged a trifle with his surprise.

"Let me tell him, Sallie," Zeb asserted. And he began the story of Lili's kidnaping from the moment that he and Bridget had come home for lunch. "We opened the door and found the cottage in a mess. And Lili missing! And Sallie wasn't here."

"My God!" gasped Ira. "I know full well that you suspected Matt Dye's dirty work."

"You know it. Dye had tried several times to buy Lili Tu from Sallie. He's tried different ways to scare her including Voodoo magic. He's tried to steal her. He's tried everything," Zeb explained. "When we saw blood on the floor of my house, we were infuriated. That's when my kennel man, Tyler, and I went over to Matt's Pub, looking for Lily Tu. Both of us were incensed and we were ready to have it out with that bastard, once and for all. Tyler has a personal grudge against Matt since his father landed in jail in Jamaica because of his dealings with that drug pusher, Matt Dye."

"We had a rough time but we won the fight with Matt and one of his gorillas, named Bubba. Matt pulled a gun on us but Tyler was able to disarm him before knocking Matt unconscious. I have the gun and will give it to you so you can check on it to see if it's legally licensed. Otherwise, we have Matt on another charge of possessing an illegal gun."

"Good work" Ira said, while taking another sip of the fragrant coffee. "Go ahead with the rest your story."

"We've been watching Dye for some time now, Ira," Zeb said. He told him about Faye and Suzanne. "We'd brought Faye over to stay with us so that Dye couldn't harm her. She could blow the whistle on his drug connections." Zeb stopped and thought for a moment. "We figured he'd try to harm Faye."

"Her word against his," Ira said.

"There's more," Zeb continued. "Suzanne is on our side too. She is at the Rehab Center undergoing withdrawal from cocaine and other drugs that Matt Dye fed her. She was his hostess at drug parties in the Happy Day Club and will tell you all about them. Dr. Sewell is cooperating with us and has a 24 hour security team protecting her. Matt's henchmen have already tried to break her out from that place but the security team chased them off but couldn't apprehend them."

"Yes?" Ira questioned. "We'd like to learn more about the Happy Day Club. There was a mysterious death out there last week. A leading citizen, Dan Vankiger O. D'd. on cocaine,"

Zeb continued. "David Smith, a college boy that works part time for me, got solid evidence for you about Matt's Pub. David bought a Special Baked Potato at the Pub, which had a good belt of cocaine tucked inside. We kept the capsule of coke and swore out an affidavit and signed it on the night he got it"

Zeb pulled open a drawer in his filing cabinet and pulled out the cocaine capsule that he and David smith had hidden there. "Here," he said. "I thought it was time to give you this. David Smith bought it in a very special baked potato at Matt Dye's Pub." He held out a paper. "And this is the written statement that David and I swore out together."

Ira looked it over. "Yes, this is evidence all right," he stated. "But we'll need more than this."

"I know," agreed Zeb. "I have some witnesses too. But I do know that you'll have to do some looking into it yourself."

"You're damned right I'll look into it. But go on with your story." "Okay," Zeb gathered his thoughts. "We can show that Dye hides cocaine in his Special Potatoes and sells them to select customers. We've seen young folks—many students- in there. We've seen them high on something. I used to think it was just marijuana but I believe it is something stronger. They sing ditties without tunes. They drink and eat anything Matt will sell them. And they try to stay high. Some of that crowd wear their hair dyed crazy colors, purple or green. Some of them have pierced nostrils with rings attached. And they wear strange clothes. And they act weird. You can tell at a glance that they are not normal."

The chief entered the conversation by saying, "You sound as if you know what you're talking about."

"Yes. And there's the Happy Day Club, don't forget," went on Zeb. "This really tears it, Ira. We found out what really goes on there. It's both women and drugs. We have two live witnesses. Just now I have to protect them, because Matt Dye would like to kill them. But I think—at least I hope-that they're safe from him. They can tell you all you need to know about the so-called Happy Day Club. It's just a whore house. And a pretty sinister one at that.

"That place is outside my jurisdiction, Zeb. I'm only chief inside the city limits. That narcotics stuff will be a state and federal matter. I've already notified the FBI and they're on the case. They can find drugs—they've got dogs trained to sniff it out for them."

"Bully for dogs," Bridget muttered. "We've been sniffing out things about Matt for days."

"I thought that we'd pretty well established that Matt brings in the drugs in the mouths of the fish he trucks in from the coast," added Zeb.

Ira nodded. "The FBI will have to make sure of that."

Bridget nodded at Zeb. "Yes, those fed's dogs will help do that."

Ira looked at Bridget. "Your dog is amazing, Zeb. She looks like she's trying to join into our conversation."

Zeb laughed. "Dogs can surprise you, Ira. Just today, a client told me that her dog is hooked on soap operas on TV. That's the only way she can keep him from wrecking the house. She leaves the programs on that he likes all day long."

"Maybe her dog should join the FBI," Ira said as he rose to leave. "The authorities are working on the case at this very moment. Matt Dye has a 24 hour a day surveillance on him and his phones are all tapped. When they have enough evidence on him, they'll make their move. Not until then. I'll call on you when I need you."

"Great! Pour it on that evil man.

"Can you depend on these folks to testify?"

"I promise," Zeb said. "They all despise Matt Dye."

"We'll have to find out where Dye gets the stuff—who his suppliers are."

"We even have a lead on that," Zeb said. "He goes to the shore every couple of weeks to buy seafood. We know that the dope is smuggled in by stuffing capsules into the mouths of the fish. Only Matt's specially paid assistants are allowed to clean those fish when they come back to the Pub."

"How did you learn all this? The Chief asked, suddenly very intense and eager.

"Ye Gods, Zeb!" Bridget whispered. "You can't tell him that a dog told you—Matt Dye's dog at that!"

"What if I said that a little dog told me?" Zeb asked, trying to suppress a grin.

"Be serious, Zeb!" Ira snorted.

"Call it a hunch," Zeb countered.

"Gee, Zeb," Bridget said with relief "You sure got out of that neatly."

"Bridget sounds like she's trying to talk again," Ira said.

"If people could understand dogs," Zeb said, "It would be wonderful. I have clients who have to spell in front of their dogs and some of the little beasts learn to spell better than their humans.

Scientific research has proven that the average dog can understand at least 200 words and commands."

"Little beasts indeed!" Bridget snapped. "Every day in every way, I get prouder and prouder of being a dog."

"Chief, I haven't told you the best news yet. When Jimmy Wang escaped from the clutches of that evil man, he brought a fish in his mouth. He carried it over the fence so that we might have some evidence against Matt. I'll get it out of the refrigerator right now so that we might all examine it together."

He returned with the foul-smelling fish and a long forceps that he had retrieved from his medical bag. With deft fingers, he inserted the probe into the fish's mouth and soon came out with a plastic capsule full of a white powder.

"Here you are, Ira. Enough evidence to hang that SOB. Take the capsule to your lab for analysis. I'll keep the fish here if you don't need it for evidence."

"Good idea, Zeb," Ira said, as he turned his head away from the putrid odor.

Ira Carter seemed to relax and he broke into a smile. Comfortably full of ham and cheese and good black coffee, he rose to take his leave. "I'll get back to the station and start working on all this information that you have given me. When I'm ready for your evidence, I'll drop by and ask for it. In the meanwhile, I'll keep in close contact with the federal narcotics people and keep the investigation rolling. They'll have their lab check that capsule out."

"Just a minute, Ira" Zeb interrupted. "Before you go, I'd like to tell you our plans about Jimmy Wang. We are never going to let Matt Dye get his hands or feet on that poor dog again. I intend to have Sallie's uncle take care of him until this mess is over."

"What dog?" the chief smiled. "I don't see any strange dog here. And I definitely do not want to know where you hide Jimmy out. I'd do the same if I were in your place-but please don't quote me."

Zeb walked Ira Carter to the door and gave him a warm handshake before he left. He walked slowly back to his big easy chair and sank into it, relaxing his weary frame for the first time in many days. The battle with the big goon had tired him, though it had lifted his spirits.

"I'll just rest a minute before I go back to work and soak my hand in icewater to prevent more swelling. Bubba had a hard jaw."

"You sure fooled the chief about talking to dogs," Lili said.

Bridget leaned toward Lili and whispered. "I think Zeb could talk to us without his amulet. I think the little shamrock just gave him confidence. He could have tuned in on us any time if he'd just tried."

"Maybe you're right, Bridget," Lili said. "But I hope he never loses it."

Zeb sipped a chocolate liqueur and talked quietly with Sallie for a few minutes after Ira Carter left. He loved to look deep into her cornflower blue eyes and listen to her sweet voice. He finally said, "I hope the Chief doesn't wait too long to arrest Dye."

"Your evidence will be a big help," Sallie said.

"Yes, I suppose so," Zeb answered. "But there's so much he needs to know. Where does Matt buy it? All kinds of things. We'll have to let Ira do it in his own way. You know the old bromide about the slowness of the law—goes back to Shakespeare's time."

"Right," Sallie agreed and curled up on Zeb's lap and planted a long kiss on his ready lips. "I wish you didn't have to go back to the hospital."

Zeb felt warm all over as he held her. "Me too. Your lips are so soft and sweet," he said. "But I do. And here I go. Right now, before it gets any more difficult." He got up and quickly walked out the door before he succumbed to temptation. The grassy path rustled under his feet.

The doctor walked reluctantly into the reception room at the hospital and found it filled with clients. They were seated like spectators at a show. Ms. Incorminies, a retired clinical psychologist, was entertaining the ladies waiting with their pets. Zeb only knew the woman slightly and was shocked to see her lying flat on the floor in the middle of the room. She had made of herself an avenue for her cat's afternoon stroll. Ms. Incorminies uttered sounds of ecstasy and pleasure each time the cat's soft paws touched the sensitive parts of her body. Zeb hurried to Norris' desk. "Please send the lady with the cat in to me before the police raid the place," he ordered. And as an afterthought. "Think twice before you ever give her another appointment."

"Oh don't be such a killjoy, Doctor. The old lady was putting on such a great show that everybody seemed to be enjoying," Norris smiled.

Zeb would have liked to consult Dr. Sewell for advice about that eccentric old lady. He often wished for a consulting psychiatrist on his staff to attend to all the eccentric dog owners that he encountered every day in his practice. Now might be the time to buy that couch the newspaper had joked about a few weeks ago.

CHAPTER XIX

Early the next morning Zeb called Tyler, Lib Nelson and Ken Peters into his office.

"You all know that I have to go to the Tobacco Road Dog Show in Raleigh," he announced. "It seemed so far in the future—but here it is. Time's just collapsed on me."

Lib nodded wisely. Freckles shone on her freshly scrubbed face. "That's life, Doctor," she said. "Everything happens at once, ready or not."

"And it's usually before a man's ready," said Tyler. "How can we help?"

I want to let everyone in on a secret that no one outside of this room should know about. Jimmy Wang escaped again from Matt Dye and he is here with me in my house. David Smith is going to drive him to Sallie's Uncle Milt in Woodbine. Jimmy is going to stay in his kennels for a while until this mess here is all cleared up. But remember, everyone must play 'Micky The Dunce.' If anyone asks, you never heard of Jimmy Wang. It could be a matter of life or death so be careful. Jimmy could be a valuable asset in putting Matt Dye behind bars." Zeb didn't go in detail how Jimmy could tell Zeb all about Matt's underhanded dealings.

"Now, as for the dog show," he continued, "Lib, you know that we'll need some goodies to help keep Lili alert. I'll ask you to prepare liver for bait. You know how to cook it, cut it up and dry it out. And please prepare an ice cooler. Then get Lili plenty of food. She's a good eater. We'll need dry food and cans of her favorite meats."

"I can handle that," Lib promised. "How many days rations do we need?"

"Two days. We'll stay there for the whole time not come back home until the show's over."

"I'll be there with you," Tyler said. "I can come back here if there's a need." he suggested. "That is if we've forgotten anything."

"Okay, Tyler. I know I can depend on you," said Zeb. "And please Lib, pack food for Bridget. She'll be with us." Zeb turned a serious face to Tyler. Now, about Faye?"

"She'll come with me," declared Tyler. "I can't let her out of my sight."

"Fine, I'll reserve another double room."

Ken Peters had sat quietly, listening. Now he spoke up. "What can I do, Doctor?"

Zeb grinned. "You've built up a clientele," he said with a smile. "Those young ladies admire the way your fair hair drops below your ears. And they think your big blue eyes simply heavenly—that's their word, not mine. Good looks aside, though, everyone, old and young alike think that you're a fine veterinarian, very capable indeed. And I agree with them wholeheartedly. You're a good one, Ken. But on a lighter side, will all these young ladies leave you time to devote to all the sick dogs and cats?"

Ken shrugged. "It's really not that bad. The ladies like you too. How do you explain the lady with the transparent blouse?" Ken thought this might be the first skirmish he's ever won with Zeb.

"I'll call in a relief man to help you," Zeb told him, calmly changing the subject. "I'll get Dr. Emmett Cross from Raleigh. Now that he's retired, he likes to do relief jobs sometimes."

"Great," said Ken. "And of course, you and I can consult by phone."

"Now, Tyler." Zeb turned toward his dignified kennel man. "You'll be with me in case Matt Dye decides to perform more of his island tricks. Who'll you leave in charge of the kennels?"

"Dave Smith can do that." Tyler assured him. "He's a smart young man. All our boarders know him and he knows them. There's no need to worry with him in charge."

"Yes, I have confidence in David," Zeb nodded gravely. He thought of the little capsule of white powder that David had managed to buy at Matt's Pub.

"All right. I think we've covered everything. Wish us luck at the dog show."

Norris was on the intercom to say that a client was waiting for him. She ushered a well-groomed young woman into Examination Room One. The lady's lavender linen suit was the obvious work of a top designer. Her thick dark hair had been artfully styled and blown dry into a neat cap. She looked as though she had been veneered. In her arms she carried a drooping Boston Bull terrier.

"My little Tanya has developed some dreadful disease, Doctor," she said tremblingly. "You must heal her. She means so much to me—I don't know how I'd live without her."

Zeb put the Boston on the examination table. "How old is she?" "She's only two years old, Doctor. My name is Watts—Joan Watts. I've had Tanya ever since she was born. She's so intelligent. She's really a genius!"

"Let me have a look at her."

Zeb made a careful examination. He found that Tanya had a fever, enlarged tonsils and a running nose, but otherwise her condition seemed good. He gave her an injection of an antibiotic and prescribed some pills. "I don't think it's anything serious—just an infection of her sinuses and tonsils. You can pick up the medication at the desk She should be better in a few days—if not, just give me a call."

"Oh, thank you Doctor," Miss Watts bubbled. "She means so much to me. She's so smart that she's even learned to use a potty chair-and she plays with the beads on the rod while she sits there—uh—waiting."

Zeb couldn't resist asking, "Does she add or subtract?" His gray eyes twinkled.

Miss Watts ignored him and went on with her dissertation. "Why she's so spoiled she won't leave the bathroom until she's been properly wiped with toilet paper. I realize that some people think that I'm nutty because I treat Tanya as a child, but please be tolerant of me. Tanya takes as much love and discipline as the two legged kind. She also doesn't smoke pot, get drunk or lie to me about where she's been. When I was sick, Tanya stayed by my side the entire two months providing me with comfort and love. I cannot imagine a child as devoted and selfless. Our pets are our children. Sometimes the pamparing seems excessive, but it is harmless. This dog gives me more pleasure than anybody I know."

And the lady walked out fairly glowing with pride in her dog's nearly human intelligence.

As soon as they left, the intercom buzzed again and Norris announced that his next patient was a special one that she knew he would be proud of. Zeb was intrigued by trying to guess which one of his thousands of patients would evoke such an emotion when the door opened and Matilda walked in. Matilda was a miniature Dachshund who eagerly wanted her doctor to see her walk in her new custom-made wheelchair which was strapped to her hind legs. She wheeled herself into the room propelling herself with her strong front legs. She ran up to Zeb and he bent down to rub her ears and exclaim, "Why, Matilda, I'm so glad to see you running around again."

She replied by saying, "Thanks to you, doc, I'm happy again. I can get around wherever I want to go- once I learned how to manipulate this contraption."

At that time, Mrs. Haskins walked in with a big smile on her face. "Dr. Zebulon, I want you to see two very happy and appreciative people for your good care. Once the veterinary neurosurgeon told us that the spinal cord was damaged beyond repair, we though that she would drag herself around the rest of her life. But you put her on a program of rigid water therapy with massage. We take her once a week to a hydro-therapy center, complete with a physical therapist Then you recommended a company who made wheelchairs for dogs. Matilda loves her new legs and she goes almost everywhere she went before the accident. All of the treatments have cost us about ten thousand dollars but it was worth every cent. My husband, Jim, is retired but he says he would gladly go back to work to help pay for Matilda's happiness. After all, she is a very important part of our family. I brought her here today so that you could be proud of her recovery. You helped us get through a family crisis. Thanks from the bottom of our hearts."

"Mrs. Haskins, I appreciate that you rewarded me by coming here to help share your joy. God bless you and your husband for being so loyal to Matilda. It is situations like this that makes me happy that I'm a veterinarian."

After they left, Zeb called to Bridget, "Come on, let's go home and see what's good to eat." The big dog rose from her corner and stretched lazily. They headed back through the trees to the cottage. Zeb felt hungry after his busy morning and knew that the afternoon would be just as busy. A cheese omelet, he thought, wouldn't come amiss just now.

They ate their lunch and Zeb spread his length in the big easy chair while he slowly sipped a cup of coffee. Bridget, watching, thought how much a good nap would help her friend. But they must return to the hospital.

Zeb and Tyler spent the evening loading the van and making final preparations for the show. There was food, grooming table, brushes, bathing supplies, lanolin spray, soft cloths, all sorts of things to make an ugly little wrinkled face more beautiful. Lili must be the best looking dog in the show.

"Optimists!" teased Bridget. "Nothing could make darling Lili beautiful."

"Please don't tease me," Lili begged. "We can't all be as gorgeous as you think you are."

"Sorry, Lili Tu," Bridget replied. "I wouldn't hurt you for anything."

"We all love you, Lili," Zeb said. "Beauty's in the eye of the beholder and we behold beauty in you!"

"Thanks, Zeb." Lili gave him a soft lick on his outstretched hand. "I think we're finished. Let's get a good night's rest."

"So right, Doctor," agreed Tyler. "We'll need to get started early. Maybe at daylight."

Tyler went off in the direction of his little home with Faye. Zeb and his little family started toward his cottage. They walked through the lush grass, stirring up insects that sang and whispered. "Step carefully, Zeb," Bridget warned.

"The snakes are all in bed now, old girl, don't worry."

CHAPTER XX

Summer had gone its more or less merry way. Autumn brought its usual quickening of life in Chapel Hill. Once more students were literally everywhere. The trees along Franklin street, Rosemary street, Cameron avenue- and every side street and lane- began to blaze with color. The town was indeed clothed in beauty.

A mockingbird awoke Zeb early the morning of the show. It was singing loudly just under his window. Glad to be drawn from an unhappy dream, Zeb opened his eyes at Sallie asleep beside him. Her blond hair was tousled and a half smile on her sweet lips made him wish he could stay at home the next two days, right there with her. The moon was still high, lighting his house with a silvery glow as he tore himself out of bed and went to the kitchen to start the coffee brewing. They must leave soon for Raleigh.

Bridget stirred and began lazily stretching, then jumped to her feet and joined him in the kitchen.

"Gosh, I haven't gotten up this early since our trip to Uncle Milt's house," she said and yawned loudly.

"Let's give Lili and Sallie a few more minutes while we cook breakfast," Zeb said. "I feel pretty well organized, Bridget." The van was loaded with everything that did not need refrigeration. Tyler and Faye should be through with breakfast and ready to leave by the time they arrived at the front of the hospital.

"I just hope Matt keeps out of our way for these two days," Bridget said as she trotted about the kitchen.

"You can bet your bottom dollar he'll be there—at the dog show, I mean," Zeb said emphatically. He struck his fist on the counter as he spoke. "He'll have a dog or two in the show. If you smell him be sure to tell me. We've got to be on our guard every minute," he warned Bridget.

"Good morning," came Sallie's trill. "You thought you were being so quiet, didn't you?" She came into the kitchen and put her arms around Zeb. She drew him close to give him a long loving kiss. "I didn't sleep a wink all night—with all the excitement. I want to win with Lili Tu."

"Oh, ho," chided Zeb. "We heard you sleeping. Didn't we Bridget? Bridget just looked wise. "Watch it, there old girl," Sallie warned. "If you want me to brush you ever again."

Bridget tried to look innocent. "She doesn't know how much I understand," she thought.

"Lili! Come and get your breakfast!" Sallie called. "It's your favorite—bacon fried just right—it'll keep your coat nice and glossy for the show ring."

At last, fed, dressed and glowing with anticipation, the four collected scattered belongings and got into the van. Lili and Bridget took the back seat and Sallie snuggled close to Zeb in the front. They found Tyler and Faye ready and waiting to help load the perishables. They followed Zeb in their car.

Finally they were on the highway. The sun began to paint the sky a brilliant rose color as it came over the horizon. Sallie's spirits were high. "It's going to be a wonderful day," she said, flashing her sweetest smile at Zeb. She was a very happy woman whether she won at the dog show or not.

The driving kept Zeb busy on the road to Raleigh. The highway was crowded with early morning traffic. "It looks as if everybody who lives in Chapel Hill works in Raleigh and everybody who lives in Raleigh works in Chapel Hill," he said-his favorite tired old joke. Add to that, the Tarheel students headed for school and you had a fine strew of cars, sometimes more than a just a scattering. Often there were accidents stopping the flow.

"You can't trust those young people to drive carefully," Zeb complained.

"I sure wish they'd be more careful," Bridget said. "We wouldn't have so many poor hurt dogs to patch up."

"Well, there's the Happy Day Club—what Matt calls a club for gentlemen." Zeb announced scornfully. "I wonder how long before the FBI shuts it down."

Sallie gave a sardonic guffaw. "Not long I hope. After the way he treated Faye and Suzanne—that wasn't very nice."

Talking With The Dogs

"You can say that again," agreed Zeb. "Chauvinist or not," giving Sallie a sly look. "Matt should try treating those women like ladies."

Sallie kept silent. She could only think of the show. Although she had been in many dog shows exhibiting her own Collies, this was different. She was showing her Uncle Milt's prize and glory, Lili Tu, an extremely fine specimen of the breed. Milt had told her that Lili was the best dog he had ever raised. "This is Lili Tu," he had said.

"She should go all the way for you. Number one Shar Pei in the country."

Lili Tu studied Bridget with her tiny eyes. "I think this show might be fun, Bridget," she whispered.

"I heard you, Lili," Zeb said. "Don't get swept away with the fun of it. We'll be seeing Matt there and we've got to keep our wits. He'll probably have a blueprint for our defeat."

For the next few miles everyone sat quietly, deep in thought. Before Zeb realized it, he saw the big Coliseum looming ahead. Already cars were turning in to the parking lot. There was a hushed suggestion of barking from the vans and trailers. A feeling of suspended excitement hung in the air. It felt like the atmosphere before a vicious thunder storm. Bridget could feel the fur on her back rise as she noticed Matt's dog-van across the lot.

"There he is," she told Zeb. "He's here ahead of us!"

Zeb found a parking place for his van near the entrance and got out to take a look around. "Wait here a minute, everybody," he ordered and went to the doorway to make inquiry. Back again, said, "Everything's ready for us. We've got a reserved space for our crates. Now we can all go in."

Tyler and Faye parked next to Zeb. Immediately Tyler began unloading. "The first class is at nine o'clock. We'll have to get a move on," he said.

"Tyler," Faye said uneasily. "I'm getting scared, having to face that man again. I never wanted to lay eyes on him ever again."

"Don't you worry, my love," Tyler answered as he patted his silver dagger. "Just stay close to me. That man will never get near you. I'll see to that."

"The puppy classes will come first. They'll take quite a while," Zeb assured him. "Uncle Milt is showing some puppies. We'll cheer him on."

"Good. Let's grab a cup of coffee while we're setting up," Tyler answered.

As they went into the big arena, Sallie's eyes grew larger and a deeper blue with wonder. The large hall had been stripped of all vestige of basketball games or rock concerts. The huge main floor was opened up. Three rings were formed in the center. Along the edge of the rings were spaces reserved for contestants to locate. People were milling about in small groups. The room buzzed with their voices. High pitched nasal voices from up north, thought Bridget. Soft southern voices—neighbors, she thought. And voices with mid-West or Western twang. People had come from everywhere.

"Isn't it exciting!" Sallie said. Her cornflower blue eyes glistened with anticipation. She ached to hug Zeb for bringing her here.

"It always does something to me. Right here," Zeb pointed to his lean stomach. "I don't know how many dog shows I've gone to. But I get a funny feeling every time."

Zeb's love for Sallie shone in his face. He looked at her proudly. She looked smashing in her silk blouse, opened low at the neckline with a tiny standup collar. And the tight pants she wore accented those thighs, which he hoped the judges would notice. "I'm glad you're here with me today," Zeb said. He felt a little guilty that he could wish to influence the judge by Sallie's good looks.

Tyler came hurrying up to them, changing Zeb's thoughts to more urgent matters. "I've found our spot—right over there." Faye clung to his hand and gave him an adoring, frightened look. "It's right across from Matt," she whispered.

"Don't worry, honey," he assured her again. "We know Matt's here and we are watching him and his goons very closely. We won't let him hurt you." He nodded his dark head comfortingly at her and his hand stroked the silver knife at his waist.

Bridget nudged close to Faye. She wished she could talk to her as she talked to Zeb. She could trust Tyler, but she could only give Faye a loving look. She hoped that Faye understood.

Sallie decided that she would like to walk about the arena. "I want to get a closer look at everybody," she said.

"Okay, but take Bridget along with you, please," Zeb insisted. "Matt isn't far away." He leaned over and kissed her lightly on the cheek. "But remember, you have to keep Bridget on a leash while at the show."

"Really, Zeb," Sallie laughed. "It would take more nerve than Matt has to try something in this crowded arena."

"I'm not sure, not so sure," Zeb said. "Please play it safe—for me. Do it for me."

Sallie attached a leash to Bridget's collar, somehow feeling that she was unfair to this intelligent animal to put her on a lead. Bridget seemed to be so worldly wise. But rules were rules. Tyler and Zeb busied themselves setting up their stand and organizing everything for Lili Tu.

Bridget pulled on the leash. She had seen Bosco across the room. He was an old friend who had visited their hospital in Chapel Hill many times. His lady left him with Zeb whenever she left on trips and he and Bridget had become good friends. They arrived at the grooming table where Bosco's lady handler, Bess, was setting up.

"Good luck in the show today," Bridget yelled to Bosco as she passed.

"Thanks Bridget. I needed that," Bosco retorted. "I'm a little nervous today with all these good dogs here."

Across the room, Bridget saw the lady who had worn a lacy net blouse with nothing under it during one of her visits to the hospital. Zeb hadn't fallen for it. Maybe the judges wouldn't fall for it either. But it seemed that these dames would stop at nothing to get a ribbon for their dogs. Somehow the whole thing disgusted Bridget and she hoped that Sallie would get back to the stand where Zeb and Tyler waited. Bridget thought, "It's a good thing that most dog show people are honest and try to win fair and square. Most people show their dogs because they like the competition and are proud of their dogs.

They arrived back at the stand to find Lili Tu happily stretched out on the grooming table with Tyler brushing her. "Hi, Bridget," she greeted her. "I'll bet you wish Tyler would brush you."

Zeb patted Bridget's head and said, "She gets plenty of attention, Lili. It's your turn today."

Just then Uncle Milt arrived. He was leading four puppies. "These are Lili's cousins." He turned to Sallie and said, "I gave you Lili Tu because I wanted you to have the best in the breed. "But these little fellows are apt to be winners, too, someday. We'll see."

Bridget somehow considered this to be a challenge. She lifted melting brown eyes to Milt and said, "They won't be half as good as Lili." And she wished desperately that he could have understood her as Zeb always did.

"Hush, Bridget," Zeb said, half scolding. "Let's keep open minds."

Bridget's fur began to rise on her back. A nasty, rank odor that had become familiar to her in recent months had reached her nostrils. "Oh, oh," she said to Zeb. "There's Matt and two of his uglies." She shot a glance toward them that was sharp enough to cut.

"He can't hurt us here, Bridget."

"I hope you're right," she said. "But I bet he tries."

Tyler stopped brushing Lili for a moment and peered about the room. "There's Matt, all right. Be right sure that we're prepared for him. Lili can't wear her silver chain when she's in the ring. Tyler checked his waist to make sure the silver knife hung ready. "We'll have to trust the Lord and our magic silver, Doctor." He nodded his close-clipped dark head wisely, his brown eyes were fixed on Matt's station.

Sallie and Bridget decided to continue their stroll about the room. The air was charged with the excitement of the dog show. The noise from the basketball games and rock concerts was gone, but the murmuring of dog handlers and the whisperings of judges filled the room. They all were discussing the handsome dogs that had come from all parts of the country. Sallie wanted to share in all the excitement.

Bridget spotted an old friend, Rambler. Bridget felt sorry for poor Rambler. An ignorant owner hadn't known how to hold a leash properly and she had gripped it so tightly that he had almost choked to death. It had given Rambler a phobia—now he wouldn't let anyone

Talking With The Dogs

lead him except his own beloved handler. He trusted nobody else, especially his owner.

Bridget and Sallie studied many of the Shar Peis who would be shown. "I wish I could count the wrinkles on all of them," Bridget thought. The uglier and more wrinkled they were, the prouder their owners seemed to be. "Beauty's in the eye of the owner," paraphrased Bridget.

The room was gradually filling with dogs of all sizes and shapes. Zebulon recognized that dogs speak in many different voices. The small dogs had high-pitched tones eminating from their mouths while the larger dogs uttered deeper and resonant sounds from theirs. He realized that each breed had distinctive speech mannerisms, vocabularies, and slang expressions. A high-strung dog talked in short, abrupt sentences. A mellow dog took a round-about route with many digressions before getting to the point. A hunting dog used lots of action verbs and hunting metaphors. A lap dog used lots of references to current tv shows. Yes, Zebulon had come to accept, even enjoy his newfound ability to talk with dogs.

"We've got the very best Shar Pei in the place, Zeb," Bridget said when they returned to their station. "That's my considered opinion."

"I've got very good news for you, Sallie," Zeb announced. "Our good friend Daniel Clancy is going to judge Lili Tu's class. But remember what we promised him at the Westminster Show in New York. We told him we would name our first child after him, Daniel or Danielle, whichever the case may be."

"Oh goodie," Sallie responded joyfully, "Maybe the old adage-it's not what you know but who you know- will come true. Every little bit helps in the dog show business."

"Everything's fair in love and war," Zeb reminded her.

CHAPTER XXI

Zeb and Tyler had arranged their stand while Sallie and Bridget walked around the arena. The dried liver—for baiting to keep Lili Tu alert during the promenade-was placed near at hand in a cool place. They were ready to give Lili every support possible. Zeb held a list in his hand and had checked off item after item. There were folding chairs to keep the party comfortable. There were many grooming aids to keep Lily Tu attractive. Zeb smiled as he thought the word 'beautiful'—a special kind of beauty was Lili's and only Shar Pei lovers would recognize it.

Tyler had placed Lili on the table and brushed her tawny coat and sprayed her with lanolin. She shone. Lili enjoyed every minute of it. "It isn't just cats who like to be brushed, Zeb," she whispered to Zebulon.

Sallie had come back to the stand with Bridget. "Well, Jacob," she laughed. "I seem to have timed it just right to get out of work."

"You've got plenty to do, don't worry," Zeb said. "Better relax so you'll be ready for it."

Bridget brushed against Zeb. "Look at Matt and his hoods," she said. "One of them looks like a toughie that I've seen at Matt's Pub."

Zeb wanted to forget Matt. Sallie looked so lovely. The early sunshine glinted red lights in her hair and her eyes were alight with anticipation. She looked better than chocolate cake.

Suddenly the air was shattered by the public address system. A harsh masculine voice said, "Get ready for the Puppy Class. Center ring please."

Milt Porter handed Tyler the leads of two wiggly puppies. "Please keep an eye on these for me," He said. "I'm just going to show the other two in the puppy class."

"Glad to help," Tyler assured him. He took the leads of the puppies and said, "How can you decide which ones to leave behind? They all look great to me."

Uncle Milt just grinned.

"Sallie, will you walk one of these little fellows for me?" he implored. "I can't possibly handle two."

"I'll do all I can, Uncle Milt."

"Sure. It's no big deal." He patted the top of her curly hair.

The line formed. There were ten little puppies—all shades of gray and tan. Sallie thought that her's was by far the prettiest, although she realized, most every owner thought the same thing about their own puppy. The puppy she held, Chen by name, was a yellow female-light in color that would probably darken as she grew older-maybe to a light fawn color. It was a lovable little thing.

Milt stood just ahead of Sallie with Su-Mei on his left. He held the lead taut enough for the puppy to feel the touch of discipline, but not tight enough to hurt. Sallie imitated him. The judge, a tall, almost skinny man with a gray military looking mustache stood watching. Milt thought he saw the judges's bright brown eyes linger on Sallie. "Oh, oh," he told himself. "Maybe it wasn't such a bad idea to have her lead little Chen."

Sallie heard a strong commanding voice. "Line up!" Sallie looked toward Milt for her cue. He pulled his puppy to attention, keeping the lead in a controlling grip. Sallie followed Uncle Milt's action after speaking softly to Chen. The puppy looked up at her as if to say she understood what was required. The puppy seemed to nod her head. Sallie told herself that her imagination was really running away with itself.

The handlers began to move slowly around the ring with their puppies. Gait was being tested. Chen's gait seemed awkward compared to Lili Tu's graceful walk. But all the puppies moved in much the same manner—Sallie must be content with it.

"If only I don't have to pass Matt's stand, I'll be okay," she thought. But all at once, little Chen came to an abrupt halt and began to urinate in front of the entire giggling, laughing crowd. "I've ruined everything for you, Uncle Milt," she gasped.

"No, my dear. Don't worry," Milt consoled her. "The judge won't fault a puppy for doing what comes naturally. Just continue on as if nothing happened."

Sallie's hot flush slowly subsided. She remembered seeing a dancing circus horse do the same thing in the middle of his act. She remembered the embarrassment of his rider, the giggles from the crowd. But she realized that nobody seemed to care what the puppy had done.

Sallie began to tire after the fourth turn around the ring. But she urged little Chen on. Uncle Milt had been a good trainer. Though Chen might be feeling bored, she wisely kept the rhythm of her gait and caught bits of dry liver that Sallie tossed to her. She lifted her deeply wrinkled head and kept it high as she came near the judge's stand. Finally, the judge called, "Stop! Now line up."

The puppies drew in a line in front of the judge. Tall, gray-haired Judge McLain bit at the end of his mustache as he knelt besides Chen. "Humph," thought Sallie. "Maybe he's nervous too."

This was Norbet McLain, an old experienced judge. He had bred and trained so many dogs. He ran his hand along Chen's back from head to tail, feeling bone contour and muscle strength. He studied posture, fur quality, color of eyes. Everything. It was almost like an expensive physical examination. He looked at Sallie from time to time through narrowed eyes, as he concentrated on Chen's points. Finally he seemed satisfied and moved on to the next puppy.

It seemed hours before Judge McLain had finished examining all the puppies and returned to his official station. When he finally made his announcement, Sallie could hardly believe what she heard.

"The first place winner is number five. Chen. Puppy owned and bred by Milt Porter of Woodbine."

Sallie couldn't hear the rest of what he said because of the roaring in her ears. "Oh, Uncle Milt," she cried. "I'm so happy for you."

Uncle Milt's bristly black eyebrows rose and fell. His big brown eyes filled. "You never get used to it." he told her. "Every time you win, it's like a brand new experience."

Sallie almost danced back to the stand where Zeb, Tyler and Faye stood waiting. "Isn't it wonderful?" she asked. "Uncle Milt breeds wonderful dogs. We already have something to celebrate."

"We're not through yet, Sallie," Uncle Milt warned her. "We came here to win first place with Lili Tu."

Bridget edged closer to Zeb and spoke softly. "I see Matt watching us."

Talking With The Dogs

"We know. Don't worry. We're ready for him." Zeb patted Bridget on her russet head as he spoke softly.

The morning wore on. Faye kept them supplied with coffee. Zeb pointed out breeders he knew to Sallie as they sipped their drinks, and he kept a wary eye on Matt's stand. There were two men with him. One had large brows over squinty eyes and another was tall, lean and thin-faced. They seemed to carry some sort of equipment in their hands—Tyler couldn't identify it—maybe intercoms—maybe weapons. Zeb strained to see, but they were too far away. "Wish I had binoculars," he thought.

It was well into the afternoon when it was time for the novice classes to begin, in which Lili Tu was entered. The loud speaker announced the call for Novices to appear in ring Two. This meant Lili Tu who had never shown before.

Tyler lifted her down from the table after he assured himself that she was sufficiently groomed. Her coat gleamed—the lanolin spray had done its work. Zeb agreed that she looked wonderful as he handed the lead to Sallie.

"Remember everything you both have practiced," he told Sallie and Lili Tu. He leaned over and kissed Sallie's rosy red lips and said, "Good luck, dear. Now give them the best performance in the house."

"What if Matt tries something to throw her off stride?" Sallie asked fearfully. "We have to go right near his stand."

"He won't dare do anything in front of the judges," Zeb assured her, trying to believe what he was saying.

Lili Tu looked up at Zeb with her tiny eyes and said, "I won't pay any attention to him, Zeb. No matter what happens."

"Bravo, just keep thinking about your own performance. And remember something very important. Win or lose, we love you very much and you are part of our family-all of us here with you today."

"Thank everybody for me. I needed that!" Lili Tu responded.

Sallie took the lead and joined the other handlers and exhibitors in the ring.

Then all eyes turned to Judge Daniel Clancy as he entered the ring to take charge of the novice class. He gave Sallie a slight sidewards glance, not wanting to show any partiality to the other contestants. He was considered an excellent judge and his experience in the ring showed it was well-deserved. He was well dressed, as usual, with a bright plaid jacket and his ever present bow-tie.

His first call was for a slow walk about the ring. Sallie took a firm grip on the lead and began to move. Lili Tu fell into position beside her and picked up her feet delicately to step in perfect rhythm for the slow promenade. They completed the circle without problems. The second turn began and Sallie whispered "Good girl."

As they neared Matt's stand, Sallie offered up a silent prayer that nothing would happen. But there was a slight thud and something landed just in front of Lili's right foot. She hesitated momentarily, then lifted her feet high to avoid the thing and moved on. Sallie could see that it was a bit of candy bar—chocolate, Lili's favorite.

"Oh, thank God that you're smart, dear Lili," Sallie murmured under her breath. "That probably was laced with drugs or something. They wanted you to be distracted and mess up."

Lili grunted quietly. Sallie didn't know whether Lili understood her words, but she was very pleased the way Lili reacted to the thrown object-cool, to say the least.

But they weren't finished yet. Now Lili must show her fast walk to the judge. Sallie feared to pass Matt and his hoods again. There he stood beside the tall lean man. This fellow had a familiar look. He stood head and shoulders over Matt. His arms looked furry with black hair—or was it a tattoo? She had seen him or someone like him at the Pub not long ago. The men Matt sent to pick up fish at the shore were probably just such men. Zeb had mentioned that one of them had a naked lady tattooed on his arm. Sallie ignored Matt's group of men while Lili held her head up high as they passed.

As they came in front of the judge, a loud noise like a gunshot rang out. Lili Tu froze for an instant. Then she realized it was not a danger-only a scare tactic from Matt—and she continued on, hardly missing a beat in rhythm. "Good girl!" Sallie said. "You're doing wonderfully well, like an old veteran of the show ring."

When they returned to the starting point and stood in front of Judge Clancy, Sallie sensed Daniel Clancy's eyes on her, but she avoided looking at him. *I hope my slip doesn't show. I hope my lipstick's on* straight, she thought. But the judge wasn't looking at her face. He obviously relished the shape of her body. Zeb had been right about those tight pants.

Finally it was time for individual examination of each dog. Clancy approached Lili to study her bone contour, teeth and muscular definition. Sallie wondered if her trembling legs could possibly hold her. Her hands shook as she held the leash. But Lili stood bravely. She seemed to understand what was needed at each point, and submitted gracefully to the judge's exploring hands. He finished his study of Lili and gave Sallie a smile of encouragement. He moved down the line to the next dog.

Zeb watched Clancy nervously. "I hope he doesn't feel guilty in giving her a first if she deserves it," he fretted to Tyler.

Bridget grunted. "Humph! Any judge in his right mind could see that Lili Tu is the best dog in the ring."

"I hope you're right. I surely hope so." Zeb said.

Time ticked slowly on. Bridget smelled the rank odor from Matt's stand. "He's sweating out this decision," she thought." He wants his dog to beat Lili Tu real bad."

When Zeb's patience was almost exhausted, the announcer's voice came through the loud speaker. "Blue Ribbon winner is number three, Lili Tu, owned and trained by Sallie Predino of Chapel Hill.

As Judge Clancy presented the blue ribbon to Sallie, he whispered, "I'll see you all later tonight."

Sallie and her friends were overcome with joy. Uncle Milt applauded loudly. "I knew I'd given you the best dog I ever bred. Now watch! She could go all the way. She could take Best in Show tomorrow."

Bridget nudged Zeb. "There are some mighty good looking dogs still to show. What about Matt's big old dog?"

"We'll just wait and hope," Zeb said. "Light heart never won a dog show."

They spent the next few hours watching many dogs strut around the ring in a slow walk, fast walk and then stand patiently for rude and exploring hands to decide how well constructed they were. In the end,

Matt's dog was judged best. Zeb's group was not the only one in the arena who wondered if there had been a greasing of palms.

"I'll beat him fair and square," Lili vowed.

"I just hope it is fair and square and Matt hasn't been using uppers on him to pep him up." Bridget said. She stared angrily at Matt's corner.

"It's not to worry, Bridget and Lili," Zeb assured them. "Matt's well known here. He wouldn't dare try anything like that."

They packed up and covered everything for the night and were preparing to leave for the motel when Matt walked up, flanked by his two henchmen.

Matt sneered at Zeb and in an angry tone asked, "What did you do with Jimmy Wang? If I find out that you have him, I'll prosecute you to the fullest extent of the law."

"Oh," replied Zeb in a very casual tone of voice," I didn't know that Jimmy Wang was missing again. Maybe if you treated him better, he wouldn't be so anxious to escape from your clutches all the time. But I haven't seen hide nor hair of him. And since you mention the law, I didn't realize that you believe in law and order."

Matt snarled back, "I'll get you, you quack. Just wait and see." He turned quickly and left with his entourage.

****

It was a warm evening. Bridget and Lili Tu wanted nothing so much as a good supper and relaxation. Sallie stepped into a warm shower with a new bar of perfumed soap and wanted to stay there forever. When she came out, wrapped in a huge bath towel, she threw her arms around Zeb, "I wish we didn't have to go out tonight, darling."

"I suppose we could skip the party. But we might miss some interesting dog show conversation," Zeb said and began to rub Sallie's back with the towel. She luxuriated in his touch. "Oh, okay. I suppose so. But let's come home early," she asked.

Sallie tore herself free and began to dress. She put on a sapphire blue gown with spaghetti straps which clung charmingly to her body.

Zeb looked at her with longing. "Your eyes could stop a ten ton truck," he whispered and kissed her.

"My lipstick!" she protested.

"Who cares? Your lips are delicious!"

Bridget snickered. "You'd better get out of here and go to that party," she said. "Kiss her once more and you'll never go."

"You look great, my darling," Sallie said. "You'll be the handsomest man at the party."

"That's damning with faint praise, if the guys I saw today are any criteria."

"I saw some good looking men there, Jacob," Sallie teased. "One of them was giving me the eye."

"I'll kill him," Zeb said vehemently.

"No need," Sallie laughed. "He was old enough to be my grandpa."

Far down the hall they could hear the buzz and clamor from the ballroom where the annual dog show party was held. One woman's voice rose shrilly over the sizzle of male voices. Bodies were planted thickly at the door. Zeb politely tried to push a way into the room. He held Sallie's elbow and gently pulled her in. "I won't be able to hear a word you say. This is bedlam."

Difficult as it was, Zeb found a pathway into the huddled groups in the center of the room. The bar was surrounded and he and Sallie must join a line to wait for drinks. They stood quietly for a moment looking about them, filtering out the sounds for familiar voices.

One voice near them came through. Zeb recognized a young handler whom he'd met at another show." Look over there at Robert, the man was saying. "Looks like he's putting the make on Kenneth."

"Yeah," agreed the other man. "It's what he does every time he has a couple of drinks."

The men walked away and Zeb couldn't hear any more.

"You know it always looks like more people when they're put together into a room rather than a large arena. I've notice that before."

"Jacob!" Sallie pulled at his arm. "There's that Judge. He's the one I thought was trying to proposition Bess today. Remember?"

"Yes. Bosco's lady," Zeb remembered.

"Yes. And there's Bess," Sallie nodded her head toward a woman just coming in. "She's combed her hair full of rhinestones or something and put it in a knot on her head. But it's the same gal."

"Oh, yes." Zeb smiled wickedly. "That's a pretty sexy dress she's wearing."

"It does seem to show her curves. You're right," Sallie laughed.

"Yes. It does that thing."

"Do you think Bosco deserves to win?"

Zeb considered for a minute. He remembered Bosco well. He was a good dog, yes. But against this stiff competition—it would probably take a better dog than Bosco to win. Perhaps a dress designed to show off a beautiful body would help more than a little bit toward getting a blue ribbon. He hoped not. In all his years at dog shows, he had met all kinds of people and he thanked God that fortunately most people were honest and trustworthy. Temptation always got to a few cheaters but they were in the extreme minority. Ninety nine out of one hundred were upstanding competitors.

"I'm not sure," Zeb finally answered Sallie's question about Bess and Bosco.

Sallie felt that her smile was becoming fixed and Zeb could feel his voice tired from the "Beg your pardons" as they moved through the crowd. Bits of conversation came to them. One handler to another compared the virtues of the judges. "I think the old geezer with the gay nineties beard's is pretty fair" Others talked about their dogs. "My dog has an upset stomach, I may not get to show him tomorrow."

Sallie and Zeb stayed near the bar where they met their friend, Judge Daniel Clancy. He started the conversation quickly. "I can't be seen spending too much time with you all because people might think I'm a friend of yours and showed you partiality in the ring today. Believe me, I thought that Lili Tu was the best dog in the ring. I really did or I would never have given you a blue ribbon. I really mean that. She's a very good specimen of her breed. I'll stop by your motel room later for a drink." With that, he walked away to speak to other friends. Clancy was talkative by nature, and a glass of alcoholic beverage enhanced this propensity. He kept everyone amused with his stories about his experiences as a judge in the dog shows.

People were brushing against them on all sides. It was a happy and noisy gathering. All at once Sallie discovered Matt standing in a far corner drinking a highball. At his side were two hard looking men. "There's Matt with a couple of his hoods." she told Zeb.

"I see him. But he'll be a good boy tonight. Too many people. But I'm glad that Tyler and Faye are with Bridget and Lili Tu. I feel much better about that."

They found a place in a fairly quiet corner of the room to enjoy their drinks. Their ears began to adjust to the noise and Zeb could take pleasure in his friend's company. It was not long before he was interrupted by a young man with long blond hair and a wispy mustache. He held out a slender nervous hand to Zeb.

"Can I talk to you a moment, Dr. Zebulon?" He asked.

Zeb looked at the man and thought he would do well to find out what was on his mind. The man seemed very up tight. "Of course," Zeb agreed.

"You should know," the young man began. "My bitch won today and she'll have to compete against Matt Dye's dog tomorrow. And." he stopped for a moment, as if he needed to think how to approach his problem. "And I just heard a shocking thing. Overheard it, really."

"Yes, go ahead," Zeb encouraged him.

"I heard Matt Dye talking to one of the judges. I couldn't believe what I heard." He looked at Zeb to make sure that he could persuade him that it was true. "I heard him offer this judge five thousand dollars if he would give his dog the best in show tomorrow."

"Believe it, my friend," Zeb said. "I know Matt Dye. He'd do anything to win. But I don't know the judge."

"It was Mr. Parsons. He's a very tall red-haired man. I've seen him at other shows."

"Thanks," Zeb said. "I'm glad you told me about it. I'll report it to the A.K.C. representative and they will investigate the attempt to bribe a judge. The American Kennel club is always on the lookout for people like Matt Dye. We'll probably need you as a witness."

"I'll be glad to help," the young man said. "It's a matter of equal rights for dogs, isn't it?"

Zeb laughed. But he agreed good naturedly.

Dinner followed, uneventful enough to be almost anticlimactic for Zeb. "But thank God for that," he thought. He had had enough drama for a long time to come. The meal had been well catered—the beef was properly pink, the vegetables seasoned beautifully and the salad, with its poppy seed dressing, fit for any connoisseur. Desert came as a piece de resistance- Tiramisu- Zeb's favorite. He found it delicious.

When they got back to the motel, they found Daniel Clancy waiting for them. No self- respecting Irishman ever went home from a party without having a nightcap first. He was waiting for his drink and to catch up on events since they last met in New York at the Westminster Dog Show.

"Don't forget my friends, you promised to name your first baby after me if ever I gave you a blue ribbon in a show. But to reiterate my statement again, I do believe your dog was by far the best one in the ring. I swear it. Now give me a drink." And all three wrapped their arms around each other in a warm embrace.

While they were having their drinks, Zeb filled Clancy in with all the dramatic events in the last few months, most of it concerning their encounters with Matt Dye. Clancy was also impressed with the Irish Shamrock that Zeb wore around his neck. "Don't ever take it off. I've heard of its powers from my grandparents. I wish I had one. Then I could find out what my dog thinks of me. I sometimes wonder, when he gives me a funny look. As for that scoundrel, Matt Dye, don't ever turn your back on him. I'm glad the police authorities are bearing down on him. Good luck tomorrow in the show and I'll be leaving you nice folks-after one more last drink."

CHAPTER XXII

The morning after the dinner party, Zeb awakened to the sound of the raindrops, like chattering little mice, beating against the large glass window pane. He stretched tired muscles and thought how good it would be to lie quietly for an hour. The pounding in his head brought memories of Daniel Clancy's original drink recipe, Fish House Punch, which he had introduced to them again last night. He should have remembered the devastating effects it had on him a few months previously in New York at the Westminster. "Whoever decided to mix fruit juice with good bourbon should be strung up by the heels," Zeb had told Clancy. And this morning he thought that he had certainly been right.

Sallie moved in her sleep and threw an arm about him. "Oh, how I wish we could stay in bed all day," he murmured to her.

She grunted sleepily and yawned.

"We must get ready for battle with Matt dear," Zeb whispered in her ear and then gave it a loving kiss.

"Oh, Matt! Blazes to Matt!" Sallie said sleepily.

"You're so right." He bent over and kissed her dewy cheek. "But if he wins his class, Lili may have to compete against him."

"Blast and double blast. I'd say more if I weren't a lady."

"If it's got to be, it's got to be," Zeb said. "But we'll beat him, don't worry," he assured her.

They pulled themselves out of the bed and sat on the edge rubbing their eyes. Bridget gave forth a mighty yawn and said, "You should've stayed here with us last night. We're all bushy-tailed and bright-eyed. I wouldn't drink that snake root tonic that Clancy fixed."

Lili Tu sat up and nodded agreement. "I hope Sallie feels better than Zeb. She's got to walk me around that ring today."

Zeb rose from the bed and went to the dog's corner. "You don't have a worry in the world. Sallie will do just fine."

Filled with bacon and eggs and much black coffee, Zeb and Sallie made their way back to the arena with Bridget and Lili Tu. Tyler and Faye followed a little behind.

Zeb began looking about the arena to locate the judges for the day's showing. There were half a dozen well dressed men talking together near the judging stand and Zeb walked closer to see if a tall red-haired man was among them. He could see a military looking fellow with a crisply turned mustache and a long-haired young man with a curly beard and a soft face. Zeb thought he could guess why the young wore the beard. And yes, there was a long gangly man with short-cropped red hair, stooping a little to talk to the others. Zeb walked over to the group.

"Good morning, gentlemen," he said. "Could I interrupt a minute?" He put on his most ingratiating smile. "I'd like to speak to Mr. Parsons for a bit, if I may."

"If it's business, of course, Dr. Zebulon," the red-haired judge said.

Zeb led him away from the listening circle to the edge of the room where it was fairly quiet. "There is a problem, sir," Zeb began.

"I hope not a serious one," Parsons said. He squinted his gray eyes toward Zeb in concentration.

"Right. I do too." Zeb agreed. "But the word is that a conversation was overheard last night between Matt Dye and you."

"Go on," urged Parsons quietly.

"Matt Dye was heard trying to bribe you."

"That's a terrible thing to say," Parsons said, his voice grating angrily.

"But just the kind of thing a terrible man like Matt Dye might do."

Parsons scowled and drew a deep breath. "However—not the kind of thing old Bob Parsons would do, I assure you." His voice sounded even angrier.

"Maybe you should disqualify yourself, Parsons." Zeb tried to speak in a gentle persuasive manner. He hoped not to anger Parsons beyond reason.

"Not this old boy!" Parsons fumed. "I wouldn't touch his money with a ten foot pole! And I told him so last night. I'm an honest judge. I refuse to disqualify myself. I know all about Dye—how he gets his money—and I spit on him and his money. And I'm going to prove I'm an honest judge and stay in there today."

"Okay then. But we'll be watching Matt Dye—and you too."

"Rest easy." Parsons nodded his head. Zeb realized that everyone would be watching Matt, judges and breeders alike.

The two men shook hands and Zeb left the judge to return to his stand. He could see Matt and his henchmen across the room, busily setting up quarters for their dog. He was truly a magnificent fellow, a well- groomed Kerry Blue terrier, named Frenzy. Zeb told himself that this dog would probably be Lili Tu's stiffest competition for the Best In Show award. Matt must have really cared for this dog. Not the poor runaway, Jimmy Wang, that was hit in front of Zeb's hospital. Maybe that fellow had been too independent-minded to suit Matt, so he beat him to make him subservient. Well, it hadn't worked. In fact the dog had become an ally of Zeb's and had told him about many of Matt's illegal activities.

Tyler had put Lili Tu on the grooming table and Sallie was brushing her. She looked truly beautiful. But not nearly so gorgeous as Sallie, who had brushed her own hair until it shone with auburn lights as the sun touched it. The rain had finally stopped. Everyone's spirits had improved with the weather. Sallie looked up at Zeb and her eyes softened.

"Oh there you are," she said in her gentle way. "We missed you."

"I was taking care of some business. It won't be long now before all the seven groups have been judged and you'll be in the ring for the finals-Best in Show.

Lili Tu had already won Best in Breed and Best dog in Non-Sporting Group the previous day. She and Sallie could relax and watch the other dogs perform. Matt's big dog, Frenzy, was in the ring, stepping beautifully, high and with a measured gait. Everyone thought he was doing so well—he would be hard to beat. And so he was. He won one of the seven coveted spots by winning Best in Terrier Group.

Tyler kept busy looking after Lili's needs. The arena was warm and noisy. He must keep her quiet and comfortable with a watchful eye on Matt and his two henchmen at all times. Tyler's hand went to his waist to feel the edge of his anointed knife. The two heavily muscled men, one with a tattooed arm, stayed close to Matt at all times. And they watched over Matt's dog as if they suspected other breeders of being as crooked as they were. Tyler chuckled to himself.

Well, it doesn't take a crook to catch a crook he told himself. Things moved slowly on toward the dramatic afternoon competition for best in show. Lili Tu was rested and prepared.

Bridget had chuckled when Bosco won his Group. "Good old Bosco. He won whether he should or not. I wonder what happened in his lady's bedroom last night?"

"Don't be so vulgar," Lili Tu scolded her.

"I'm not even sure that it was the same man who did the judging, Bridget," Zeb said.

"Oh, yes it was," Bridget assured him. "I noticed specially. It was that weasly old guy who tried to look down her dress all right."

"Well, he won't be judging Best In Show," Zeb checked the list of judges in the brochure.

The usual sandwich lunch was over as well as the heavy rain when the loudspeaker rasped out its announcement, "All group winners in the main ring for the final competition."

Lili Tu's big moment had come. Tyler gave Lili an appraising look, "Her coat looks wonderful, Sallie," he said and gave Lili an encouraging pat on the head.

"Try to ignore Matt when you're in the ring, Sallie," Zeb warned. "He'll probably try something. You and Lili must be on guard against any tricks he may have in store."

"My knees are shaking so that I can hardly stand up," Sallie said.

"It'll be all right as soon as the promenade starts. You'll see."

Sallie took the leash in her hand and she and Lili walked to the center of the ring where the ring steward pointed her. Just ahead of her stood Matt's handler, Jon Roberts, with the handsome Kerry Blue, Frenzy. Jon Roberts stood tall and straight in Mr. Laurent's casual clothes, hair barbered by a stylist and posture won in a gym. Sallie looked at him and wondered. But she was reminded of what Zeb had told her. "Matt has hired the most capable and expensive handler in the business to show his dog. But don't worry, the winner is picked for being the best dog in the show, not the best handler."

Frenzy turned and looked at Lili Tu just for a moment. The handler flicked the leash to bring him round. "No foolishness, Frenzy." he warned. "That's not how you become best in the show."

Sallie smiled to herself. She tried to ignore Matt who stood some distance away, still guarded by the two muscle men. She felt for her silver chain. Lili could sense the odor that always spoke of Matt's evil ego, but tried to concentrate on her posture.

The order finally came for the slow walk to begin. Lili lifted her feet in a measured slow tempo and thought only of how she placed each foot in front of the other. "I'm doing pretty well," she thought. Suddenly something almost hit her in the tiny left eye.

"Oh, my God!" Sallie said. "Pay no attention." Sallie saw that a piece of dried liver had fallen besides Lili after hitting her. "Good girl, ignore it. They're just trying to spook you."

Zeb, watching, said to Tyler in an angry undertone. "That's their first attempt. I wonder what'll be next?"

Tyler's brown hand twitched toward his silver knife. Bridget wanted to go to Matt and bite him. "I smell him. I tell you I smell that nasty man," she repeated.

Zeb soothed the two of them. "Just keep watching them. We don't need to do anything yet."

The order came for a fast walk around the ring. Bernie, a Standard Poodle, behind Bosco, had become tired. He had won in the morning after performing in two classes and was showing signs of fatigue. His exhibitor was a young woman. Sallie could hear her trying to encourage her dog. "It's just a little longer now, Bernie. Be brave and toughen it up." Sallie thought how lucky they were that Zeb and her dogs understood each other so well. It was definitely an advantage for them to be able to converse with one another.

Did Lili hear that encouragement to Bernie? Sallie wondered. She's probably tired of being on show herself. I know my face is tired from smiling. But it can't be much longer. "Keep up the good work, Lili," she whispered.

Lili nodded her head wisely as if she understood.

During the fast walk, Sallie's heels became entangled in something that had been dropped on the path just behind Frenzy. She shook free from it, not quite losing the rhythm of her walk and Lili bravely kept her rhythm. "That trainer showing Frenzy must be a crook too," Sallie thought. "Of course. Or why else would he work for Matt Dye? He's just following instructions."

As they neared the spot where Matt stood, a large boom came from a bass drum, or some such instrument. Lili felt it echo through her head. It hurt but she stared straight ahead trying to ignore it. Sallie felt the throb of it too. Will the judge notice notice what's happening? She wondered.

But nobody seemed to notice. Not even the handlers coming behind her. Maybe this was all part of that evil magic that Matt had learned down in the islands.

The fast walk finally ended and each dog was asked to stand for physical examination. The judge would feel the entire body for bone contour and muscular development. And he would grade for behavior during the entire showing.

This judge, the one selecting the Best in Show, was a stranger to Zeb and he could hope that he was honest. It had not been Parsons judging after all. This was an elderly man with gray hair and a closely clipped gray beard. He had a professional look and seemed to study the dogs in a scientific manner. Zeb crossed his fingers.

The judge stopped besides Frenzy and spoke to the handler. Then he stooped over the dog and began to run his hands over the dog's back, beginning at the head and working down to the hindquarters. He spent a very long time feeling the bony structure and musculature. He talked quietly in a deep bass voice to the dog while he examined him. Frenzy seemed to pay no attention, simply held his stance and kept his head high.

Sallie muttered her breath, "Watch Frenzy, Lili. I think you should act like that when the judge comes to you."

Lili heard the whisper but showed no reaction.

After what seemed hours, the judge finally came to Sallie. "Now young lady," he said to Lili, "Let's see how you look at close quarters."

The judge's knowing fingers touched Lili's ears and he peered into them. He opened her mouth and checked her teeth. He pulled at the skin on her neck and felt the bones. It tickled a little bit and Lili had to struggle to remain quiet. Then his hands, like a masseuse, traveled down her back, feeling every inch of muscle and bone. Lili kept perfectly still. It was an effort. Sallie watched, fascinated, her blue eyes wide.

The judge finally straightened to his full six feet and stretched tiredly. It was a long journey down to those dogs and he wasn't as young as he'd like to be. Sallie wished she could read his mind, but his gray eyes told her nothing. He moved on down the line to repeat the entire process with the remaining dogs in contention. All that Frenzy and Lili Tu could do was wait and hide their impatience.

When all the dogs had been examined, the judge returned to his stand to wipe his brow and drink a tall glass of water. He looked a bit world-weary. Then he took a deep breath and announced in a strong voice, "I now choose the winner for third place. Bosco, owned and bred by Bess Boone......" Sallie couldn't hear the rest of it for the roaring in her ears.

"Bessie with the big boobs," Bridget said disgustingly to Zeb.

"It was an honest choice, Bridget," Zeb assured her. "That wasn't the bedroom judge."

"Well, you'd better hope he's an honest judge," Tyler broke in. "Matt's dog is still in there with Lili Tu."

"Rub your anointed silver sword and hope," Zeb said.

Judge Fitzsimmons stood tall and asked that Frenzy and Lili Tu walk the ring again at slow tempo. Sallie looked wistfully ahead at Matt's handler. Not a hair on his head was out of place. His suit was impeccable. He must know something. As to Sallie, she felt worn and dusty.

Lili Tu lifted her head high and began her walk behind Frenzy. She seemed completely at ease and her feet fell into the proper rhythm without a break. "What a wonderful girl you are," thought Sallie. "You're born for this show business. You're a natural." Just then a large piece of delectable candy fell just in front of Lili's nose. She could smell it. It was her favorite, a chocolate cream. But, no matter, she could have one out of Zeb's kit after the show—he promised her one if she behaved properly now. Matt Dye never stops trying.

Then the fast walk, with the judge watching, peering, seeking some kind of error. Both dogs went through the pace beautifully. "I don't see any choice," Zeb said to himself. "Lili's the best," Tyler thought. Sallie didn't dare guess.

Judge Fitzsimmons picked up the huge silver trophy, the Best In Show award. He held it in his hands, looking at it for a moment. He wrinkled his brows in thought. Then he walked toward Frenzy. He hesitated and looked over toward Lili Tu. He reversed himself. Now he walked to Sallie and Lili Tu with sure tread. He handed the trophy to Sallie. She grasped it in hands that trembled so much that she almost dropped it. Then she bent forward and kissed it heartily.

Mr. Fitzsimmons deep bass voice rang through the arena. "First prize, for the best in show goes to Lili Tu. Bred by Milt Porter of Woodbine and trained by Miss Sallie Predino of Chapel Hill.

CHAPTER XXIII

Sallie walked to the stand where Zeb and Bridget waited. Her legs felt weak under her and her ears rang as though she might faint. "It's over," she told herself. "I can't believe that we really won."

"Congratulations, Sallie," said a smooth, almost oily voice in her ear. It was the tall, sleek handler who had led Frenzy around the ring. Sallie accepted his limp hand and hurried on toward Zeb.

Congratulations flooded her ears. Other exhibitors came to her with their smiling faces. Most of the male handlers came with moonstruck eyes to tell her how proud they were for her. One of the handlers said, "God, she's beautiful.' Zeb, overhearing, wondered whether he meant Sallie or Lili. "The judge probably looked harder at Sallie than at her dog," said one female exhibitor angrily.

Matt watched quietly from his distant place. He shifted his weight from one foot to the other. He clenched his fists, unclenched them. His cheeks moved with the gritting of his teeth. He was thinking to himself, "I'm not through with that bunch yet." Zeb was completely aware of him and could guess what was on his mind.

Tyler and Faye quickly packed everything loose at the stand and gathered up the cooler and bags of supplies. They carried a load outside to the van while Zeb folded table and chairs and prepared to follow. Soon everything was ready to go. The party filed into the van, weary but proud of their accomplishment. Lili Tu curled up beside Bridget and said she'd like to snooze on the way to the motel.

Uncle Milt pulled away from the arena and hurried to a Gourmet Shop to buy the snacks he had ordered and then to the motel to open chilled bottles of the best champagne. This must be a night of celebration. His two puppies had proven to be winners and Lili Tu had beaten dogs from all over the country. He had bought everything good that money could buy—and Uncle Milt had plenty of that. All of it was loaded into his limousine for the big party. He arrived at the motel ahead of Zeb and Sallie and was there to open the door for them.

"Enter!" He greeted them. His teeth shone in his face and his bushy eyebrows rose high. "We're going to have a real celebration.

We'll make this a night to remember!" Judge Daniel Clancy was already in the room, glass in hand and ready for the party.

Sallie threw her arms around Uncle Milt's neck. "Oh, thank you for Lili Tu," she said. "You gave me the most wonderful dog in the world."

"I'm taking full credit for Lili Tu," he said, laughing. "I raised her ancestors, remember."

"Okay, you dear man," Sallie said. "Those wonderful genes came from your kennels."

Zeb came in behind Sallie. "Matt was still there when we left," he told Milt. "He had his fists balled up as if he'd like to punch out Frenzy for not winning."

"Maybe he'll take it out on that wimpy handler."

"Don't judge that guy by his clothes," Zeb warned. "Matt would never hire a wimp. He was probably as crooked as the rest of them. As for Matt, men like him never quit easily. I'm afraid we haven't seen the last of him or his bag of tricks."

"Well, let's have some champagne and forget about him." Milt pressed his thumb under the cork and the cork went flying with a clunk toward the door.

"We can't forget him. Matt could try anything," Tyler said. "One good thing-I saw some men in the crowd at the arena who looked like FBI people to me. Maybe our friend, the Chief, put them onto him."

"Chief Ira Carter is on his trail," Zeb answered. "We put him onto the Happy Day Club and the cocaine filled Special Potatoes, just before we left for the show."

Tyler agreed. "Yes. Especially after that man died from free-basing some of Dye's cocaine."

A loud fizzy sound filled the air. Milt caught the amber liquid in a flute glass and handed it to Sallie. Then one to Zeb. Tyler and Faye held out glasses and Milt filled one for himself. "Here's to a wonderful dog," They clinked their glasses.

Faye had begun to load the table with delicious morsels. And now She passed cheese-filled biscuits to the drinkers. There were several different kinds of meat layered artistically on a tray, topped with pink slices of roast beef. And unusual kinds of bread. Everyone made sandwiches and began to eat. Lunch had been sketchy and peanut butter had long ago lost its charm. Their appetites were quickly sated and they began to eat for the enjoyment of the flavors.

Dusk had fallen and the rooms held a gray light. Zeb turned on the shaded lamps in the room and it was bathed in a romantic glow. The patio outside their picture window was gently lighted by muted lamps. "It's been a good day," Zeb whispered to Sallie.

"Really. I've loved it," she replied.

Suddenly the fur on Bridget's back bristled and she said hoarsely. "I smell him!" She breathed deeply and rushed over to the picture window. She growled softly.

Zeb and Tyler followed to the window and peered into the dusk. Eyes like glowing fire showed in the near distance. They moved slowly closer, like lights on an eerie plane. "Look," Zeb said. "It's Matt's voodoo man. I can see his dreadknots and multicolored robe and this time he's carrying a big wicked-looking stick."

"That smell!" Bridget snarled. "There's that smell again!"

The figure approached the room.

Zeb and Tyler rushed out the door to confront the Obeah man. He turned to face the oncoming men rushing at him. Both men came in low with heads crouched as the monster man lumbered toward them. Both began throwing punches which rolled off the thing's body as if they were the flutter of moth's wings. The monster man sent great awkward blows toward the men who were quicker but the creature was stronger and much bigger. Zeb's blows were like mosquitoes annoying the big man but he kept throwing them. Finally a roundhouse blow at Zeb's jaw knocked him down and he lay still on the ground.

In the meanwhile, Tyler was hitting the monster man with all his strength, trying to throw him off-balance. Drool fell from the monster's lips as he muttered and growled words that were not recognizable. He then picked up the very large stick he brought with him and went after Tyler with a vengeance. Tyler watched for an opening. At last he found one. He pulled out his silver dagger and while yelling, "This is for what you did to my father," he dodged under the large stick and thrust the knife into the heart of the Obeah man. Blood gushed out over Tyler's hand and wrist. The weakened man fell to the ground and lay still, forever.

"Voodoo didn't help him this time," Tyler shrieked.

Zeb looked around and spotted Matt Dye a few yards away. Zeb and Tyler were about to go after him when an entourage of men came running up and surrounded Matt Dye on all sides. They were FBI men and Chief Ira Carter of the Chapel Hill Police Department. The FBI men handcuffed Matt and read him the proper legal terminology of his arrest and the numerous charges against him. When some of the men led him off, Chief Carter and Special Agent Frank Morrow came up to Zeb and Tyler. Zeb was on his feet by now and his head was clearing from that knockout blow he received.

Chief Carter exclaimed in a loud voice, "We watched the whole thing and it looks like a simple case of self defense. That monster man was trying to kill you both."

Agent Morrow of the FBI agreed with the Chief. "I'll back you up on that. That voodoo man had a lethal weapon in his hands. I would have done the same thing to save my own life. You guys did a great job. He was a big one!"

Everyone smiled and relaxed now they knew that Zeb and Tyler had come through the battle unscathed. Chief Carter asked," What shall I put down as a cause of death?"

Zeb and Tyler exchanged a weary smile. "Let's just say he died of unnatural causes," Zeb said.

****

The End

ABOUT THE AUTHOR

Dr. Louis Vine attended Cornell University and Middlesex University. He has been practicing veterinary medicine in Chapel Hill, North Carolina for forty years and is a frequent lecturer and demonstrator at veterinary symposiums on the subject of corrective (plastic) surgery on the ears of dogs. Professional journals carry his articles on varied subjects in veterinary medicine. Dr. Vine is a member of the American Veterinary Society of Animal Behavior and a member of the International Animal Behavior Society. He is a member of the Dog Writers Association of America.

Dr. Vine's first book *DOGS IN MY LIFE,* was widely acclaimed in the United States and Great Britain and has been translated into several European languages, as have many of his subsequent books. Dr. Vine is also the author of *THE TOTAL DOG BOOK,* which was acclaimed "Best Technical Book of the Year" by the Dog Writers Association of America. His book *COMMON SENSE BOOK OF COMPLETE CAT CARE,* was selected as an alternate selection for the Literary Guild Book Club and was revised and republished. His book, *TRAINING PROBLEM DOGS,* was nominated for an award by the Dog Writers Association in the Behavior and Training class.

OTHER BOOKS BY DR. LOUIS VINE
PUBLISHED IN THE UNITED STATES
Common Sense Book Of Complete Cat Care,
Your Neurotic Dog,
Your Dog, His Health and Happiness,
Dogs, *Devils and Demons,*
Behavior and Training of Puppies,
Breeding, Whelping and Natal Care of Dogs,
A Vets Advice to Puppy Owners,
Training Problem Dogs,
Dogs are People, Toot!
Dogs are my Patients,
Dogs In My Life, 1961,

Problem Cats and Their Owners
Problem Dogs and Their Owners
Voices of the Dogs At The Westminster

PUBLISHED ABROAD
Mon Chien A Des Problems, France
Hunde Meine Liebsten Freunde, Germany
Dogs are my Patients, Great Britain
Leilkibeteg Kutya, Hungary
Vas Neuroticky Pes, Czechoslovakia